PRAISE FOR GUNNAR STAALESEN

'Undoubtedly, one of the finest Nordic novelists in the tradition of such masters as Henning Mankell' Barry Forshaw, *Independent*

'The Varg Veum series stands alongside Connelly, Camilleri and others, who are among the very best modern exponents of the poetic yet tough detective story with strong, classic plots; a social conscience; and perfect pitch in terms of a sense of place' *Euro Crime*

'Hugely popular' *Irish Independent*

'Norway's bestselling crime writer' *Guardian*

'The prolific, award-winning author is plotting to kill someone whose demise will devastate fans of noir-ish Nordic crime fiction worldwide' *Scotsman*

'Intriguing' *Time Out*

'An upmarket Philip Marlowe' Maxim Jakubowski, *Bookseller*

'In the best tradition of sleuthery' *The Times*

'Among the most popular Norwegian crime writers' *Observer*

'Dazzling' *Aftenposten*

'Ice Marlowe' *Thriller* magazine

'Gunnar Staalesen and his hero, Varg Veum, are stars' *L'Express*

'An excellent and unique series' *International Noir Fiction*

GUNNAR STAALESEN was born in Bergen, Norway in 1947. He made his debut at the age of twenty-two with *Seasons of Innocence* and in 1977 he published the first book in the Varg Veum series. He is the author of over 20 titles, which have been published in 24 countries and sold over two million copies. Twelve film adaptations of his Varg Veum crime novels have appeared since 2007, starring the popular Norwegian actor Trond Epsen Seim. Staalesen, who has twice won Norway's top crime prize, the Golden Pistol, lives in Bergen with his wife.

DON BARTLETT lives with his family in a village in Norfolk. He translates from Scandinavian literature and has translated, or co-translated, books by Per Petterson, Karl Ove Knausgaard, Lars Saabye Christensen, Roy Jacobsen, Ingvar Ambjørnsen, Jo Nesbø and K.O. Dahl.

Cold Hearts

GUNNAR STAALESEN

Translated from the Norwegian by
Don Bartlett

ARCADIA BOOKS

Arcadia Books Ltd
139 Highlever Road
London W10 6PH
www.arcadiabooks.co.uk

First published in the United Kingdom by Arcadia Books 2013
Originally published by Gyldendal Norsk Forlag, Oslo as *Kalde Hjerter*
Copyright Gunnar Staalesen © 2008
English language translation copyright © Don Bartlett 2013

Gunnar Staalesen has asserted his moral right to be identified as the author of this work in accordance with the Copyright, Designs and Patents Act, 1988.

A catalogue record for this book is available from the British Library.

ISBN 978-1-908129-43-7

Typeset in Garamond by MacGuru Ltd
Printed and bound by CPI Group (UK) Ltd, Croydon CR0 4YY

Arcadia Books gratefully acknowledges the financial support of NORLA.

Arcadia Books supports English PEN *www.englishpen.org* and The Book Trade Charity
http://booktradecharity.wordpress.com

Arcadia Books distributors are as follows:

in the UK and elsewhere in Europe:
Macmillan
Brunel Road
Houndmills
Basingstoke
Hants RG21 6XS

in the USA and Canada:
Dufour Editions
PO Box 7
Chester Springs
PA 19425

in Australia/New Zealand:
NewSouth Books
University of New South Wales
Sydney NSW 2052

in South Africa:
Jacana Media (Pty) Ltd
PO Box 291784
Melville 2109
Johannesburg

1

I WAS DANCING THE BRIDAL WALTZ with Beate, but I was not in heaven; I was at Mari and Thomas's wedding in Løten one boiling hot day in June, 1997.

I had met her at Oslo Station. She had come from Stavanger, I had come from Bergen. Since the last time I saw her she had had her hair cut short and there were red flecks in it, but her eyes were as I always remembered them: cornflower blue with a touch of aggrieved sorrow. She was dressed in a youthful style: jeans, pale green T-shirt and a light reddish-brown summer jacket. She gave me a quick hug, flashed me a wry smile and said: 'Event of the year? Our only son getting married ...'

The train journey north passed in amicable conversation. It was more than twenty years since we got divorced, four since she was widowed and soon two since I myself almost followed her second husband, Lasse Wiig, to the happy waiting rooms in the sky, if lecturers and private detectives were indeed on the same floor.

The wedding had run according to plan, even though several of the veteran cars transporting the bridal party from church to reception had begun to overheat. Indoors, the temperature was well over thirty degrees. When Odd Sverre Midthun, the bride's father, stood up and removed his suit jacket for everyone to see, the relief was tangible. Within two seconds, every single male in the room had done the same. The women around the long tables regarded us with envy, but it may have created a greater stir if formal dresses and traditional costumes had like-wise been abandoned.

We were in the café rooms of what had once been Løiten Dis-tillery, where the fumes of artificially spiced potato schnapps still resided in the walls. NON AGUNT NISI FLUIDA, it said on the wall outside, which Mari's father had translated for me as 'nothing works without liquid', and for that matter they may well have been right, from water and blood to petrol and aquavit.

Dancing with Beate was like being transported back thirty years in time, to when we were young and in love. Stavanger was the town and the future lay before us like an endless red carpet; all you had to do was take a run-up and launch yourself. We hit the wall soon enough, but something always remained, if no more than dancing with each other on a timeless dance floor in a rhythm we had never quite forgotten, however long ago it had been.

Perhaps that was why it happened. Late at night, standing with keys in hand to our separate rooms in Miklagard, where we were staying, and glancing at each other.

'Lonesome sleeping alone,' I said.

She gave a mischievous smile. 'If I'm not much mistaken we allowed ourselves to be tempted on another occasion as well.'

'What about a repeat performance. Back by popular demand?'

'Well, a repeat performance anyway,' she said, putting the key in her pocket, coming over and standing close to me.

An hour later she lay in the crook of my arm, hot and sweaty. With infinite care, she caressed my two scars, one at the front and one at the back of my left shoulder, which the surgeons at Ullevål Hospital had patched up on that September night almost two years ago.

'How did it feel to be at death's door?' she breathed.

'Like a swallow dive,' I answered. 'The most perfect swallow dive of my life.'

When I had opened my eyes I was lying in a bed with drips in my arms, four thick tubes sticking out of my chest, upper body and bandaged left shoulder and a numb sensation throughout my body. The doctor treating me had explained how lucky I had been. If the bullet that hit me had been a few centimetres lower it would have gone straight through my heart. It had probably been a ricochet as the trajectory of the shot had been upwards. I had lost quite a lot of blood, which would soon have proved fatal if they had not got the flow under control. The left lung had been punctured, and I'd been bleeding fresh blood into the chest cavity. They had separated the sternum lengthwise to reach and stem the bleeding. The top of the left lung had been removed, I had one broken rib, and on its way out the bullet had taken with it something he called the scapula. He had obligingly explained to me what the scapula was: the bone at the back of the shoulder. 'You can thank your lucky stars,' he had concluded, 'that this happened in Groruddalen and not on some islet far out at the mouth of a fjord. And that someone had rung for an ambulance so that we had you on the operating table before much time had elapsed.' 'But,' I had said, 'I was with someone. How did he fare?' The doctor looked down and said: 'Not as well as you, I'm afraid to say.'

The day after the wedding I took Beate to the churchyard where he was buried. The cemetery in Oslo Old Town lay in the shadow of Ekeberg Ridge. Standing there, we were surrounded by trees on all sides. A goods train passed on the nearby railway line, its wheels squealing on the track. The first time I went, there had been a rudimentary wooden cross on the grave. Now it had been exchanged for a rock. On it was carved his name, year of birth and year of death, and last of all three simple words: *Dead For Ever*.

She read out his name and looked at me. 'Who was he?'

'A sort of client. I met him so long ago that you and I were still married. Later I bumped into him on several occasions, more's the pity. A sad twist of fate. One of our failures.'

She took my hand and squeezed it lightly. 'I'm sure it wasn't your fault, Varg.'

'I hope not. But for some reason we always feel just as guilty, we who strictly speaking are no more than casual passers-by in their lives.'

'I know what you mean. I've often felt the same myself.'

I nodded and raised my eyes. A plane was flying in silence towards Fornebu. Soon that would be history too. In a year or two Oslo Airport would be somewhere else.

We shared a taxi there and sat waiting for our planes, she to Stavanger, me to Bergen.

'You look so pensive, Varg … Have you got any regrets?'

'No, no. We should make this a tradition, once every five years or so.'

'Ha ha. So what is it that's bothering you? Not the grave still?'

'No. It struck me that … it was a case I was working on. Six months ago. In January … For some reason I can't get it out of my head.'

'Why's that?'

'Do you remember Hege?'

'Hege … You don't mean Hege Jensen, the girl Thomas …'

'Yes. She …'

That was as far as we got. Her flight was called, and I accompanied her to the gate. We didn't do goodbye kisses. We weren't that young. But she got a hug for her journey and I got a caress to my cheek from a soft hand.

Three quarters of an hour later I was sitting on my plane, not only on my way to Bergen, but six months back in time, to the day in the middle of January when everything changed in one fell swoop from being a beautiful, white winter to slush and rain and chaos.

2

IT HAD BEEN A PALE, colourless January day. I stood by my office window staring out.

Before the weekend, the weather had been wintry and frost-clear, and skiing conditions in the mountains had been excellent. On Friday evening I had done a few turns on the illuminated ski trail myself, beneath a starry sky and along a track bordered by snow-laden trees; an experience that was so Christmas-card beautiful I wished I had someone to send one to. But I did not, and by the early hours of Saturday the weather had changed, with strong winds from the south-west. The rain washed away the snow, formed cascades of water, flooded cellars, caused chaos on the roads and turned life upside down for twelve hours.

On Monday morning everything was back to normal. Down at the fish market there were just a handful of sellers who had bothered to open their stalls, but none looked as if they were expecting a great invasion of customers. The fare on the counters looked somewhat lean and they stood flapping their arms at regular intervals to keep warm.

For private detectives who refuse divorce cases January is a meagre month. There was a single message on my answer machine when I entered the office, and in the postbox there had not even been so much as a window envelope. Companies sending invoices reckoned that most people were scraping the bottom of the barrel after Christmas shopping, and advertising brochures that had not had an effect in December would be hard put to have any in January.

I held a cup of freshly brewed coffee in my hand. The draught from the window was cold, and I wrapped my fingers tightly around the cup to keep them warm.

I had read the day's newspapers from front to back, and there was not much to get your adrenalin flowing there, either. Everyone was writing about the storm at the weekend. A house had been set alight in Mathopen, and the police feared it was motivated by racism. In Italy there had been a train crash killing eight people. Børge Ousland was approaching the end of his trek across the Antarctic. Ole Gunnar Solskjær had scored in Manchester United's 2–1 defeat of Tottenham at White Hart Lane. A man had been found badly beaten up in Skuteviken and had been taken to A&E by a passing taxi driver. The duty doctor had informed the police, but the man had refused to report the case. According to police accounts, the injured man was an old acquaintance of theirs. They assumed the incident was the settling of old scores between criminals. At the same time the Chief of Police announced that the force was planning a clampdown on the town's drug community. Several head teachers reported a large, and in part covert, drugs problem at their schools.

I sat down at my desk and watched some coloured windows hovering aimlessly against a black background on my computer. I had learned it was called a screensaver.

My stay in Oslo had been drawn out for longer than I appreciated. In the days following the operation I contracted a serious infection that sent me into a two-week transport of feverish fantasies and intensive treatment. I was not discharged until the end of October, and was still sleeping on the sofa in

Mari and Thomas's flat for a week before the doctors would risk letting me slip back over the mountains. During the winter I went for a number of check-ups at Haukeland Hospital, all of which were positive.

After four months of sick leave I had gone back to the office in February, still sore around the shoulder, but it improved by the day as I did the recommended exercises. From the convalescence period I had returned with a technological advance, a PC tower that hummed away on the floor under the desk, a keyboard that was a great deal easier to use than the old typewriter had been and a screen that was literally a window onto the world. The small mouse lay beside the keyboard like a cleft tortoise, and I was no more than a key or two away from the world's infobahn. I had my own email address and had taught myself to travel on the internet's highways where, not infrequently, I ended up on a side track that culminated in the darkest electronic forest, with no other solution than to press Control, Alt and Delete and start again.

Even after a year there were not many people who had my email address, and there had not been many messages in that postbox, either. Not surprising therefore that I raised both eyebrows when I heard the door to the corridor opening. Cautious footsteps crossed the waiting room floor, and there was a knock on the office door. I went over and opened up, flashing my warmest smile to the potential client, as warm as I could muster for a Monday in January.

She eyed me with a kind of experienced distant gaze, without saying a word.

I met her gaze and said: 'Come in. I have some fresh coffee on the go.'

'Thank ...'

She stepped inside and scanned the room with wary vigilance.

At once I saw there was something familiar about her. She was in her late twenties, not altogether attractive, but conspicuous make-up emphasised her beautiful eyes, yet failed to hide the bitter expression in them. Her hair was black, perhaps not a gift of nature, and there was something tight and bitter about her full lips as well. She had no smiles left to spare, and not one for me. She was dressed in a large, practical puffa jacket, dark red in colour, and a not quite so practical pair of grey, skin-tight jeans. Her high, black boots had heels that would have required quite a bit of training to master balancing in them.

I held out my hand. 'Varg.'

With a limp handshake she said: 'Hege.'

'We've met before, have we not?'

She looked away for an instant. 'Yes, maybe.'

I studied her features. Deep inside I saw a younger face, a young girl of fourteen or fifteen with a saddened expression on her face even then. 'From …'

'Mind if I smoke?'

'If you have to.'

She produced a pack of cigarettes from her copper green shoulder bag, poked a cigarette between her lips and lit it with a small lighter. After which she looked at me through the smoke. 'I was in the same class as Thomas. At secondary school.'

'Yes, now I remember you! Hege …'

'Jensen.'

'And you lived …'

'In Nye Sandviksvei.'

'Right … please, take a seat.' I ushered her to the client's chair and fetched a clean cup from the cupboard above the sink. 'You did want a coffee, didn't you?'

'Yes, please.'

I poured her a cup, and she smiled with gratitude. A coffee and a cigarette. For some, little more was necessary.

I sat down behind the desk with my back to the window, spread my hands and said: 'So what brings you here?'

She looked at me, mistrustful. 'I don't know quite how to …'

I responded with a friendly smile, leaned over for a biro and opened my notepad. 'You could start by saying what you do.'

'What I … My job, you mean?'

'Yes, that sort of thing.'

She looked past me. Her get-up and the expression around her mouth had caused me to draw some swift conclusions, and I had not been mistaken. 'I, erm, sell myself.'

'I see.' I tried to give her a sense that in this office it didn't matter. 'Most of us do when it comes to the crunch.'

'It's not that simple, believe you me,' she snapped, as though she had been expecting a stronger reaction from my side.

'Listen, Hege …' I leaned forward. 'I'm a social worker by training and in the course of my career I've come across a great variety of human situations. I don't judge anyone.' After a tiny pause I added: 'But I am keen to hear what you want from me.'

'It's about a … colleague of mine. A girlfriend. She's gone missing.'

'When did that happen?'

'Before the weekend. I haven't seen her since Friday.'

'And she's not in the habit of taking long weekends away?'

She rolled her eyes. 'Long weekends? In our profession? That's our peak business period.' As I didn't respond she continued:

'Maggi and I always made sure we told each other if anything happened. After all, we know the risks we're exposed to.'

'Yes, of course. Her name's Maggi?'

'Yes, Margrethe in full. But we called her Maggi for short. She couldn't walk the streets with the same name as the Queen of Denmark, could she!'

'No?'

'Eh?'

'It might have added a frisson for some.'

'For you perhaps?'

'No, I don't frequent prostitutes or such circles, if I may put it like that. What's her surname?'

'Monsen.'

I made a note. 'And she lives …?'

'She has a little flat in Strandgaten.'

'Does that mean she also takes clients home?'

'I suppose she does.'

'That's where you have your base?'

She nodded in silence and stared stiffly at me.

Hege Jensen … I tried to remember her. If she was the same age as Thomas she would be twenty-five or six. So it would be ten to twelve years since I had last seen her, and then in all probability *en passant* or at some school function. I didn't remember her parents at any rate. I had a vague memory that she might have been one of four girls who had performed a pop song at an end-of-school social, but I was not certain.

'Has anything special happened of late that gives you cause for concern?'

'Yes, that's just it. It was Friday evening. She turned down a trick.' Then, as though I might not have understood the jargon, she added, 'Refused a customer.'

'I see. That must happen from time to time, I would imagine, mustn't it?'

'Yes, it does, but her reaction was so violent. And then Tanya said she would take him instead.'

'Tanya?'

'Yes, one of the others … out there.'

'What happened next?'

'Well, she went with him and came back a few hours later, in floods of tears, battered and beaten. She had bruises everywhere and looked absolutely terrible! She said she would report him, not to the police but to … well, you know, and if either of them showed their face out there another time she would kill them herself, if she got the chance.'

'Them? She said *them*?'

She nodded.

'How did Maggi react to this?'

'Well, she wasn't there. Not then. She must have had a trick of her own. I don't know. I haven't seen her since!'

'You haven't seen her since this Tanya returned from her trick. Have I understood you correctly?'

'Yes, you have understood me correctly!' she exclaimed with impatience, as though she were talking to someone hard of hearing.

'OK, have you considered going to the police?'

'The cops?' She looked at me with contempt. 'Well, you know how they treat cases like this when it's about people like me and Maggi. Why d'you think I've come to you?'

'Did you know it was me? Thomas's father?'

She nodded, and for a moment or two a glimpse of childhood innocence seemed to flit across her face. 'He … We were walking along Strandkaien once and he pointed up to one of these windows, and then he said: "My father's got his office up there. He's a private detective."'

I felt a stab of melancholy in my abdomen, a sudden yearning for the son who had walked past underneath with a school friend and had pointed up to my window, but who dropped by all too seldom.

'Haven't we met at some point?'

'No, I don't think so. I never went to your house. And I remember his mother better than I remember … you.'

'Well … not so strange perhaps. But … back to the case. If she has in fact gone missing the police have quite a different set-up from mine.'

'Really? Don't you believe me?'

'Yes, I do, indeed I do. But … it hasn't been that long, has it. There may be a natural explanation for the whole thing. She didn't have any plans for the weekend, did she, for example?'

'No, imagine that. No, she did not! If she had she'd have told me beforehand.' She pushed back the chair as though intending to get up. 'Now tell me, are you going to take the job or not?'

I cast a glance at the expensive screen and reminded myself that there were still a few instalments to pay.

'Yes, I am. I can always try. But then I'll need some more information.'

'OK, shoot!'

'I need the precise address in Strandgaten. You wouldn't have a key for her flat, would you?'

She nodded. 'That's the reason I know she isn't there. We kept each other's house keys, in case something like this happened. That one of us might go missing.'

'Let's take a look afterwards then.'

'Us?' She threw me a quizzical glance.

'Yes, or I'll go alone.'

'That wasn't because … I was thinking more about you and … your reputation.'

'It's pretty tarnished already. One migratory bird more or less won't make much difference. What about her family, do you know them?'

She heaved a sigh of despair. 'You know girls like us don't exactly receive family visits at our workplace, and if we did it would spell trouble.'

'You mean …'

'No. In fact, brothers, fathers and uncles do show up out there to buy services, and then they bump into a little sister or a daughter or a niece. And that's not the half of it. When one of them comes to return their little darling to the nest there's a real rumpus.'

'But Maggi's family …'

'We talked about the hells we have come from now and again. What she came from was nothing to boast about, either. The father drank and the mother whinged. One brother's in the clink, and she said only the big sister has sort of coped.'

'Which part of town did she come from?'

She hesitated. 'From somewhere in Minde, I think. I'm not sure.'

'Is she on drugs?'

'What do you think? Why the hell do you think we're on the game? Because it's such great fun being fucked up the arse?'

I held my hands up in defence. 'Alright! But I do have to ask, don't I. You've given me a job to do, haven't you?!'

'Oh, yes? So you're taking it, are you? Positive?'

'I'll do my best anyway.' I made a few more notes. 'So that's the address, drugs, family … How do you go about it? To be blunt … I suppose you've got a pimp, have you?'

She eyed me with the same distance as when we started the conversation. 'We have someone who takes care of us, yes.'

'That was what you had in mind when Tanya threatened to report what had happened, someone different from the police.'

'They protect us when it's necessary, yes. There can be other groups who try to muscle in on our patches. Or crazy folk. They're queuing up out there, I can tell you that. Everything from drivers of trucks as big as mountains to embarrassed office workers in their tiny Starlets, so cramped it's tough to do a blowjob inside. And you never know who you'll meet, you never know who they are when they remove their masks.'

'These people who protect you, have they got names?'

Her eyes widened a fraction. 'I can't tell you that.'

'No?'

'No. You'll have to accept that.'

'Are they Norwegian?'

'Yes.'

I ruminated. 'These people Maggi turned down but Tanya agreed to go with … Do you know any more about them? Did she say anything? Tanya, that is.'

'Nothing in particular.'

'The name suggests … Is she Russian?'

'Yes.'

'Can you put me in touch with her?'

Suddenly she grinned. 'I'm sure she'll turn you a trick if that's what you're after …'

'No, that's not what I'm … How will I recognise her?'

'She's very red-haired, let me put it like that.'

'Dyed?'

She responded with arched eyebrows.

'Of course I'll pay her for the time it takes. While I'm on the subject …' I listened to the hum of the expensive hard disk under the desk. 'How will you pay?'

A fresh attempt at a smile, but stiffer this time. 'In kind?'

Her cynicism hit me harder than I had anticipated. I could have been her father. She had been in the same class as my son. Nonetheless she was willing to open the goodie bag, however well-used, even for me.

'Thanks, but no thanks. I prefer cash payments. Or I can fill in a banker's draft for you.' It would give my bank a minor shock if they noted some movement in the account, which had been drained down to rock bottom over the last few months, but I took the risk.

She nodded. 'Just fill it in and you'll get the money.'

'I'm afraid I'll have to ask for a small advance.'

'That's what we do, too. Afterwards you can never be sure.'

'Sounds like our professions aren't so far removed from each other.'

'No?'

'No.'

She opened her handbag and produced a few thousand-krone notes. I took them and gave her a receipt. Afterwards she gave me the key to Margrethe Monsen's flat in Strandgaten. 'You'll see *M. Monsen* on the door.'

'Thank you. I'll start there. How can I find you?'

She looked past me, towards Bryggen. 'Round and about.' She took out a mobile phone. 'You can have my number.'

I tapped it into mine.

'And here's mine.' I gave her a business card.

She read it and stuffed it in her bag. After a short pause she asked, somewhat hesitantly: 'How's Thomas?'

'He lives in Oslo. Goes to university there. They're planning to get married this summer. He and his girlfriend.'

Her mouth contorted, half smile, half grimace. 'Did you know we dated for a while?'

'No, I …' I rolled my chair back half a metre and gave a laconic smile. 'I could have been your father-in-law, in other words?'

'If a lot of things had been different, yes.'

'Why did it end?'

'Well …' She shrugged. 'I suppose these things happen.'

For a moment we sat in silence. We finished our coffee. Then she sighed and got up. 'So we've got a deal?'

'We have.'

I accompanied her to the door. Hege Jensen from Nye Sandviksvei. A migratory bird that had flown off course, much too early in her life, and way, way off course.

I met her gaze one more time. Then she walked towards the lift while I returned to my office, skimmed the few notes I had made, put my computer into hibernation, grabbed the notes and went out into the gloomy January daylight without any great hopes of success.

3

STRANDGATEN IS ONE OF Bergen's oldest streets. From one century to the next, it has wound its way from Torgallmennin-gen to Nordnes, followed buildings across the peninsula and been shaped by fires and other catastrophes.

The apartment block where Margrethe Monsen lived was in one of the quarters that had lain in ruins after the great explosions of 20 April 1944. I had grown up a few stone throws from there, and if my memory served me well, these blocks were built towards the latter end of the 1950s. At least there was an unmistakable 1950s feel to the entrance: black slate tiles on the floor, locked covers to the refuse shaft on each floor and blue doors with a narrow vertical window in matt wire glass. The front door was locked, but the flat key worked on this door as well.

I found the *M. Monsen* sign on the third floor. I could have taken the lift, but preferred the stairs. I rang the bell several times and stood waiting for a response. Nothing.

I heard someone come into the downstairs entrance and the lift machinery buzz into action straight afterwards. The lift stopped on the third floor, the door opened and a young woman with long, blonde hair pushed a little turbo-pram carrying an eighteen-month-old child in through the door.

She glanced at me, curious.

'I've just rung my sister-in-law's bell.' I nodded to the door. 'But she doesn't seem to be in.'

'No, it's a while since I've seen her.' She opened her bag and took out her key to the door on the opposite side.

'Mm, do you have any contact with her?'

'No, no, no,' she said without drawing breath. 'Besides we've only been here for a few months. And as you can see, we've got a tiny tot here to concentrate on.'

Tiny Tot responded at once with a few impatient grunts and movements, suggesting that he wanted to be out of the pram as soon as possible and to get started on the daily razing of the flat.

'I see.' I took out the key. 'I'll let myself in then to make sure everything is as it should be.'

She looked at me with a combination of suspicion and anxiety.

'My wife always keeps a spare key in case of emergency.'

'Yes, I suppose that would be wise.' She opened her door, pushed the pram in, nodded quickly and closed the door behind her. At once I heard the shrill howls of pleasure from indoors. The tiny tot was free: Run!

I inserted the key in the lock, twisted and stepped inside. For a moment I stood sniffing the air, but I couldn't smell anything suspicious and closed the door quietly after me.

I was in a very small hall, furnished with an old dresser. Above it hung an oval mirror and as I flicked on the light switch a flattering reddish glow descended over the room.

I opened the door to the right of me. It led into an oblong bathroom with a shower cabinet, toilet, sink, a medicine cupboard with a mirror at the front and a plastic basket for dirty laundry. I peered down. There were a few things there: panties, bras and a couple of blouses. At the back in one corner was a combined washing machine and drier. The door was open, and there was nothing inside.

I opened the medicine cupboard. Shampoo, ointment, hair lacquer, various boxes of painkillers, none of them prescriptions, nail varnish and varnish remover, mascara and lipstick. I found a box of propolis granules and opened it. The contents might appear to look like tiny concentrated lumps of hash, but when I gingerly tasted one of them I soon recognised the sharp flavour of the real McCoy. Beyond that there was nothing unusual present, more the opposite.

I went back into the hall. The next room I came to was the kitchen. It was small and narrow without space for much more than a unit, sink, fridge and dishwasher. Attached to the wall by the window was a small table, the kind that can be flipped up and secured with a bolt. There was a folding chair by the wall, but neither the chair nor the table seemed to have been used of late.

I opened the fridge. Not much of interest there, either. A few jars of jam, an unopened packet of sheep sausage, a dried-up bit of brown cheese. I closed the door at once. This was not where she put her heart and soul.

Through the hall I entered the sitting room. It was like most sitting rooms. The sound system was not as dominant as if there had been a man living here, and the TV was not the latest model. She had a few shelves of CDs and cassettes, but no books. There were some weekly magazines and a couple of newspapers strewn over the floor beyond the shabby coffee table, and the chairs looked as if they had been collected from the Sally Army shop, Fretex, one rainy day fifteen years ago. But the stains were more likely to be from beer and spirits than rain, I feared.

It struck me that there was not a single picture hanging on the walls. There were a few plants in the window, but when I went over to inspect them I saw that they were artificial and covered with a thin layer of dust.

Out of habit I cast a glance behind the threadbare sofa. Someone had stuffed a blue Fjord Line bag there. I bent over, picked it up and peered inside. It contained some scrunched-up plastic bags, the type you get in supermarkets. SuperBrug-sen ones, not that I was any the wiser, all I knew was that at some point she had caught a ferry to Denmark and had been shopping. Perhaps she had even been working on it, an activity that was far from unusual, according to what I had been told. In the bar on the Danish ferry morals were free and wallets even freer. If you were the diligent kind you could fit a handful of cabin visits into a journey.

The door to the adjacent room was ajar. I opened it wide and paused in the doorway.

This was the room where she had invested most of herself. The bed was broad and large. There was a soft carpet on the floor, and the walls were covered in red velvet wallpaper with a silk lily pattern. In the corner of the room was a tall, dark brown wardrobe. I walked over and turned the key. Two doors unfolded. There was a tall mirror on the inside of each one, and from the poles hung a variety of outfits, most black, imaginatively designed and with a selection of openings, all according to your taste.

I went to the bed and folded the quilt to one side. The linen looked nice and fresh. But even here there were no pictures on the walls. To me this seemed more like a workplace than a home. The first thing I had to find out was whether she had another address.

There did not seem to be any personal effects in any part of the flat, unless ...

I went back to the hall and opened the drawers in the dresser, one by one. The top ones contained nothing more than a couple of headscarves and some handkerchiefs. The bottom one contained what I was looking for: several large envelopes, a small photo album, a pile of prescriptions, certificates and other papers.

I riffled through the papers. I was unable to find a driving licence, if she had one, a passport or any other kind of ID. Most were old invoices, prescriptions for a selection of medicines, some of them names I knew, others I didn't. Most seemed to be sedatives and sleeping tablets of various strengths.

I opened the small photo album. It had a dark red plastic cover and an old Tourist Office photo of Bryggen, the German wharf area of Bergen, on the outside. With a text: *Greetings from Bergen.*

Most of the photographs were black-and-white, some newer ones were colour. The same woman appeared in the majority of them. As a young girl she had been photographed in a street I could not immediately place, but seemed to be somewhere in Bergen. Further in, there were a few photos taken in booths and a handful of very shaky pictures of her sitting in festive company in what must have been Børs Café. A couple of beach holiday snaps from somewhere in Southern Europe, with her sitting at a little table in front of an umbrella cocktail, smirking at the photographer.

In some of the early pictures there were other children, but whether they were brothers and sisters or friends was hard to say. Many of the photos were taken on a slope with a white building in the background. If I was not mistaken it was Lea Park with Lea Hall in the background, or Solhaug School, as it was called in my days. In which case Hege was right when she thought Margrethe came from the Minde district of Bergen.

The solitary photograph showing adults was a summery shot taken somewhere in the country, in front of a cabin and with high mountains in the background. It could have been anywhere in Vestland from Ryfylke, south of Bergen, to Nordfjord, north of Bergen. The small girl I assumed to be Margrethe was sitting with two other children, a boy and a girl, at a long wooden table, with five adults, three men and two women, all in their late thirties. It was a fair assumption that two of them were her parents, the others perhaps uncles and aunts, and the two children were her brother and sister. Everyone was smiling for the photographer, and there was a relaxed atmosphere of sun and summer about the small photo, snapped at a time when everything appeared to be better and no one was looking fifteen to twenty years ahead.

The little album was the right size to fit in my coat pocket, and I decided there and then to take it.

I was casting a final gaze around the room when I saw shadows through the windowpane in the apartment door. A second later there was a long, shrill ring at the door.

I held my breath. What should I do? Who could it be? And what did they want? I hoped they would go away if no one opened up. But they did not. They did the same as I would have done. They let themselves in.

4

FOR A MOMENT we stood gawping. One of them closed the door behind them, hard. 'And who the hell do we have here then? Father Christmas?'

The other grinned. I knew the routine. Abbott & Costello. And they always came in two formats.

The taller of the two spoke. He was approximately forty years old, one ninety tall, broad-shouldered and wearing a dark, half-length winter coat, as though he had just come from the latest board meeting at the bank. The one grinning looked more like his gofer. He was wearing a leather jacket and blue jeans and had a thick, greyish scarf knotted around his neck. Neither was a charmer, in my book.

I realised that in this situation it was important to take the initiative. I stepped forward, proffered my hand and introduced myself as Henriksen from social security.

Big Boy regarded my hand with disdain, as though his greatest dream would be to break it in half. 'Social security. And what the hell …?'

'Do you know *frøken* Monsen, by any chance? Since you have the key to her flat, I mean.'

He came one step closer, and I became aware of the strong, somewhat too sweet aroma of his aftershave. 'Let's see some ID then, *herr* Henriksen from social security.'

I met his gaze. 'What was your name, did you say?'

The lean gofer glanced nervously at Big Boy.

'That's none of your bloody business.'

'In that case, my ID is none of your bloody business. But we can phone the police if you're uncertain about which of us has most to lose.'

'Kjell,' said Little Boy.

'Shut up!'

Kjell glowered at me. Then he placed his hands flat on my chest and pushed me hard. 'And what is social security doing here?'

I regained my balance and retreated into the sitting room to have greater freedom of movement. Both of them followed. Little Boy positioned himself in the doorway. Kjell followed me in.

'There are reasonable grounds for suspicion,' I said. 'To assume an illegal income, for example.'

He widened his eyes. 'Illegal income?'

'Do you know *frøken* Monsen? Do you know how she makes her living?'

'You, Henriksen ... I don't think the authorities have any business sniffing into ...' He came to a halt. 'How did you get in by the way?'

I knew that I was skating on thin ice. 'I was lent a key ... by the family.'

'Rolf ...'

The signal he gave had been clear enough, but Rolf was faster than I had expected. He circled round behind his friend. In an instant he had a flick-knife in his hand. He came straight for me, pushed me to the wall with one arm and placed the blade against my larynx, so firmly that I had difficulty breathing. 'Don't move!' he wheezed into my ear. 'If you do ...'

Kjell arced round behind him. 'Slash him if he makes so

much as one unexpected move!' he ordered. 'In the meantime let's check out who he is, whether he likes it or not.'

He stuffed a hand inside my jacket and groped for inside pockets. He unzipped one and fished out my wallet. Then he took a few steps back and began to rifle through it.

It wasn't long before there came a protracted whistling sound. 'Henriksen, hm, as it were. From social security.'

He held up my certificate and Visa card. 'In which case, who do these belong to? Have you stolen them?'

Rolf glanced to the side. 'What do they say, Kjell? What's his name?'

'Veum, it says. Varg Veum. And here he even has some business cards. Varg Veum, private investigator, Strandkaien 2. Social security, my arse!'

'A private dick? What the hell he's doing here?'

'Well, we can ask him.'

'Yes, you haven't quite cut my vocal cords yet,' I garbled in a forced voice, then felt the pressure from the knife blade relax a touch.

'What the hell are you doing here, Veum?'

'The same as you, I would guess. Looking for Maggi.'

'And under whose instructions?'

' … The family's.'

'The family? Don't make me laugh. They've never given a toss.'

'The sister,' I said.

'The sister?' Kjell looked at Rolf, who shrugged. Then he turned back to me. 'And what was it that caused her to miss darling Maggi all of a sudden?'

'If Rolfie boy could shift the knife a little perhaps it might be possible to have a rather more civilised conversation.'

'Veum, the conversations we have are seldom very civilised. Especially not when people get in our way.'

'I could ask you the very same question. What the hell are you doing here? Who gave you the right to break into other people's property?'

Kjell sneered. 'Other people's property? And who the hell do you think owns this property? Maybe you would like to see the rental contract?'

'So you're the person responsible for these inviting interior furnishings?'

'What's that supposed to mean? Don't you like it here? This wonderful ...' He broke off as his gaze fell on the blue Fjord Line bag which I had left on the sofa after establishing that it was empty. He strode over, opened it and drew the same conclusion. When he turned back to me, his eyes were small and menacing. 'Tell me ... It wasn't you who emptied this, was it?'

'Emptied what? It was empty when I came.'

'Sure?'

I looked at Rolf. His eyes were alert and sly. 'Would you mind removing the knife?' The nature of his gaze changed. A flash of humour appeared, and he recited: '*He who fain the blood of another must early go forth; the wolf that lies idle shall win little lamb meat, or the slumbering man success.*'

'Eh?'

'Did that go over your head, Veum?' Kjell said. 'Rolf is well read, you know.'

'At any rate, I am not looking for lamb meat.'

'No? What for then?' He held the blue bag in the air. 'What do you know about this, Veum?'

'What is there to know?' When he didn't answer I added: 'Nothing.'

'What do you know about Maggi?'

'Listen to me … She's been missing since Friday. The family is worried.'

'The family doesn't give a flying fuck!'

'A woman friend then!'

'Ah, I see! Now we're getting closer. One of the other girls?'

I shrugged. 'Anyway, it's my job to find her.'

He fixed me with a stern look. 'But we're worried too, Veum. She hasn't paid her rent, let me put it like that.'

'And how often does she pay? Every day or once a week?'

'We have a fixed agreement, and she hasn't kept her part of the bargain since …'

'Friday?'

'Something like that.'

'Is subletting allowed in this housing co-op?'

He snorted. 'Now let me give you a piece of good advice, Veum.'

'I can't afford it.'

'Eh?'

'I already know what you're going to say.'

'And that is?'

'*Witless man lies awake all night, thinking hither and thither,*' Rolf interrupted.

'That'll do,' Kjell said. 'He doesn't understand anyway. Press the knife into his neck a little harder so that he understands the seriousness of what I'm about to say.'

Rolf followed orders. He pressed the blade in and up so that I had to climb onto my toes to avoid being cut. 'Stop!' I groaned.

'Listen carefully, Veum. You can go back to whoever gave you this assignment and say you're calling off the whole thing.

You couldn't find Maggi anywhere, her flat was empty and she's bound to get in touch when she returns from … wherever it is she's staying.'

'And where's that supposed to be? A holiday? You are aware, are you, that a punter scared her a couple of days ago?'

Again his eyes narrowed. 'A punter? How do you know?'

I didn't answer.

'How do you know, I said! Rolf …' He motioned to Rolf to press harder. I could feel my skin was on the point of giving.

'You saw my card. I'm a private investigator. This is how I work.'

'You've been sniffing round the area?'

'I heard that Maggi had been frightened by a punter, so frightened that she refused a trick with him. If there weren't two of them, that is. Another woman took her job and was beaten black and blue.'

'Another woman? Who?'

'I wasn't given a name.' I saw no reason to give it to him.

'And when was this supposed to have happened?'

'On Friday.'

'Friday.' He looked at Rolf, who relaxed the pressure on the knife a little. 'Have you heard about this?'

'No. *Witless man who strays …*'

'That'll do, I said!'

'In other words … If we could start by finding out who the guys were …'

'You, Veum, won't be finding out anything at all. If people hear that there's a private dick snooping around the district, the place'll be as deserted as the far side of the moon.'

'People?'

'You've been warned. If you set foot here again …'

'At the moment I walk around Nordnes at least a couple of times a week.'

'If you try to contact any of the girls …'

'Ah, you've got more tenants, in other words?'

'In short, if our paths cross again you'll be up shit creek. Is that clear?'

'As clear as *The Moonbeam*, but not quite as wonderful.'

'Rolf, slice him!'

Again Rolf demonstrated his agility with the knife. The pressure on my larynx went for a second or two as the knife was swung round and I felt a smarting pain down my neck, where with one fast, efficient slash he had cut a line down from my ear to my collarbone. Not deep. Not serious. But sharp enough for me to have to use my handkerchief to stem the flow.

Kjell slung my wallet over, at such a speed I had trouble catching it. He grinned. 'Got the message, Veum? Next time it'll be deeper. Right to the hilt. Show him out!'

Rolf did as his lord and master instructed. On the way out I mumbled: '*Cattle die, kith die …*'

'*… you die too in the end,*' he mumbled back, then opened the door and shoved me roughly onto the landing.

Before I had turned he had slammed the door behind me.

5

I HUNG AROUND FOR A WHILE until the blood on my neck had dried. Behind the door on the opposite side I heard irascible screams coming from the tiny tot, but not irascible enough for me to ring the bell and demonstrate my childcare background. Behind M. Monsen's door I heard muffled sounds that suggested they had already started putting the flat in order for the next tenant. Or were they searching for something? But I didn't ring to offer them a helping hand.

I sauntered down the stairs and back into the most sterile part of Strandgaten. In the quarter between Nykirken Church and Tollbodallmenningen there was little to feast your eyes on apart from the sale at the vinmonopol on the opposite side, and I supposed that would not be for long, sad to say. A plaque on the wall beyond announced that Edvard Grieg's childhood home was here. Sontums Hotel had been situated in Tollbodallmenningen, where Ibsen had been accommodated when he moved to Bergen in 1851, but there was not much cultural life in the area any more, apart from the odd buck-ride with a forlorn Anitra. Nowadays it was ticking parking meters that characterised the streetscape. I was glad I was on foot and didn't have to keep an eye on my watch.

I took out my mobile, rang Karin Bjørge's work number and asked if she fancied a meal out today. She riposted: 'And what are you after this time then?'

'Well, I was wondering if you would mind checking a name for me.'

'What a surprise. And it would be …?'

'Margrethe Monsen, born around 1970, I would guess. Grew up in Minde possibly.'

'You're as precise as always, I see. What do you need?'

'Most of all, factual details. Addresses and whatever you can dig up about closest family.'

'How many generations back?' She made no attempt to conceal the sarcasm.

'Parents are enough.'

'And where were you planning to invite me, did you say?'

'Pascal's?'

'Let's go for that then. After work.'

'Half past four?'

We agreed and rang off. I looked at my watch. That gave me a few hours. But until I had something concrete to search for there was little I could do.

I decided to check out Kjell and Rolf a bit more. I glanced at the front door I had just left. I assumed they were not going to spend the rest of the day there. But this part of the street did not offer much in the way of shelter or camouflage, unless you were a car or a traffic warden. I could have crossed the street and queued outside the vinmonopol of course, and shifted places in the queue until Kjell and Rolf emerged, but the problem was that early on a Monday morning in January there were no queues, so I would have stood out like a sore thumb.

They solved the problem by making a personal appearance. Catching sight of me, they came to an abrupt halt. Kjell said a few words to Rolf before making a beeline in my direction.

He stopped in front of me. 'Didn't I tell you to hop it?'

I pointed to the pavement at our feet. 'This is public

property, Kjell Boy. The flat up there belongs to you, doesn't it?' I pointed again, to avoid any misunderstandings.

'And don't call me Kjell Boy!'

'But Kjell Boy … We haven't been properly introduced. Tell me your surname and I'll address you according to conventional etiquette.'

A large, black Mercedes pulled up. With a grinning Rolf at the wheel.

Kjell looked deep into my eyes once more. 'Veum … I am warning you for the last time. Don't tread on my toes. You will regret it!'

He turned around, strode over to the car, tore open the rear door and plumped down heavily on the commodious seat. Rolf saluted with a neutral hand to his forehead, and the car shot forward.

I made a hasty note of the number, first of all in my head, then on my notepad. Before they had passed Nykirken Church I had rung the Vehicle Licensing Agency.

The car was owned by a firm called Malthus Invest. What they invested in was not clear from the name, but it was obviously everything from property to what they would no doubt prefer to call the entertainment industry.

I walked through the pedestrian zone back to my office. I looked out of the corner of my eye at the black screen, which had now allowed the dancing windows to rest, wondering vaguely whether the Internet could have assisted me here. However, I found it safest to get out the telephone directory and leaf through. That, it transpired, was enough.

Malthus Invest had an office in Markeveien. Thus they could have saved the Mercedes the trip to Nordnes. They also had a central switchboard number, but I considered it inappropriate to bother Kjell Boy any further at this juncture, so I was content to store his number on my mobile for possible later use.

There was one person in Bergen with the surname Malthus. Oddly enough, his first name was Kjell. His home address was in Fyllingsdalen. Street called Storhammeren, although that didn't mean much to me.

The telephone directory was a tool I had used a lot during my years as a private detective. I sat flicking through it.

I couldn't find anyone called Margrethe Monsen. Nor, for that matter, Hege Jensen. Either they didn't have a landline or they had a private number. I glanced at the screen again, but still I didn't feel competent enough to use the Internet for detective work. A meal at Pascal's was much more my style.

That may have been why I arrived half an hour before the agreed time. It gave me a chance to have a glass of beer and skim through one of the day's newspapers. I read that the number of Norwegians with access to the Internet had passed a million. Around two hundred thousand people were online every day. In other words, I was not alone out there. In some miraculous way my office had become connected to the rest of the world, and a familiar refrain had been buzzing in my head for some time: *You'll never walk alone* ...

Karin did not have far to walk either and she entered from Valkendorfs gate on the dot. She was wearing a coat and boots, with nothing on her head. She had shaken her umbrella before entering, and bridled at the terrible weather. 'My God, Varg! Have you seen the floods!'

I nodded. The water was streaming down the gutters, and the last remnants of snow from the morning were now gone.

I gave her a hug, helped her off with her coat and pulled out a chair for her. I was so conspicuously gallant that she peered up at me and said: 'And just what is it you're working so hard for?'

'What have you got to offer?' I grinned, taking my place opposite her while an observant waiter dashed up with a menu.

'I thought *you* were treating *me*?'

'Here, yes, I am.'

Our eyes met, the way two old friends pass on the street and stop for a chat because it has been such a long time.

We soon decided what we wanted and agreed to share a half-bottle of red with the meal, as we were in a French mood. While we waited for the food to arrive she pulled out a print-out of some notes. 'This is what I found.'

I looked at her expectantly. 'The info did the trick?'

'The info? A shot in the dark I would call it.'

'But …'

'Yes, you fusspot. I found one Margrethe Monsen with a Minde address, born on 14 April 1970. Falsens vei, if that means anything to you.'

'Vaguely.'

'Parallel to Inndalsveien. A friend of mine lived there once years ago.'

'Right. Is that her present address?'

'She hasn't officially moved at any rate.'

'No address in Nordnes?'

'Not officially, as I said.'

'And her parents?'

'Frank and Else Monsen, née Nybø. But her father's dead, died four years ago. An older sister, Siv, born in 1968, and a brother, Karl Gunnar, born in 1972.'

'Addresses?'

'The mother has the same address as Margrethe. Falsens vei.

Siv lives in Landås, in Kristofer Jansons vei, and the brother's in prison.'

'What?'

'At any rate he has an address at Bergen Prison, and that's what it tends to mean.' She passed me the sheet across the table. 'You'll find everything there.'

'Thank you very much. If I didn't have you I don't know what I would do.'

'Find something else to do maybe.'

'Yes, perhaps.'

The food arrived, and we dug in. She had ordered pork fillet, I chose salted beef. I told her about the little I had to go on, so far. She listened attentively, with a sad expression on her face. I knew why. She was thinking about Siren. We were both thinking about Siren, Karin's sister who had taken the same route as Margrethe and died of it, ten or eleven years ago.

'I hope you find her, Varg.'

'I hope so, too.'

'Alive.'

'Yes …'

After the meal we drank coffee, and at length she said: 'Are you coming back to my place?'

I caressed her hand. 'If you could let the offer stand for a few hours.'

'By which you mean?'

'I have to drive to the red light district first.'

She arched her eyebrows. 'What have they got that I haven't?'

'That's what I intend to find out. But I'm interested in the information, nothing else.'

'And you think you'll get it for nothing?'

'Doubt it.'

She sighed. 'Well, well. I suppose it's a kind of job, too.'

'But the offer's still open?'

'Till midnight, if you're still interested.'

I paid the bill, and we parted by the sixteenth-century building known as Muren. She walked down Strandkaien to catch the bus. I headed for C. Sundts gate to see if I could get a nibble. To each his own, said the proverbial fox, and in Norway he ended up skinned.

6

THE RED LIGHT DISTRICT in Bergen had moved over the years. In olden times it was around Øvregaten where seamen, monks, members of the Hanseatic League and the town's own citizens had beaten a path up the back stairs to the first floor of the local taverns and hostelries. In the nineteenth century most of the goings-on were to be found in Nøstet until the very last brothel was closed by the police during a major raid in 1875.

In the 1950s and 60s the most obvious signs of street activity were in Strandgaten. After the number of cars increased and the circle of clients became more mobile, business moved out further to Nordnes, to C. Sundts gate, where there is still an abundance of freelance working girls to be seen, from early afternoon to late at night.

For someone who had frequented this area more often than most, though for strictly professional purposes, there was nothing glamorous about this industry. The number of young girls I had found there was not small, from my time in child welfare to the years as a private investigator. For some of them, things had worked out fine. A depressingly high number had been immune to help. So as to get money for the daily dose of drugs they did whatever had to be done with whomever, often for a lower price when competition became too fierce. Market forces held sway in this business as well.

The furthest end of C. Sundts gate was Bergen's answer to

Ålesund – or vice versa. The area from Muren to Holbergsall-menning burned down in 1901, Ålesund in 1904, and several of the same architects were involved in the reconstruction. Art nouveau-style dominated. The construction work did not start until after the Second World War as the explosion of a Dutch ship in April 1944 had flattened the whole area.

A solitary man driving at a snail's pace down C. Sundts gate one windy night in January aroused the fullest attention on all sides. No sooner had I opened the window than I had the day's hottest offers raining down around my ears, in loud falsetto to drown the competitors.

The women gathering round my car were plastered with make-up, wore skirts so short they were damaging to their health and were aged from seventeen to thirty-something, as far as I was able to judge. The youngest was the most modest in self-promotion; the others cackled like a coven of witches on their way to the Midsummer Eve celebrations on Mt Lyderhorn.

'I'm looking for Tanya,' I said.

'Tanya! The Russian slut!'

'What the hell d'you think she's got …'

'… that we haven't.'

On that point they were in total harmony, the whole bunch of them. But their hasty looks further up the street betrayed them. On the quay outside Nykirken Church there was a girl standing on her own, thin with very red dyed hair.

'Thank you for the offers,' I mumbled, rolling up the window to the accompaniment of displeased rejoinders and slighted bangs on the car roof.

I accelerated and pulled into the kerb by her. I rolled down the window on the opposite side. She bent forward and peered in. Her eyes were nervous. Even though she had not stinted with make-up there were clear marks of punches to her face, round her eyes and on her chin, still swollen from the beating.

'Tanya?'

'What d'you want?' She spoke Norwegian with a slight accent and clear influence of Finnmark dialect.

'Hege said I should talk to you.'

'Talk?' She opened her mouth and ran her tongue lingeringly over her lips in a way that made it clear she was ready for a lot more than talking.

'I'll pay the full price.'

'Full price for what?'

I sent a silent prayer to my contact at the City Treasury who would be assessing my claim. 'A trick.'

'Wow! Have you won the lottery?'

'Are you coming?'

She measured me with her eyes for a few more seconds. Then she changed her intonation. 'I'm comin'! Course I'm comin'!'

She opened the door, pulled her short skirt so far up that I could have checked whether she still had an appendix, and spread her legs. I glimpsed black panties with dark red lace and a slit with a dark red border.

'Seat belt. Safety comes first,' I said.

'Not with me it doesn't,' she said, revealing a row of tiny teeth with brown edges.

I shrugged and put my foot down. She grasped my thigh, high up. As I went to move her hand she resisted. 'Gotta have something to hold onto!'

'Yes, but not the gearstick, alright?'

'Bastard!'

I didn't drive far. At the top of Nordnesbakken I turned

right into what once had been the terminus for the Nordnes bus. The square was dark, lit by a few scattered streetlamps. In the summer, benches were put out here so that people could sit with a view across Byfjorden. Now it was winter, dark and cold, and the sole view there was the smashed diadem above Askøy bridge and the distant lights.

She looked as if she had been there before. 'Where do you want to take me? On the back seat?'

I unfastened my seat belt. 'I'd like to talk, I said.'

'Yes, but I didn't bloody believe that! Talk!' She closed her legs at once, made a vain attempt to pull her skirt down and glowered at me. ''Bout what?'

'About the trick you had last Friday. The trick Maggi refused.'

She was out of the door almost before I could think, but I grabbed her arm, yanked her back in and held on tight.

'What the hell do you want? You a cop or what?'

'No. Calm down! I'm not going … to do anything to you.'

She wriggled like a wild cat in my arms, detached one hand and struck out at my face with sharp nails. I grabbed her wrist and twisted it round. The horn went off, and I pressed her head against the car door, locked her in a half nelson and forced her down. Despite this she continued to fight. 'I'll scream! I will!'

'I said I'd pay you for Christ's sake! Full tariff! What I need is some information.'

'I'm not saying nothin'. I want double!'

'OK, OK! I'll pay you double!' The tax collector will rub his hands with glee when he reads my expense claims.

She calmed down. Slowly I released my grip, and she sat up. She glared at me and held out a palm. 'I wanna see the cash!'

I gave her what she demanded, thereby emptying my wallet. 'Can we make a start?'

'How do you want to take me, I asked. On the rear seat?'
But this time there was a scornful glint in her eye.

'You're fine where you're sitting, aren't you?'

'So so.' She pulled up the edge of her skirt so that I could see
what I was missing.

'The trick. You remember it, I gathered.'

She nodded. Her mouth tightened.

'Maggi refused it. Have you any idea why?'

She shrugged demonstratively and thrust out her arms.
'What do I know! I told her. If the boys hear she's got so uppity
she turns down a trick she's in serious hot water!'

'The boys?'

There was another contemptuous glint in her eyes. 'I think
you know what I mean!'

I nodded, and she went on: 'But she stuck to her guns, and
then she said she wouldn't be here long. She was slinging her
hook, she said.'

'Uhuh! Did she say anything else?'

'Nope. Just you wait and see, she said.'

'And maybe she was right, quicker than anyone imagined.'

Again she shrugged. 'What do I know?'

'But the trick … Tell me about it.'

Once more her mouth tightened, and her face seemed to
darken, as if a shadow had fallen over it. She sat hushed, staring
down.

With some circumspection, I said: 'Are you … afraid?'

She glanced up at me. 'Afraid? Me?'

'Listen, Tanya. Even today you're still carrying the marks of
your ordeal. I know you were beaten up. It's important you tell
me what happened. Who were they?'

Another shrug of the shoulders, but not quite as energetic

this time. 'Two guys.' After a brief pause she added: 'But only one did me. The other one waited, round the next corner. When I found out I tried to get away, but the one in the front seat held me down, and the one who got in the back slipped a rope round my neck and threatened to tighten it!'

I could feel myself beginning to boil with anger. 'Were they Norwegians?'

'As Norwegian as Satan himself!'

'How old?'

'Mm … Two old fellas. Way over fifty.'

'Thank you …'

'But not criminals, not as such. No competitors for the boy. No, these were two fine old gents out on the town to beat up a tart because they can't do it to her indoors.'

'Where did they take you?'

'Not far. Down to where the Hurtigruten cruises go, one of the quays there. The one at the back tightened the rope while the one at the front pulled up my skirt, tore my panties off and raped me, with his fist. "You need a real whammer, you do," he said. "What? Can't you get it up?" I said, but I should never have said that because that was when he started on me. He hit me again and again, while the one at the back breathed into my ear. I think he was getting off on it from bloody watching. Afterwards they dragged me out and shoved me onto the back seat, face down, and one of them took me from behind. I thought I was going to tear. Because a girl's a prostitute they shouldn't bloody treat you like shit, should they? Eh?'

'Not at all. But this isn't the first time this has happened, and it won't be the last. You know that.'

I thought of Hege, who had been in the same class as Thomas. I thought about Siren whom I had known once, and

Eva-Beate. The number of women who had been subjected to the sort of treatment Tanya had described was not small. They were in the grey area between law and law-breaking and as such easy game for brutes of all kinds, from notorious criminals to top civil servants with an unfulfilled need to make their mark.

'The one that took you … like that, was that the person in the front of the car?'

'I think so. Because I had to give the other one a blowjob in the end, and he was a real limpdick, I'm tellin' you. Not much bloody life in 'im.'

'And then …?'

'Well, in the end they closed up my eyes with a few punches and said if I breathed a word to anyone they'd be back to kill me, I could be damn sure of that! I was scared out of my wits. For a while I thought they were gonna do it there and then, but then they gave up, kicked me out of the car and screeched off. I ambled back down the street, but I didn't take any more soddin' tricks that night, I went home and took a massive dose of pills so that I could sleep.'

I looked at her battered face. She didn't look so cocky now, after being reminded of her terrible experience.

'But … did you ask Maggi who they were? Could she have had the same done to her before?'

'I haven't seen 'er since, have I! She took off like a rabbit!'

'Right … What about the car they were driving? Would you recognise it?'

She rolled her shoulders. 'It was black. That's all I remember. Oh, and the three first numbers.'

'Ri-ight! And they were …?'

'There was an SP first, followed by 523. I remember that

because the last two add up to the first number, if you know what I mean. I'm not a hundred per cent sure about them, though.'

I noted down the numbers on my pad. 'Tell me, Tanya. These boys you were talking about, are they the same ones that take care of Hege and Maggi?'

She tossed her head; that was her response.

'Kjell and Rolf?'

I could see in her eyes that I had hit the bullseye, but she didn't answer.

'If so, have you told them what happened?'

She hesitated. 'That Rolf came and asked. They'd heard a rumour, and he could see the state I was in.'

'OK. How did he react?'

'Well, a bit like you. Asked questions, did some digging, about who they could have been and what car they drove. Said if they came again I should refuse to go, but take their number and they would deal with them.'

'Exactly.'

'Yes!' She almost looked indignant. 'They're s'posed to be looking after us! It's their job!'

'What a job!'

'Tell me about it. Who are you anyway? What have you got to do with all this?'

'Name's Veum, and I'm a private investigator.'

'Private investigator!'

I took out a card and gave it to her. 'I'm looking for Maggi.'

'So she has gone missing?'

'Looks like it. When she told you she was going away … did she mention where?'

'No. I thought she was just dreamin', the way we all do from time to time.'

'Mm.' I fastened the seat belt again and pointed to the card in her hand. 'Should you remember something later, you can find me there.'

She glanced at the card and nodded.

'I'll drive you back then. If that's where you want to go.'

'Yes, unless you want … after all you've paid!'

'Not tonight, thank you,' I said with a crooked smile.

As we were driving back I asked: 'How long have you been in Norway?'

'I've got a work permit, if that's what you're wonderin'!'

'Oh yes? In the fish filleting industry?'

'Exactly!'

'You speak good Norwegian anyway!'

'Thank you. I picked it up using the natural method, as they say.'

'Yes, it's supposed to be the best.'

I dropped her off at Tollbodallmenningen. I remained in the car and watched her until she disappeared round the corner towards C. Sundts gate. I didn't like the thought of what she was going back to, but there was nothing I could do, not tonight. It was a free country, for most of us. Freedom had a price, though. Some paid the highest rates, and it was seldom those who could best afford them.

Then I put the car into gear and drove to Fløenbakken, where Karin was waiting for me with hot tea and a little something extra. But I was not in the mood. Not for that either. I had an uneasy feeling inside, an icicle in my heart.

Before we went to bed, I borrowed her telephone directory. I couldn't find Else Monsen. There was an entry for Siv Monsen at the address Karin had found. I rang the number, but no one answered. I left a message on her answer phone, without saying what my call was about, but she didn't ring back.

I let it go at that, but I was impatient to get started. I knew from bitter experience that time was a thief. When you arrived where you wanted to go it was often too late. The following morning I got up with Karin and was in my office before eight o'clock.

7

THE FIRST THING I DID was to ring Siv Monsen again. This time she answered, out of breath, as though she had been running. 'Yes, hello. Siv here.'

'My name's Veum. I tried to get hold of you last night, but …'

'Yes, I got the message, but it was too late to ring back. What's this about?'

'Your sister, Margrethe.'

Silence for a few seconds. 'Yes? Is there anything the matter?'

'I hope not. You haven't heard from her?'

'… not for a few days, no. What … What was your name, did you say?'

'Veum. I'm a private investigator.'

'Private …'

'Could she be at your mother's?'

'My mother's? I doubt that.'

'Hasn't she got a telephone?'

'Who? Margrethe?'

'Your mother.'

'No. We've … She's never had one. Listen, I'm on my way to work, and I've got a bus to catch.'

'Could we meet?'

'Meet? I'm going to work. I've just told you.'

'Where do you work?'

She mentioned the name of the same insurance company

in Fyllingsdalen I did assignments for now and then.

'Well, I'll drop by. Perhaps we could have a chat during your lunch break?'

'No, not there, but ... There's a café in the Oasen mall. Right by the market. We can meet at twelve.'

'Great. How will I recognise you?'

'I'm blonde and have a red coat. I can sit with *Bergensavisen* open in front of me.'

'Not the most original idea, that, but fine. I'll find you. I'll be the middle-aged man with grizzled hair desperately looking around.'

'I have to get my skates on.'

She rang off, and I sat with the receiver in my hand for a moment, before putting it down gently as if it were a raw egg.

So far, so good.

The next call was to the Vehicle Licensing Agency. Where they were not as accommodating as they had been on the previous occasion. The lady answering the phone was as cheerful as a funeral director on Good Friday. Although I claimed I was ringing about a collision it was impossible for her to give me all the car registrations beginning with SP-523. She invoked the Data Protection Act and recommended I contact the police first. If an accident had been reported and they had received an enquiry, she might view the matter in a different light. I tried to argue but before I was halfway into what I had planned to say she had put the phone down. No funerals at Easter; we appreciate your understanding.

The third call I made was to an old colleague in social services, who was now in the Norwegian Correctional Services, Per Helge Brubak. At once he sounded a bit more cheerful. 'Hi there, Varg! To what do I owe the honour?'

'I was wondering if you knew a fellow called Karl Gunnar Monsen.'

'KG, yes.'

'KG?'

'That's what they call him. In his community.'

'And he's in prison?'

'For the time being, yes.'

'What's he in for?'

He hesitated. 'What's this about, Varg?'

'I'm really just collecting background information. He's got a sister who's gone missing, and … well, some people are worried.'

'Which of the sisters is that?'

'You know them?'

'By repute alone. Through KG.'

'This one's called Margrethe and she works on C. Sundts gate if you get my drift. Not at one of the offices, though.'

'OK. I'm with you.'

'Well, as I said … what's he in for?'

'You'll remember the case if I mention it, but his name was never made public, so … the Gimle case.'

'Gimle as in Gimle School?'

'Yes, there was a teaching assistant who was pawing some of the boys in PE, and one of them – KG – reacted with violence. Over-reacted some would say.'

'He killed him, didn't he?'

'Yes. Hit him on the head with a dumbbell until … well, he was left lying there. With his head caved in.'

'How old was he?'

'KG? Sixteen and a half.'

'How long ago was that?'

'Eight years.'

'And how long was his sentence?'

'He's been in therapy for the whole period, and he's approaching the end of his sentence now. He attends classes in town and his rehab is almost over.'

'I see. Do you know if he has any contact with his sisters?'

'With the elder one, yes. But not much. You know where the other sister has ended up. I would guess we're dealing with a relatively difficult upbringing here.'

'Do you know any specifics?'

'No, he's always been quite closed. Hard to get close to. Unless we talked about football.' He sang the Bergen football song refrain: '*Hei-a Bra-ann!*'

'Do you think he would talk to me?'

'What about? I cannot imagine he knows what's happened to his sister.'

'I suppose not, but could you ask him for me?'

'By all means! I can ask.'

'Thank you. Ring me when you have an answer.' I gave him my mobile phone number and then, as an afterthought, my email address.

The last person I rang was Cathrine Leivestad, with whom I worked for the last year at social services. She had changed offices and was now in the Outreach Centre for prostitutes. I asked if she would have any time if I popped round.

'What's the problem?'

'Maggi Monsen Margrethe. Does that name mean anything to you?'

'I know who she is, yes.'

'She's disappeared.'

'Really! But what …?'

'You know the type of milieu she grew up in, and one of her

– let's say colleagues – has initiated a search for her. I thought you might be able to give me some background details, about her and some others …'

'And you were thinking of …?'

'Two guys I bumped into. One called Kjell Malthus, the other Rolf.'

Her voice took on a bitter edge. 'Great. We know both of them as well.'

'In a nutshell …?'

'I'm afraid I don't have any time until tomorrow, Varg. I've got meetings until late evening today.'

'When tomorrow then?'

'Can you be here at eight?'

'In the morning?'

'Yes.'

'If I'm not there my alarm clock will have let me down. As well. See you!'

Hardly had I put the phone down when it rang. It was Per Helge Brubak. 'I played it by ear, Varg. Rang the prison to talk to KG. But … it turns out he's done a runner.'

'A runner!'

'Yes. He had a pass this weekend and should have returned on Sunday night, but he didn't turn up.'

'Oh yes? How long has he been out?'

'Since Friday after class. He left school at three. Since then no one has seen him.'

'Well, I'm damned. The same day as his sister went missing.'

'Exactly.'

'But … I suppose an alert has been put out?'

'An internal one, that's all so far. He's not thought to be dangerous to anyone apart from himself.'

'Himself? You mean he's suicidal?'

'No, no, no. What I mean is … he's not dangerous, not to anyone else, that's what I mean.'

'Anyone got any ideas as to what he might have done? Did he have a girlfriend on the outside? Good friends? Something like that.'

'Not as far as I know, I'm afraid to say. He was a lone wolf. No contacts outside prison of which I am aware.'

'But where did he live when he had a pass?'

'With his sister. The elder one.'

'Siv?'

'Yes. At least that was the address he gave.'

'Well … thank you very much. If he contacts you, could you let me know?'

'Will do.'

He rang off, and I sat looking into middle distance. Two of the three had gone missing, and both on the same day. That was not a coincidence. All I needed now was for Siv not to appear as arranged in the Oasen mall. There was only one way to find out. I locked the office door and walked up to Skansen for my car.

8

FROM THE EARLY 1970S the first real shopping mall in the Bergen area was Oasen. Sletten shopping centre was older, but it still had the traditional market square formation you also found in Landåstorget and other places in Bergen's ever-increasing circle of satellite towns. Oasen was completely covered by a superstructure. It protected the public from rain and goods from the sun in a perfect symbiosis, and it was no surprise that the mall with its location in the centre of Fyllingsdalen became a magnet for the ever-growing population there.

Since that time there had been enormous competition from other shopping centres in new districts, and it had itself increased in size, the last time three or four years ago. Nonetheless, it had maintained its status in the locality, and the café in the middle of the mall by the large square was the scene of regular battles for unoccupied tables. The surest victors were very mature women who used their bulging handbags as sledgehammers during the marauding invasion, and God help anyone who sat down on a coveted seat if they could not marshal their defences. They were on the ropes before they knew what was going on, and they needed more than a count of ten to stagger to their feet.

Siv Monsen was sitting, as I had assumed, with a lot of other people reading today's *Bergensavisen*, but the way she was holding the paper, very high up and visible, as in a commercial, drew me in her direction, and she met my quizzical expression with confirmation in her eyes.

'Siv Monsen?'

She nodded.

'Varg Veum.'

We shook hands, and I went to the counter and ordered the same as she had: a cup of coffee and a cinnamon twist. I balanced the feast on a tray back to the small table and a free chair she had succeeded in defending, and sat down.

Siv Monsen was an ordinary, attractive young woman, in her late twenties according to my mental notes. She had removed her red coat and was wearing everyday clothes: dark blue trousers and a plain turquoise blouse with long sleeves. Her hair was blonde and short, except for a seductive curl that fell over her forehead and she kept flicking to the side. Her make-up was discreet, and her face bore clear, compact features surrounding a fleshy nose. The tiny smile she sent me was brief and professional, as though we were located on separate sides of a barrier.

'What do you do in there?' I asked by way of an introduction.

'At work?' As I nodded, she answered: 'I'm a consultant.'

'Which means?'

'I generally sit answering the phone and advising customers.'

'I've had lots of assignments for your company. Nils Åkre is my contact.'

She sent me a chilly look, as if to say that if I wanted to inform her about my acquaintances I had come to the wrong person. 'I see.'

'But … today I'm interested in Margrethe.'

She cast a quick look around, raised her coffee cup to her mouth, took a sip and set it down again. 'So I gathered.'

'It looks as if she's disappeared.'

'Yes … how long has it been?'

'Well … how long is it since you last saw her?'

She twirled her cup. 'A week. New Year some time.'

'Are you often in touch?'

'We meet on a regular basis, yes.'

'So you know how she makes her living?'

Sharp, angry intake of breath. 'Of course I know! And don't you ask me if I've tried to talk her out of it. What good does it do? You can't be the big sister all your life. People have to make their own decisions.'

'Your mother?'

'Yes? What about her?'

'Does she know?'

'I doubt it. Impossible to say.'

'Your brother? Are you in touch with him as well?'

'Our Karl? Not very often.'

'No? But he used to stay with you when he had a pass out.'

'Now and then, yes, he did. He …'

'I know he's in prison.'

'So why are you asking me then?'

'Because, as of now, he has gone AWOL.'

Her face twitched. 'What? Him as well?'

'Him as well? Do you mean that Margrethe has … gone AWOL?'

'I just mean … gone missing. Him, too.'

'At about the same time in fact. Last Friday.'

'Friday,' she repeated, as though finding it difficult to assimilate the word.

I nodded.

She leaned forward. I caught a faint whiff of her perfume, as discreet as the rest of her. 'But … The police have organised a search, I suppose?'

'Only departmental for the time being. Neither of them has contacted you, I assume?'

'No. Neither Karl nor Margrethe. I had no idea about this until you told me.' Her reaction was visible now. There were two red patches at the top of her cheeks, and I could see her pulse throbbing in her throat.

'Could they have contacted your mother, do you think?'

'I doubt it.'

'She hasn't got a phone, I've been led to believe. Should I go round and see her?'

'Have fun, if you do!'

I produced the small photo album I had taken from Margrethe's flat in Nordnes. She regarded it with suspicion. Next she made a show of glancing at her wristwatch. 'I have to go back to work soon.'

'Won't take a moment.' I opened to two pages. 'This is Margrethe, isn't it?'

She took a quick look and nodded.

I flipped through until I found the photograph of the three children and the five adults outside a cabin somewhere in Vestland. I held it out for her. 'And this is all of you?'

She screwed her head half round, as if to view the photo from the right angle. Then she nodded.

I pointed to Margrethe, then to the second girl and at length to the boy. 'Margrethe, you, your brother. Which ones are your parents?'

She moved her head from side to side. 'They're not there.'

'Aren't they? Who are *they* then?'

She shot to her feet. 'Now I do have to go.'

'You didn't answer my question.'

She cast another swift glance at the photograph. 'They were some neighbours. We had been invited to their cabin. What's that got to do with all this?'

'Nothing, I imagine.' I gave her my business card. 'Look, if either Margrethe or your brother contacts you, would you let me know?'

She accepted the card without looking at it, shrugged and left.

I ate the rest of the pastry, drained my coffee cup and went in the same direction as she had gone. Instead of descending to the car park I turned right by the exit, headed for the reception desk at the insurance company and asked if Nils Åkre was in. He was. He could even speak to me. I had a sticker bearing my name attached to my lapel and found my way to his office under my own steam, as usual.

Nils was sitting behind his desk, in the middle of a phone conversation. He motioned me to a free chair with a wave of his hand and carried on talking. When he had finished he cradled the receiver, looked at me quizzically and said: 'What brings you here? Run out of assignments, have you?'

'No, today in fact I'm here as a kind of customer.'

He arched his eyebrows. 'Is that right? If it's life insurance you're after I'm afraid the incident in Oslo sent your premium through the roof, however good a business contact you are in other ways.'

'Now I have no close relatives and Thomas has become self-sufficient, so if you had been following, Nils, you would have known that I don't actually have any life insurance with you any more, and the personal accident and sickness insurance I was offered I couldn't afford.'

'Well, there you go. If you can't keep away from the fireworks in Tiger Town then … But that's not why you've come, is it?'

'No, it's not.'

Nils Åkre and I had a nice line in patter from way back, and the number of jobs he had pushed in my direction over the years was not so small. Apart from that, we were as different as it was possible to be. He was an ardent family man, a little overweight and had no ambitions in life other than to reach pension age in good enough shape to cash in on all the benefits from the insurance policies he had taken out over the years. I guessed that then he would emigrate to Provence, a class higher than Costa del Sol, to enjoy his retirement there.

'This is about a colleague of yours. Someone called Siv Monsen.'

He looked at me blankly. 'I see.'

'She told me she worked here. As a client adviser.'

'That may be correct. Have you spoken to her?'

'Yes.'

'In what connection, if I might be so bold.'

'In total confidence, of course.'

He gave an indulgent smile, and nodded.

'A family matter. Her sister has gone missing … and perhaps also her brother.'

'Mm … that sounds dramatic. Why come to me?'

'Well, I thought you might have something to say.'

He raised his eyebrows. 'What about?'

'Well … Sometimes you chat to your colleagues, don't you. Also about private matters.'

'Varg, Siv Monsen and I are not exactly bosom pals.' He swivelled his chair towards his computer screen, clicked a couple of times and searched down a list until he came to her name. He nodded, moved the mouse and nodded a second time.

I couldn't read the text from where I was sitting, but I assumed that some personal details had come up.

'Employed four years ago. Customer adviser. No other remarks apart from the purely factual.' He swivelled his chair back towards me. 'Since I don't know her in person I'm afraid I can't help you with any further information, Varg.'

'Fine … but if anything comes to your ears, you know where to find me.'

He smirked. 'Outside Lido Café, begging from passers-by?'

We got up. I looked at him. 'Aren't you curious? Don't you want … any more details?'

'Goodness, no, Varg. I have more than enough to think about with our everyday stuff without worrying about one of our employees' private relationships.'

'Well … Give my best regards to the Good Samaritan, if you should bump into him in the lift or wherever.'

'Same to you. I'll get in touch whenever we have a case for you. One of our own, that is.'

'Thank you. Without you all I doubt I would have survived.'

'To tell the truth I'm not entirely sure if that's a compliment.'

'Nor me.'

I strolled down to reception, handed in my visitor's badge and out to the car. I sat leafing through my notepad before I made a decision. Next stop would have to be Else Monsen in Falsens vei in Minde. *Terra incognita* for a Nordnes boy.

9

MINDE WAS A PART OF TOWN I had never really got to know, for a variety of reasons. It may have been due to a traumatic childhood experience, of course. In November 1954, when we were twelve years old, Pelle and I, in our capacity as the detective bureau Marlowe & Spade tailed Sylvelin – a girl we were both wild about – from Nordnes to Minde, where, under cover of autumn darkness we had seen her being kissed by a tall, gangly boy at least two years older than us, and from then on neither Pelle nor I suggested undertaking any more excursions to Minde or surrounding areas. I never even went to Fanahallen cincma until I was grown up. We could see the films on show at the Eldorado, without having to fork out for an additional tram ticket. The closest we came to that part of town was when we were at Brann football stadium, but then the stadium was closer to Fridalen than what we considered to be Minde, and Brann FC gave us enough traumatic experiences to repress any further thoughts of Sylvelin. Pelle later moved to Frederikstad, and on the whole I had nothing to do with Minde, for no other reason than the serendipity of Fate.

I turned up the heavily trafficked Inndalsveien and thence to Falsens vei, the much more peaceful parallel street, bordered by small houses of a somewhat British design with small gardens at the front. I parked by the playground at the crossing with Jacob Aallsvei and glanced up at the park around Solhaug School. I could just make out the old white timber building that used to be called Lea Hall after the then owner, Erik Grant Lea. In the playground were a handful of children engaged in loud games, suitably dressed for the rainy weather, while two mothers stood huddled in one corner, each under her own umbrella, each with a cigarette in the centre of her mouth, as if to keep warm.

The Falsens vei address pertained to one of the houses roughly midway in the row. I opened the gate and crossed the handkerchief of a garden. The front door was locked and there were two doorbells, the top one for *Monsen*, written in blue biro and rather childish letters on a label behind a small glass plate. Someone called Torvaldsen lived on the floor below.

I rang the top bell and stood waiting. Nothing happened. I walked back a few paces and gazed up at the house. There was a dim light behind one window at the top. The other was dark. On the floor below, both windows were lit.

While I was waiting a taxi stopped outside the gate of the neighbouring house. A woman alighted, together with the driver who opened the boot and removed two suitcases, which he placed in front of the gate. They exchanged a couple of words, the woman opened the gate and the driver carried the cases across the lawn to her front door. She thanked him for his help, and the driver returned to his car, got in and drove off as the woman rang the doorbell. For a moment we stood looking at each other. She nodded a cautious hello, and I recip-rocated. As far as I could see, she was in her fifties with shiny, blonde hair, but the large padded olive green coat obscured any further impressions of her appearance.

She turned to the door, annoyed. No answer there, either, I could see. I pressed the first-floor doorbell once again. While waiting I noticed her take out a bunch of keys and unlock the door.

I waited a bit longer; then I rang the ground floor instead.

Soon I heard footsteps inside. The door was opened, and a well-built man of medium height, sixty-ish at first glance, stood in the doorway. He had greying hair, pronounced eyebrows and an oblong face. The look he gave me was neutral, though not unfriendly. 'Yes?'

'My name's Veum. I apologise for the disturbance, but I've been trying to ring the first floor and there's no answer.'

He automatically peered up the inside stairs. 'At Else's? Yes, she seldom does. Answer the bell, I mean.'

'But there's a light on.'

'Yup. I've heard her upstairs. I can hear her padding around. After my wife died it's so quiet in the house that even the tiniest noise resounds.'

As an immediate comment on this we were interrupted by a protracted howl, like the cry of a wounded animal caught in a trap it could not escape. However, it did not come from upstairs but the house next door.

I turned towards the noise, and the man I assumed was Torvaldsen stepped onto the front doorstep and looked in the same direction.

'What's going on? Lill?'

The woman I had seen arrive had come back out. She was tearing at her blonde hair while staring around wildly and continuing the long, incoherent scream.

Torvaldsen raised his voice. 'Lill! What's up?' He dashed past me and through the gate towards her. I followed, thinking only that I might be able to help.

The scream died. Now she was sobbing. Long, whimpering sounds while sending Torvaldsen and me incomprehensible stares and clinging to the gate, as though she had no idea how to open it.

'What's up, Lill?'

She studied Torvaldsen. 'Alf?'

'What's happened? Has something …?'

Her gaze was pure apathy. 'I-it's Carsten. He's in there. I think he's dead.'

'Dead!' Torvaldsen opened the gate and looked towards the front door. 'But have you informed …?'

'No one! I haven't informed anyone.'

He turned to me. 'You … ring for an ambulance. Report a possible death.' Then he turned back to the distressed woman. 'Come on, Lill!'

'No! I can't. It's a terrible sight.'

He glanced at her in astonishment. 'Stay here with …' He groped for my name.

'Veum.'

' … for the moment.'

She sent me an uncomprehending look. I smiled in as reassuring a way as I could muster and called A&E. I got through directly, and even though I was unable to supply any more detail than that there was a possible death, they noted down the address and decided to treat it as an emergency.

I rang off, stepped inside the gate, approached the woman warily and patted her back in consolation, a gesture which led her to throw herself around my neck and shake with profound, despairing sobs.

Torvaldsen came to the door, his face ashen grey. 'I'm afraid we don't need an ambulance, Veum. We might just as well ring the police straightaway.'

10

'AMBULANCE'S ON THE WAY,' I said. 'We can leave that part to them.'

When he joined us, I said: 'You take care of her and I'll have a peep inside.'

'Really?' He sent me a bemused look, but did not resist. I carefully moved the woman he had called Lill from my embrace to his, gave him an encouraging nod and left them there, inside the gate.

I crossed the garden path. The tiny garden was well tended, but now in January there was nothing but the withered remains of roses. On a couple of the rhododendron bushes buds protruded between the evergreen leaves, and there were new, fire-red shoots on a leafless Japanese quince.

I went into the porch. Unlike the adjacent house, this looked as if it had been converted to a house for one family. Even in the entrance there was a homely feel with pictures on the walls and green plants in corners. The stairs to the first floor were covered with pieces of red carpet that had been fitted and secured with large brass nails.

From the porch the door was open to what had been the original hall on the ground floor, now an extended cloakroom. On a coat hanger hung the large, olive-green coat. One suitcase stood on the floor; the other she had carried indoors.

I entered the sitting room. Standard furniture, and not very tidy. There were several unwashed coffee cups and glasses, and piles of magazines, newspapers and mountains of advertising brochures. An unpleasant stench hung in the air, as though it had been a very long time since anyone had done any cleaning.

As I moved closer to the open door of the neighbouring room the smell became stronger. I stopped on the threshold. Now I understood her reaction. It was not a pretty sight. I could feel the nausea rising in my chest, and recoiled a couple of paces. I had to clench my teeth not to vomit and stood breathing slowly in and out through my nose.

The man lying on the floor in front of the big desk had his face turned to one side, his mouth hung open and his eyes stared as far as it was feasible for any human to see. The face was swollen and huge, the skin wan with large, bluish bruises. At the side of his head, beside his left ear, there was a long, open wound, black with dried blood and dotted with something greyish-green that I assumed, from previous experience, was cerebral matter. I couldn't see a murder weapon anywhere.

The room was a kind of office-cum-library. Someone had ransacked the shelves. A swathe of books was strewn across the floor, many lay open, spine up. The door to the big cupboard in a corner of the room was open, and I saw heaps of papers scattered across the floor in front.

Outside, I heard the sound of sirens, which were switched off suddenly. I waited for the two paramedics to come in. There was a man and a woman, both in their late twenties, dressed in Red Cross uniforms.

'He's in there,' I said, pointing.

The man, who had short red hair, looked at me with suspicion. 'Who are you?'

'I'll wait outside. We can deal with all that afterwards. You'll have to phone the police anyway.'

The dark-haired young woman had already walked past me. Behind me I heard her reaction. 'Oo-er!'

I nodded to her companion. 'I couldn't have expressed it better myself.'

Then I joined Torvaldsen and Lill to await events.

There was not much conversation. Lill had stopped sobbing. Torvaldsen looked pale and shaken.

The two paramedics came back. The man nodded to us. 'We've called the police.'

The woman went over to Lill. 'Is this …?'

Torvaldsen nodded. 'His wife. Lill Mobekk. The man inside's Carsten.'

'Carsten Mobekk?' asked the paramedic.

'Yes.'

'And you are?'

'Alf Torvaldsen. I live next door.'

He turned to me. 'And you?'

'Veum.'

He waited, expecting more, but I said nothing else. There would be enough to talk about when the police arrived.

They arrived in two cars, a white patrol vehicle and a civilian Volvo 850. A group of curious onlookers had gathered by the parked ambulance outside the fence. Schoolchildren were on their way home. I had noticed one of the young women at the playground, now with a child in a small buggy. There were a few older men and women, some of them obviously married couples. Several had their heads together. Squinted at Lill Mobekk and Alf Torvaldsen and commented in, for the most part, low voices.

I sighed with relief when I saw the good-natured Inspector from Voss, Atle Helleve, shifting his considerable body out of the Volvo, while Bjarne Solheim, the young officer with hair permanently standing to attention, got out on the opposite side. They were met by two uniformed officers from the patrol car, exchanged a few words and then came in our direction, all four of them.

Helleve ran a hand through his thick beard when he caught sight of me. 'Veum?' he exclaimed, almost resigned.

'Yes, but today I happened to be passing by.'

Solheim smirked.

Helleve sent me a sceptical glower. 'We'll soon see.' He turned to the ambulance driver. 'Where's the deceased?'

'Inside.'

The woman said: 'This is his wife.'

Helleve imparted a gentle look in Lill Mobekk's direction. 'I see. Would you like to come in with us? Then you can sit down.'

I coughed in admonition. 'Not sure if that's wise.'

Helleve sneered. 'Oh no? You've already examined the crime scene, I assume.'

'I did pop inside, yes. The whole house needs to be checked out.'

He met my eyes with a kind of dejection. 'Yes, it is possible we may have to assess circumstances first.' He motioned to one constable. 'Pedersen. Stay here with these.' Meaning: '*Don't let any of them leave the scene.*' 'Stavang and Bjarne, you come with me. You wait here.'

Solheim nodded, and the other three went into the house.

I glanced at Torvaldsen. 'Did you know each other well?'

'God, yes! I've known Carsten since we were in the military together, and we've been neighbours for nigh on thirty years. It was Carsten and Lill who brought this unoccupied flat to our attention.'

'Carsten grew up here,' Lill Mobekk drawled, as though forcing the words out. It was only now I noticed she was from Østland, eastern Norway.

'We went hunting together every autumn. Sometimes we went on holiday together.' He shook his head, as though to emphasise how inconceivable the situation was for him.

'Hunting? What for?'

'Deer. We've got a deal with a landowner in the Gulen area.'

'Dalsøyra, to be precise,' Lill said.

Torvaldsen met my eyes and nodded. 'Carsten and Lill have got a cabin, not so far from the sea. We used to stay there when we went hunting in the mountains.'

'When did you last see him?'

He sent Lill Mobekk a fleeting glance and half-turned to the side. 'Just before the weekend,' he said in a low voice. 'We had a long, cosy evening together last Friday. After Wenche, my wife, died last autumn ... She had a protracted, painful death and was rendered pretty lethargic by the medicine she was taking. It was cancer. She couldn't do much during the last six months before she found peace. At this time Carsten and I became closer again. I talked and he listened. Or vice versa.'

'A long, cosy evening you say.'

'Yeah.' He smiled wryly. 'We had a few drinks. Lill was away, had been for more than a week, he said.'

I turned my gaze to her. She had somewhat pointed features, which gave her face a V shape. Her eyebrows were plucked, but her tears must have removed the make-up she had been wearing. There were streaks of mascara down her cheeks and at the corners of her eyes, and her half-open mouth sagged, reflecting the shock she must have experienced on finding her husband in such a state.

I would have liked to ask her when she had last spoken to him, but I knew that was a question I should leave to the police.

Again I focused on Torvaldsen. 'In other words, when did you see him last?'

'Friday night as he left to go home.'

'So you were in your flat?'

'Yes. I was away at the weekend. I get very restless at weekends. I took the car and went for a drive, up to Sandane and back. Wenche loved trips like that, at any time of the year. Doing things we did together brings back memories.'

I nodded.

'I came back Sunday night, but I didn't talk to him. Nor yesterday.'

'I wish I'd come home a bit earlier!' Lill blurted.

He looked at her with melancholy eyes and tilted his head, without saying a word.

Then Helleve and Solheim re-emerged, affected by what they had witnessed. Helleve said: 'In fact, I agree with Veum. In principle the whole house has to be considered a crime scene. Solheim will stay here until the SOC officers arrive. As soon as we have some snaps of him and we've marked the position he'll be removed. He shouldn't be there much longer now.'

'H-how long has he been there?' Lill asked in a faint voice.

Helleve sighed. 'In fact that's what we'd like to talk to you about.'

'But I haven't a clue! I was away for more than a week, and I wasn't in touch with him from the moment I left. When I rang yesterday to say I was coming home today there was no reply.'

He nodded, and I could see he was formulating his own ideas. He shifted his gaze to Torvaldsen. 'Could we perhaps adjourn to yours since we can't stay here?'

'Naturally. No problem at all. Come with me.' He opened the gate and went into the street. Helleve and Lill Mobekk followed. I brought up the rear.

Helleve eyed me doubtfully. 'Er, Veum … We can talk later, can't we?'

'I'm sure we can, but … The reason I'm here at all is that I have to see someone in Torvaldsen's house.'

'Uhuh?'

'There's a woman on the floor above with whom I'd like a little chat.'

'Fine, fine … But you're not with us.'

'No, no, I understand that.'

We had reached the gate, which had been left open after Torvaldsen and me. I went into the entrance and while Torvaldsen was finding the key I started up the stairs to the first floor. Torvaldsen looked up at me. 'Knock on the door. She'll open.'

'OK. Thank you.'

'Get in touch tomorrow, Veum,' Helleve said. 'I don't want to miss hearing your version of this story. If nothing else, consider yourself a witness.'

'I'll give you a buzz.'

'Good.'

Torvaldsen and Helleve disappeared into the ground-floor flat. I stopped in front of the door on the first floor and knocked. Some time passed before I heard faint, shuffling steps inside. Then the door opened, slowly and hesitantly.

11

THE WOMAN IN THE DOORWAY was about fifty years old and drained of all colour. Bluish-grey smoke rose from an almost burned-out cigarette in the corner of her mouth. Her skin was pale bordering on transparent, her eyes watery blue, her hair grey and dishevelled, and she was wearing a beige jumper over a pair of un-chic brown trousers. There wasn't a trace of make-up on her and she had a flat-chested, sunken posture that made her seem almost genderless. The look she sent me was vacant, blank, and she stood watching me, as though leaving the entire initiative to me.

I grabbed it. 'Else Monsen?'

She nodded in silence.

'The name's Veum. Can I come in?'

'What's this about?'

'Your children.'

She blinked a couple of times. Then she retreated indoors, but left the door ajar as a sign that I could follow.

The air in the dark hallway was heavy and stale. The clothes hanging on a stand smelled of mould. She gestured with an arm towards a door leading into the sitting room. I followed her.

There was something empty and lifeless about this room, too. It was deafeningly quiet. There was a TV in one corner and an old-fashioned portable radio on a worn, brown varnished dresser, but both were switched off. The only sound we could hear was the distant shouting of children in the playground by Jacob Aallsvei.

There was a parish bulletin and a couple of magazines on the low coffee table, and visible rings left by bottles, cups and glasses on the wood. Along the wall there was a sofa and by the table two chairs. None matched, and they looked tatty and uncomfortable. In the middle of the table was an ashtray piled with cigarette ends. Before she sat down on the sofa she stubbed out her cigarette, took another from a packet she had in her pocket and lit it with a cheap plastic lighter. She made a vague motion towards the two chairs.

I chose the one closest to the door and let my gaze drift across the faded, nicotine-brown walls. No family photgraphs. No gypsy ladies. No elks in the sunset.

Else Monsen watched me expectantly. She appeared to be someone who was used to anything and everything from public services, and all the signs suggested that was where she had pigeonholed me.

I took out my notepad and a pen to appear more official. 'As I said, this is about your children. That is, two of them.' I paused for dramatic effect, but she did not show any signs of wanting to say anything. 'How long is it since you last saw Margrethe?'

She frowned, to demonstrate that she was giving the matter some thought. Then she shrugged. 'Don't remember. Several years.'

'Really?'

'I never see any of them.'

'You don't?'

She gently shook her head.

'So that applies to Karl Gunnar as well?'

'Our Kalle? But he's in prison.'

'Yes, but he gets out on a pass now and then. He's almost served his sentence.'

'Mm?' She didn't sound very interested.

'He hasn't been here then, I take it.'

She didn't respond, except with a vacant look.

'Not even in the last few weeks?'

'I haven't seen him since … we were in court.'

'And no one else has been here asking after him? The police, for example?'

'The police? He's in prison, I told you.'

'Yes, he is.' I paused before continuing. 'But Siv … you've had some contact with her, haven't you?'

In her eyes she was miles away. 'No.' After some thought, she added: 'But she went to Frank's funeral. Frank's my husband.'

'Yes, but surely they were all there, weren't they?'

'No. Just her.'

'Siv was the only one at the funeral?'

'Yes. In the chapel.'

'So you didn't have a get-together to celebrate his memory?'

'Yes. In the chapel. At Møllendal.'

'But afterwards. Nothing private?'

'No.' She sucked the smoke down deep and coughed it up again, a thin, fragile sound.

'And that was three to four years ago, wasn't it?'

'1993.'

'Does that mean … have I understood you correctly … you haven't seen your children since 1993?'

She shrugged.

'You're not sure.'

'No.'

'And you haven't got a telephone, I've been told.'

'I cope fine without. No one rings me anyway.'

'No, if you haven't got a phone, then … but that could of course be … Alright. How do you make time pass then?'

'Well, I sit here thinking.'

'What about?'

'Well, everything and nothing.'

In a strange way, it was as if she wasn't reacting to why I was asking her all these questions. I just asked, and she just answered. That was how it was, today.

All of a sudden, I felt deeply depressed, as though Else Monsen's stagnant life and meaningless existence had infected me as well. I let out a heavy sigh, and said: 'So you know nothing about what your children are doing? What professions they have chosen?'

She shook her head.

'Have you any idea why two of them didn't turn up for their father's funeral?'

'Couldn't be bothered, I suppose. I don't even know if they were told. We didn't have a death notice until … afterwards.'

'But Siv went, didn't she. She must have spoken to the others about it?'

'Yes, perhaps.'

'OK. I don't know if I …' I got up from the chair and looked around. A side door led into another room that must have been her bedroom. We had passed the kitchen door in the hall. 'Are these the only rooms?'

'Yes, and the loft.'

'The loft?'

'Yes, we had a room for the children up there when they were small.'

'I see. Is it used now?'

'No.'

'May I have a look?'

She looked at me in the same passive, subservient way she had done the whole time. Then she nodded. 'I can show you.'

I followed her through the hall and up the stairs. We came into a drying loft beneath a slanting roof. The light angled down from two windows. In a recess there was an old-fashioned mangle. In a corner there were some suitcases. At the opposite end there was a wall with two doors, as if to two storerooms. One was padlocked. The other was ajar. Beside the half-open door was a large wardrobe.

Else Monsen went straight there, opened the door wide and stepped aside so that I could see in.

It was a cramped children's bedroom, with two bunk beds along one wall, a single bed along the other. There was a dormer window that looked out onto Falsens vei, and on the sill some old, faded girls' magazines. A green dresser, and on a chair some forgotten clothes they had outgrown. On the floor there was a pile of comics, as far as I could judge from the 80s. The room left me with the impression that this was a hastily vacated childhood, a period of life no one had bothered to tidy up after.

'So they grew up here?'

'Yes.'

'Not much room.'

'That was all we had.'

'But where did they do their homework?'

'They didn't have so much … homework.'

'No?'

'No.' After a pause she added: 'But when they did, they sat in the kitchen. Or else they did it at school.'

Again I felt the depression taking a firm grip around my

heart. Once again it was as if I were being inexorably transported back to my time at social services and the frequent dispiriting home visits I had made in those days.

I turned away. 'That door …'

'No, that's Torvaldsen's storeroom. *Fru* Torvaldsen helped them with their homework now and then. She was a teacher at their school.'

'Fridalen School?'

'Yes.'

'Well, well, well … then I won't disturb you any further.'

'You're not disturbing me.'

'No, I …'

In fact I did understand. It had been a long time since anyone had disturbed Else Monsen. Much too long from what I could glean.

I trudged back downstairs. We said goodbye, and she closed the door without waiting for me to leave the building. For a moment I stood outside Torvaldsen's door, undecided whether I should intervene in the conversation between him and Helleve, but I concluded it was safest to keep out of it. Anyway, I had arranged to ring Helleve the day after. Furthermore, I had my own investigation to conduct.

I closed the front door quietly behind me and walked into Falsens vei. If nothing else, it had stopped raining. The police had cordoned off the front part of the neighbour's house with red and white tape. There were still some small groups of inquisitive onlookers watching what was happening. The door was closed, but inside the windows we could see SOC officers in their characteristic white overalls inching their way forward.

There was not a lot for me to do here. I walked back to where I had parked my car, got in and drove back to the town centre. It was time to get myself something to eat. I found a parking spot in Markeveien and ambled down to Børs Café. I ordered a steak, medium done, the safest option on the menu if they didn't have potato dumplings. The waiter raised his eyebrows in scorn when I ordered a Clausthaler instead of a pils, but he did not make a comment.

However, the tall, ungainly guy who appeared from nowhere in front of my table with a freshly pulled, foaming half-litre in hand, did. 'On the wagon, Varg?'

'I wouldn't say that.' I met his eyes. 'Take a pew, Lasse. Long time, eh?'

12

LITTLE LASSE we had called him for as long as I could remember, despite the fact that he measured one metre eighty and was not so little with respect to age either. I seemed to recall that Ludvigsen was his real surname. With his shoulder-length, grizzled hair he looked like an ageing hippie, but in all probability that was down to the fact that the money he saved at the hairdresser's he was able to use on more pressing needs.

I met him first when I was working in the social services, and he was not so many years younger than me. Somehow or other, he had managed to temper his drug addiction enough to survive. Regular consumption of beer had been one of the methods. He belonged without any doubt to the veterans of Nygård Park. At Børs Café he was part of the wallpaper.

For many years it had been the case that if I needed to know anything on the shady side of the law – west of Pecos, as it were – I had, on not so few occasions, been given useful information by Little Lasse. In total confidence, it goes without saying; otherwise he would not have been upright and entering his third decade since 1968.

Lasse sat down and drained half of his glass in one swig. His nose was narrow and pointed, as it had always been, but his cheeks looked thinner, and his neck had a network of wrinkles I had not noticed before. His teeth were yellowish-brown and stunted. It had been a long time since he had seen a dentist.

The waiter came with the Clausthaler, placed the glass on the table, poured from the bottle and said acidly: 'There you are, a driver's pils. Enjoy.' Not long afterwards the steak arrived, blackened at the edges and served with fried potatoes in gravy, a droopy leaf of lettuce and a sliced tomato that should not have left the greenhouse this side of Easter.

Lasse stared at the dish hungrily, and I offered to treat him to a portion.

He beamed with gratitude. 'Would you, Veum?'

'Anything for old pals.' I signalled to the waiter and gave him the order. 'And another half-litre,' I said. 'For my friend here.'

Lasse grinned. 'Have you won the lottery, or what?'

'I'll never win. What about you?'

He ran one hand across his forehead. 'Got LOSER written here in big letters, haven't I!'

I shrugged. 'You're not alone, if so. Anything happening in your neck of the woods?'

He leaned forward, looked left and right and whispered: 'Are you after what I'm after…?'

'After what you're …?' I said, furrowing my brow.

'Half the town is, that's my impression.' He leaned back and took another large swig of his beer. Soon there was nothing but foam left.

'I don't think I'm quite with you.'

'No?' He winked at me as though he didn't quite believe what I had said. 'Have you stopped reading newspapers?'

'No. Which article?'

'No, that's not the point. There was nothing about what really mattered in the paper. But I can guarantee you, Veum … it has not gone unnoticed in the right quarters.'

'I think you're going to have to spell it out, Lasse.'

He nodded, but went quiet when the waiter came with his steak and the accompanying beer. Thereafter he launched himself at the food as if he hadn't consumed any since the New Year. Only when the final bite had been devoured, and there wasn't so much as a scrap of meat left on the plate, did he raise his eyes and look at me again. 'You may have read in the paper about the man who was beaten up in Skuteviken?'

'Yes, I did … an old police acquaintance, wasn't it?'

'You can say that again. And he got quite a pasting later, I can assure you. A double dose, as they say at the chemist. The whole town is after those who did it.'

'I may be a bit slow on the uptake today, but I'm still not with you.'

He shook his head condescendingly, as if talking to a little child. 'No? How big do you want the letters?'

'As big as the ones you reckon are on your forehead.'

'Thank you for that!'

'And I'll buy you another beer if this is something I can use.'

'I'm not sure they're giving a reward.'

'What for?'

He leaned closer and lowered his voice a couple of notches. 'Listen here, Veum. There's a banana boat coming, that's what we used to say in the old days, but today there's a boat coming from Denmark, and it's not just bananas they have on board. The customs in Skolten have never been the most meticulous, so with a bit of cunning you can soon pass through the eye of the needle with this 'n' that.'

I nodded to show that I was with him.

'This guy, his name's Lars Mikalsen, he's probably some kind of eternal student. Anyway, he's never taken any exams, but he's still got a student card. Now and then he does odd jobs for folk with needs. A little package on the Danish ferry, well disguised, so to speak, and Lars Mikalsen has earned enough to live on for another month or two. Like so many others, that's how he covers his own needs. But this time it went wrong.'

I got the picture. 'He was robbed?'

'Indeed he was. Someone no one knows, but who will meet a sticky end when they find out, welcomed him when he came ashore, took him to Skuteviken – or wherever it was it happened – pounced on him and stole what was in his bag.'

'And that was?'

'I don't know exactly, but there is talk of a hefty lump of H, with a street value of up to one and a half million.'

'One and a half!'

'Yup.'

'I can begin to understand why he didn't want to report the assault. He would have got up to ten years behind bars himself for a cargo like that …'

'Not far off it, that's for sure.'

'And no one suspects who could be behind it?'

He shrugged. 'There's always gossip about competitors in the same branch. Somebody who wants to elbow their way in. But, if so, they have to be armed to the teeth, I can promise you that.'

'Who sent the package?'

He looked at me askance. 'I doubt you would want to know, Veum. It would not be good for your health, let me put it like that. And, as I said, I don't think a reward has been offered.'

'But this Lars Mikalsen, didn't he see who robbed him?'

'He hasn't given a name at any rate, I do know that. That

was why he was beaten up a second time, by those waiting for the goods. To knock it out of him. But it doesn't seem like it helped.'

'Where does he live?'

'Who? Lars Mikalsen? Surely you're not thinking of calling on him?'

I shrugged. 'Might be useful to know.'

He gave me the heavy look. Then he slowly shook his head. 'You've never been very bright, have you, Veum?' As I didn't answer he told me the address: Konsul Børs gate in Møhlenpris. 'Right under the roof, a kind of attic flat. But I'm warning you. It would not be wise to do any digging in this case.'

'Right ... but now you're here, Lasse. Someone who calls himself KG, do you know anything about him?'

'KG as in Karl Gunnar Monsen?'

I nodded.

'The Gimle case.' He gave a nod of confirmation. 'Well, I know of him, that's all. He's still banged up, isn't he?'

'He's supposed to have escaped.'

'Well ...' He grimaced. 'The days can get quite long out there in Åsane Prison. You can't blame anyone for wanting some fresh air now and then.'

'Not such a smart idea when he's approaching the end of his stretch perhaps.'

'No. Perhaps not. But this KG has never been known for being very smart, has he.'

'Don't ask me. I'd barely heard of him until yesterday. I'm searching for his sister. One of the women working C. Sundts gate.'

'And what's in it for you? A complimentary dip of the wick? Free season ticket for the winter?'

I raised my alcohol-free beer in a last *skål*. 'Usual rates, Lasse. Enough for another beer or two if I can find her.'

'I'm afraid I can't help you. What's her name?'

'Margrethe. But out there she's called Maggi.'

He knitted his brows. 'As you know, I am subject to other vices, so it's rare I bump into that milieu, but should she come by the park I'll give you a buzz.'

'That would be great.' I unhooked my jacket from the chair, signalled to the waiter and stood up. 'Thanks for the help.'

I paid and went on my way to the car. Before driving home I took a detour to C. Sundts gate. I kept my eyes sharpened for both of them, but found neither Hege nor Tanya at either end of the street. Perhaps they were both on a trick at the moment.

There was no shortage of propositions during this drive either, and it struck me that I should not let detours here become a habit. If I drove by too often I risked being targeted by female activists and having WHOREMONGER sprayed on my car.

13

THE FOLLOWING MORNING I was up early to make my meeting with Cathrine Leivestad at eight. I crossed the fish market before the Narvesen kiosk had opened. On Vågsallmenning a copper green Ludvig Holberg stood steadfastly staring north-west. From the old fire station in Christies gate I could hear the sound of throaty morning laughter. Along Lille Lungegårdsvann Lake the ducks were doing battle with gulls and pigeons over the remains that nocturnal kebab and hot dog diners had left. The town was coming to life after the winter night's sombre drizzle.

Bergen's Outreach Centre is located in Strømgaten, across the street from the stately old Lysverket building. It was built in 1916, in a style similar to art nouveau. Cathrine Leivestad had north-facing office space and was exposed to the eternal pounding of the traffic by the crossing outside. I remembered her as young, blonde and attractive when she started at social services a year or two before I finished. That was twenty-two years ago, and no one would call her young any more. She was still blonde, but all the sad lives she had encountered in the course of her career had made her leaner than, to be brutally honest, suited her. The skin over her cheekbones was taut, and her lips had become so thin that the smile she flashed me produced no more than a curl at the corners of her mouth.

A few years had passed since we last met, but I could hear

that she was well-informed nonetheless. 'How are you, Varg? I was told you'd been shot in … in Oslo, wasn't it?'

'More proof that moving to the capital is the most stupid thing you can do.'

'But … there are no permanent injuries, are there?'

'Couple of decorative scars, if you like the rugged look. And confirmation that not even superheroes last for ever.'

She gave a sardonic smile. 'So you see yourself as a super-hero, do you?'

'Not any more.'

'You said you wanted to speak about Margrethe Monsen. Have you found her?'

'I'm afraid not. I don't suppose you've had any recent contact with her, have you?'

'No. As a rule we don't keep in touch on a daily basis. Mar-grethe and the other girls know where to find us, and they know they'll get the support they need here. Besides, we're out on the streets as good as every night, but, for myself, I've cut down on that side of the job. I have more than enough to do with the admin. Of course, Margrethe's been in the business for some years, so I've met her … in action, so to speak.'

'Meaning?'

'No, not that … on the street. But she's disappeared, you say?'

'Yes, that is, we don't know yet for sure. It may have been her own choice. She has been reported missing though, by a colleague from the streets.'

'Who?'

'Hege Jensen.'

She nodded. 'I know her.'

'Yes, in fact I did, too.'

'Oh, how was that?'

'Former classmate of my son, Thomas.'

'She's a bright girl, bearing in mind her situation. But haven't the police been informed?'

'No, that's why she came to me. She didn't seem to have a great deal of faith in the police, and … well, I've started making a few enquiries. That was when I bumped into the guys I mentioned on the phone. Kjell Malthus and his side-kick, Rolf.'

Her gaze hardened. 'Kjell Malthus and Rolf Terje Dalby. God, yes, we know all about them, and we have talked to the police about them on several occasions. Officially, however, all they do is run a rental service, as well as a number of other business activities. Malthus does, that is. Dalby just goes along for the ride. If only you knew how frustrating this is! Even though we all know what they are up to, it requires such enormous resources to establish damning evidence against them that they will be free for years! If you can help us with that, then …'

She looked at me, and I shrugged. 'We'll have to see what we can dig up. The first priority is to find the woman.'

'Tell me what Hege said.'

I briefed her on what Hege had told me, my visit to the flat in Strandgaten, the encounter with Kjell Malthus and Rolf Terje Dalby and the story Tanya had told me on Monday evening.

During the latter part, her face darkened further. 'Some people reckon they can treat these girls like trash, just because their circumstances have led them to soliciting on the street. A black car, did you say?'

'Yes. Mean anything to you?'

'You didn't get the model?'

'Afraid not. But the car registration starts with SP-523.'

She jotted that down on her pad. 'I can ask my colleagues. Many of the customers out there are regulars, aren't they. Gradually we've got to know them by their cars. But ...'

'Yes?'

'Margrethe turned down a trick, wasn't that what you said?'

'Right. May be a blind alley, of course. But I was told she refused the number point-blank, so Tanya took her place. Margrethe may have come up against the same punter before. She may have known there were two of them. And that the second was waiting round the corner. But whether this has anything to do with her disappearance I don't know. All we do know is that what happened was out of the ordinary, and the following day she was gone. Since then no one has seen her.'

'The police can track down electronic leads.'

'The police can do a whole load of things I can't, Cathrine. But for now I'm the one with the job.'

'I really hope you find her! Safe and sound.' After a short pause, she continued: 'I should tell you something ... I've known Margrethe for many years, from long before she started working on the streets. Going right back to one of the first years in social services when we saw the initial signs of concern regarding her family. That's at least nineteen or twenty years ago.'

'I see. And the cause for concern was ... the usual?'

'Yes, but it was above all the father who was addicted. Alcohol and pills. The report came from the health visitor at the school where Margrethe started. The sister was a couple of years older, but it was Margrethe who set the whole process in motion.'

'Because?'

'Well, it was the usual symptoms. Restlessness, inability to concentrate, no appetite, weight below what it should have been. That sort of thing.'

'Did you go to their home?'

'Yes, I ... you know what it was like. I was still quite new to the job, but I suppose you remember Elsa? Elsa Dragesund?'

'Do I remember Elsa? I was trained by her as well.'

'Right. We went to the family home several times, and our conclusion was obvious. The parents were not capable of taking proper care of their children. There was a little boy there too, Karl Gunnar, also undernourished and restless. Only Siv, the eldest, seemed to be coping alright, and that's the way it has been in her later life as well, so I've been told. But that is not unusual. As the eldest in a dysfunctional family she assumed the parental responsibility for both her brother and sister. She got them up in the morning, made their packed lunches, accompanied Karl Gunnar to nursery when her mother could not, picked him up after school, in short ...'

'But the father was the drinker, didn't you say? What about the mother?'

'Cowed. Totally under the thumb of the idiot.'

'Mm, that was the impression I had of her as well.'

'Have you met her?'

'I was at her place yesterday, in case Margrethe had gone there. But no.'

'No ...'

'So what happened? About the report expressing concern, I mean?'

She tossed her shoulders, as if to illustrate her displeasure. 'A committee was formed.'

'Oh yes? By whom, and with what purpose?'

'They were members of the local church council and a few neighbours who got together to offer them support. Great commitment – no doubting that. Even the parish priest was involved and gave his consent to the campaign.'

'Campaign?'

'Yes, it became a matter of principle between us, that is, social services and them. They undertook to ensure the children were supported and the family home got all the practical and economic help it needed. We brought the case before the arbitration court, and it ended with our consenting to the committee having a go. Well, I didn't consent!'

'No?'

'Elsa didn't either. But we were overruled by ... management.'

'And afterwards?'

'Well, we tried, of course, to follow things up, but it was not easy. We were dealing with strong personalities. The parish priest, as I said, although he was not one of the most committed. But there was a central member on the council who, by the way, was a neighbour. There was a couple living in the same house as the family and she worked in the school. He worked in public administration.'

'Torvaldsen.'

'Possible, yes. Did you meet them as well?'

'No, only him. His wife is dead.'

She nodded. 'And a few more. But anyway ... I don't doubt their idealism. "It's terrible when a family's broken up," this council fellow told us. "Can you imagine anything more painful than parents having their own flesh and blood taken from them?" I felt like telling him: Yes, we can. But sometimes it's necessary, out of consideration for the children. But it was futile. We had been steamrollered, Varg, and you know how it would have ended otherwise. There would have been headlines in the press, photographers waiting outside when we went to take the children. Howling kids, distraught parents, social services as the big bad wolf. Just great!'

'We've been through publicity like that a few times, yes.'

'So, events took the course they did. For Margrethe.'

'And things didn't go too well for the brother either, I understand.'

'You've heard about that, have you?'

'I spoke to Per Helge yesterday.'

She looked almost desperate. 'So who had to pay the price for the committee's idealistic efforts?!'

'Has it been long since you last spoke to her?'

'Margrethe? Oh, yes, must be at least a year. As I said …' She opened her palms, indicating the piles of paper towering up on both sides of her desk.

'This committee. You were unsure about Torvaldsen. Do you remember the names of any of the other members?'

'What I remember most is their faces. But … Mobekk, wasn't he one of them, I wonder. Builder. I had met him before in that context.'

'Mobekk?!'

'Yes. Does the name mean anything to you?'

'You'll find him on the front page of both Bergen papers today. Without any mention of his name though. He was found dead yesterday afternoon. Brutally killed in his own home.'

'What! But you don't think that … Margrethe has anything to do with this, do you?'

'I have no idea. But Per Helge told me yesterday that Karl

Gunnar had absconded from prison. And we know he has killed before.'

'Yes, but ...' She looked worried. 'My God! You'll have to tell the police, Varg.'

'Of course. I have an appointment to see them, after this. But back to the committee. Do you think it would be possible to find out all of their names?'

'Yes, I can try. Are you online?'

I smiled. 'I am.'

'I'll send you the list if I find it. Just give me your email address.'

I gave her my business card. 'It's there.'

'Thank you.'

We stood up, and she accompanied me to the entrance. In the waiting room there was turmoil. A client was demanding to talk to a counsellor, who by some mischance was not present, but he wouldn't accept this, not at all, and his voice went more and more falsetto with every sentence he uttered. When Cathrine and I entered he looked as if he was going to pounce on us, as though everything was our fault. And in a way it was. It was always someone else's fault, never mind who. That much I had learned, in the five years I had spent under the clipped wings of the social services.

We discreetly rolled our eyes to each other. Cathrine retreated to her office. I went out in January's dying light, to the foot of the hillside.

14

THE MORNING LIGHT ANGLED LOW over the parking floor at the top of Bystasjonen shopping mall and was reflected in the sculpture of Olav Kyrre across the street from the library, giving the large rhododendron bushes opposite Kaigaten forlorn hopes of spring growth. The forecast was cloudy and changeable with glimpses of the sun during the day.

I rang Atle Helleve on my mobile, and he exclaimed: 'Bloody hell, Varg! You're up with the larks, aren't you?'

'Have you got some time for me if I drop round?'

'You've got something to tell us, I take it?'

'Yes.'

'Thought so. That's what Hamre said when he was briefed this morning: "Veum at a crime scene? Definitely not a coincidence." He was right, Varg.'

'You yourself asked me to drop by.'

'Come on over. Tell them downstairs, and I'll meet you in the foyer.'

I followed instructions, and ten minutes later I was sitting in his office. We were alone. I had nodded to Hamre through his open office door. He was embroiled in a telephone conversation and sent me a mocking look as I passed, but didn't make a big thing of it.

Helleve was a decent guy, but there was no reason to allow yourself to be duped. He was sharper between the ears than many I had met in this neck of the woods. He was no older than late thirties, but had already achieved a reputation as one of the most competent detectives in the department.

'Spill the beans then, Varg … What were you actually doing yesterday afternoon in Minde?'

'No, that isn't how it was. I'm investigating a possible disappearance, a young woman from the red-light area in C. Sundts gate. Her mother still lives in the flat above Torvaldsen, with whom you yourself spoke. It was a pure fluke that I happened to be outside their house – with Torvaldsen – when *fru* Mobekk returned home and found her husband … in that state.'

'Right. So what is it you have to tell me?'

'This woman I'm looking for … Her name's Margrethe Monsen and she grew up there. Her family had problems. The father was an addict, the mother pretty helpless. To cut a long story short, social services were contacted, but a local action committee took the initiative and looked after the Monsen family, supported by the church council.'

'Uhuh?'

'I'm being sent a list of the committee members, but I already know that Mobekk and Torvaldsen were on it.'

'How?'

'An ex-colleague from social services dealt with the case. She remembered Monsen, and the description of the downstairs neighbours matches the Torvaldsen couple.'

'Torvaldsen's a widower, as far as I've been informed.'

'Yes, but only since last autumn.'

He smiled good-naturedly, but without relinquising eye contact.

'I must say you're well-versed for a casual passer-by.'

'Torvaldsen himself told me that. She died of cancer. Furthermore, she was a teacher at Fridalen School.'

'OK, OK, Varg. You've passed the oral.'

'And one more thing. Margrethe has a brother in prison. Known as KG to his circle. Karl Gunnar Monsen. Name ring any bells?'

'It does sound familiar, I have to confess.'

'The Gimle case. Do you remember it?'

He nodded slowly. 'Ye-es. I had something to do with that one, but … A student killed his teacher, or some such thing. And this was KG?'

'Yes, and he's on the loose. He didn't return from leave on Sunday night. Neither he nor his sister has been seen since Friday. Do you know when Mobekk died?'

'Hey, hey, hey! Not so fast, Varg. All I can say is no, we haven't established a time of death yet, but the pathologist's preliminary judgement is that it happened over the weekend, perhaps as late as some time during Sunday night.'

'He didn't answer the phone when his wife called on Monday, wasn't that right?'

'Mm, and she hadn't spoken to him since she went east, more than a week ago.'

'Must have been a knot in the telephone cable.'

Helleve winced. 'Indeed. But this is nothing for you to concern yourself with, Varg. Strictly speaking, you shouldn't have overheard any of what was said. In fact, you were only …' He threw out his hands.

I grinned. 'A casual passer-by. Tell me though … Was he in work?'

He shook his head patiently. 'He had been in the building trade, but sold his business six months ago. Wanted to cut down, according to his wife. Took on consultancy jobs, as they're known.'

'And there were no jobs last week?'

'Not at the weekend at any rate.'

'So from the moment Torvaldsen said goodbye on Friday night no one saw him?'

'Not that we are aware of.' He leaned forward. 'But I think we'll draw a line there, Varg. What I'm interested in is what you can tell us, not what we can tell you.'

'OK, I think I've said pretty well everything I had to say. If I were you I would check where this Karl Gunnar Monsen might be holed up following his disappearance.'

'Why's that? Can you back up your suggestion?'

'There's a definite connection. I …'

He raised one hand. 'Just a moment, Veum.' He went to the door and called down the corridor. 'Bjarne! Can you come here for a second?'

Seconds later Bjarne Solheim was at the door. He sent me a cheery nod. 'Yeah?'

'The fingerprints we found at the scene of the crime yesterday. Have any of them been identified?'

Solheim showed him a sheet he had in his hand. 'Got this from Forensics a moment ago. Definitive answer. Apart from the wife's and what we reckon are Mobekk's own prints there was nothing that could be identified. Nothing matched what we have on file anyway.'

'And we would have Karl Gunnar Monsen's prints in the archives, would we?'

Solheim gave a look of surprise. 'And who is that?'

'The Gimle case. May have been before you came to the department.'

'If he was charged and sentenced we have got him in the archives, no question.'

Helleve turned back to me. 'What makes you connect Karl Gunnar Monsen with the Mobekk murder?'

'Nothing apart from what I've already told you. Mobekk was on the committee taking care of the Monsen kids. But … as far as I could see they were searching for something indoors where we found him. Were there any signs of a break-in?'

Helleve glanced at Solheim, extended a hand towards me and said: 'Meet our new departmental boss, Bjarne. The man with a thousand questions.'

I raised a dry smile. 'I saw what I saw. Someone had been searching for something. If so, what were they searching for, and how did they get in?'

'They?'

'Yes, they or he, what do I know?'

Helleve sighed. 'There were no signs of a break-in. Mobekk must have let whoever it was in.'

'Someone he knew perhaps? Someone who was connected with his work. In that branch there are quite a lot of …'

'Thank you, Varg, that'll do. We drew the line some time ago. Didn't you catch that? From now on this is not your case; it's ours.'

'Now, now, Atle. Let's take a rather broader view, shall we. I've been given an assignment, and I intend to complete it. If by some chance there should be a suspicious death where I'm conducting my investigation it won't stop me. I'll keep as far away as I possibly can from your activities, but I'm going to continue my search for Margrethe Monsen.'

'Alright, alright,' Helleve sighed. 'We live in a free country. You can go. But don't forget where we are if you dig something up.'

'How could I forget?'

'And don't slam the door as you leave!'

I saluted and left. As I passed Hamre's open door he shouted to me. 'Veum!'

'Yep?'

'I heard you'd found another body for us?'

'Nope. The body's wife found it. I just happened to be in the vicinity.'

He eyed me with his by now almost ingrown sardonic expression. 'Veum … Be a good boy. Behave nicely. Don't cause us any trouble.'

'Trouble? Me? The best-behaved boy in Dormitory 1?'

'Who was sent home after a week, with instructions never to show his face there again? But did he listen?'

'Probably not.'

'No.' He got up from his desk and came over to me. Patted me on the shoulder in an amicable way. 'Go home and play on your own, Veum. Make a telephone call or two. But don't trample over our flower beds. Not again.'

'I'll do my best, Hamre.'

'Your best has never been good enough to date.'

'And yours has?'

We stood looking at each other for a few seconds. Then we shrugged and went our separate ways. We would meet again. I wasn't in any doubt about that.'

15

I TOSSED THE STACK OF POST from the letter box onto the desk. Most of the envelopes had windows, but the view through them was wretched. Several of them contained payment reminders, and some threatened legal action. I placed them in a pile and made a mental note to phone some of my regular contractors, like Nils Åkre.

I went to the window and peered out, but the view from there was not much better. The good weather we had been promised had not materialised. Storms of sleet swept in over the town like biblical swarms of locusts, and we were not far from having darkness in the middle of the day. January is an unreliable month with at least two faces, like the god it is named after. Today it was the one in the surly mood. It would have been tempting to brew up a good cup of coffee, pull down the blinds, put my feet on the table and let the day drift by without announcing my presence to the world. However, this was not one of those days. Switching on the computer, I noticed a message from Cathrine Leivestad waiting for me.

I clicked it open and read:

Hi Varg!
No one I have contacted so far can identify the car you mentioned. At any rate it's not one of the ones we know.
I have attached the list of names of those on the action

committee set up in September 1978.

Hugs,

Cathrine

I opened the attachment and scoured the list:

Markus Rødberg (chair)
Carsten Mobekk
Lill Mobekk
Alf Torvaldsen
Wenche Torvaldsen
Hulda Vefring

I printed a copy of the list and put a tick by Markus Rødberg and Hulda Vefring. A quick scan through the telephone directory told me that both still lived in Minde: Markus Rødberg, verger, in Finnbergåsen; Hulda Vefring, teacher, in Bendixens vei. Neither of them answered when I rang, but it was in the middle of the working day.

For the next few hours I surfed the Net, made a few telephone calls and tried to devise a strategy. I rang Hege and asked her if she could give me some more names from Margrethe Monsen's circle of acquaintances, but she couldn't. I asked her whether she had ever met the brother, Karl Gunnar. She hadn't. When I told her that Maggi had said to Tanya that she would be leaving soon, she reacted with loud astonishment. She hadn't mentioned any such plans to her. Where then? Well, her guess was as good as mine. I didn't have an answer either …

After a couple of hours I tried Hulda Vefring and Markus Rødberg again. This time Rødberg answered. 'Yes, hello?'

'Markus Rødberg?'

'That's me.'

'My name's Veum. I'm investigating a disappearance and would very much like to speak to you.'

'To me? About what did you say?'

'Just to gather some background information. This is about a young woman called Margrethe Monsen.'

Silence for some seconds. Then he said: 'I see.'

'May I drop by?'

'Now, this minute?'

'Preferably.'

He sighed. 'Alright then. If I can be of any help. I have to say that the Monsen family ... well ... we can discuss that when you get here.'

I went to get the car. Half an hour after we had talked I was standing outside a terraced house in Finnbergåsen, a consequence of the 1920s social building programme, after the legendary founder during the employment boom, Grant Lea, had sold most of the area to Bergen City Council. The houses were similar to those in Falsens vei, but here the sunny back gardens faced Lea Park, on the days when there was sun, which made them a degree more attractive in the housing market.

I crossed the front garden and rang the bell.

Markus Rødberg's hair colour matched his surname, red, though it had faded a little. For that matter there was also a New Testament gentleness about the way in which he received me, reminiscent of the evangelist he was named after. 'Veum? Come in.'

He was in his late fifties, and rounded at the edges without seeming overweight. His hands were conspicuously small and well manicured; his thick hair had a neat parting and swept elegantly upwards from his forehead. He was wearing dark brown trousers, a green jacket, a creamy-yellow shirt and a burgundy tie with a hint of check.

He led me into the house, through a tidy entrance hall and into a rather old-fashioned living room with well-worn period furniture that gave the impression they were handed down. The same was true of the large bureau with the oval mirror and the traditional landscape paintings in the gilt frames that covered the walls. On a bookcase I glimpsed several books of a religious nature, a four-volume edition of the Bible in red leather and several classical works: the Four Greats plus Hamsun, Falkberget and Sigrid Undset. There was a 1950s style radio cabinet along one wall, but the tiny portable radio on top revealed that the luxury model didn't have FM. Hopefully, the record player worked, because there was a stand containing LPs next to the cabinet. The closest was *Ella Fitzgerald's Christmas*, a recording of carols by the American jazz vocalist from some time in the 1960s, judging by the cover.

He had set the dining table with cups and plates. There was a flask of coffee and a small coffee service ready, and a dish of dry biscuits and tasty coconut macaroons.

'I've made some coffee,' he said. 'Please do sit down.'

We sat and he poured some coffee for us both.

'Sugar? Cream?'

'No, thank you.'

When, at length, he had finished all his chores he sat down in the chair at the other side of the table. He folded his hands, quietly bent his head, straightened up again and pushed the dish towards me. He looked at me with a gentle expression. 'So … Tell me more. Margrethe has disappeared, you said?'

'Yes. I don't know h… How well did you know the family?'

He sent me an eloquent look. 'Very well. I don't know how

you got hold of my name, but I assume it was through the committee.'

'Yes, I was given a list. You appear on it as the chair.'

'Yes, I undertook that task. Are you from the police?'

'No, no, no,' I said with a disarming smile. 'I'm a private investigator. This is a private investigation.'

'Is that so?' A furrow appeared on his brow. 'But ... before we proceed any further. Has this anything to do with what happened in Falsens vei yesterday?'

'You know about it?'

'I read newspapers. It was on the front page of *Bergens Tidende* this morning, if you didn't see it. I saw from the photo which house it was, so when I made a call and enquired, my suspicions were confirmed.'

'You spoke to Torvaldsen, I take it?'

'Yes. Do you know him?'

'I was with him yesterday when we found ... the deceased.'

'But there isn't thought to be ... Was that supposed to have any connection with Margrethe?'

'For the moment I don't believe there are any specific suspicions, but everything is being checked of course.'

'Of course,' he repeated, like an educated little echo.

'You know the family, I believe. From when the children were small.'

'The Monsen family? Yes, I do. How long has she been missing? Margrethe.'

'Just a few days.'

'Ah.' He seemed to be expecting more to come, but when it didn't, he said: 'I'll tell you what I know about them, and you can form your own conclusions.'

I tasted the coffee. It was excellent. Then I took a coconut macaroon and leaned back in the chair as an indication that he should give himself as much time as he needed.

'In point of fact I knew the father best. Frank Monsen. We called him Frankie. We grew up together. That is, he was three or four years younger than me, but I remember him from our patch. From the Ritz, where we went regularly, from Lea Park, where we often played football in the schoolyard, or later, when some of us went to Årstad, to the training ground over by Rautjern. He was a little tank, even then. I remember ... often when we were sitting in the Ritz ...'

'Is that Kafé Ritz you're talking about?'

'Yes.' He looked at me in surprise, as though it was impossible not to know what the Ritz was.

'I grew up in Nordnes.'

'Ah, alright. But for those of us growing up here we went to the Ritz a lot. You know, it was a decent café. You could have lunch there, and the taxi drivers from the rank across the street, by the tram loop, were often there for a cup of coffee and a smoke. The big attraction for us kids was the chocolate counter. If you bought something you were allowed to sit there while you ate, and there was no end to the number of tiny bits we could break the chocolate up into so that we could stretch out the time. But we were sternly scrutinised by the women behind the counter, *fru* Olsen and *fru* Tarlebø, and I remember once, when Frankie had been up and down the shop like a yo-yo, without buying anything, and *fru* Olsen shouted: "Now you've all got to go home, Frank Monsen!" Another time she said: "Frank Monsen, I've spoken to your mother on the phone. You've got to go home." To which Frankie replied: "We haven't got a phone." And in fact he was telling the truth.'

He looked dreamily into the distance. In his mind he was

forty years back in time. 'And later, when we were teenagers, we often hung around there, playing music on the jukebox, eyeing up girls and so on. But … I was beginning to look for somewhere else to meet. I joined a youth club in Årstad parish, as it was called, and that determined the course of my later life.'

'You're a verger?'

'Yes, but only fifty per cent now.' He gazed at me with light blue, almost grey eyes. 'Nerves. They play me up a bit.'

'I see.'

'But … Frankie, as I said, he grew up and stayed in the district as well. Bit by bit, though, well, things didn't go so well for Frankie.'

'What happened?'

'Hm, what did happen?' He met my eyes. 'So much happens in a human life, Veum. It's not always that easy to say why. But … I believe the problem started when he was in the army. He was sent to the back of beyond, and when he returned he had an alcohol problem. He had started as a trainee electrician before his military service and continued after his return. He couldn't hold down any jobs, and had longer and longer periods of absences, and it all became … problematic. We tried to help him as much as we could.'

'We?'

'Yes, neighbours, friends. I started doing voluntary parish work early, and Frankie's parents were active.'

'So he hadn't inherited this from his parents?'

'Not at all. His father was a teetotaller and his mother the same, of course.'

'A reaction then, perhaps? Did he have brothers or sisters?'

'An older sister. Things didn't go well for her. She got married and moved, well, east. At first she was in Lillestrøm. Now she lives in Asker, I think I heard.'

'But he still lived in the area?'

'Yes, in the same house as his parents. They were very young when they married, Else and him. But they were allowed to rent the first floor, where they still live. That is, Else does. Frankie's dead, of course. And then the children started coming.'

'Right. And the parents had gone, both of them?'

'Yes, they died young, sad to say. Now Torvaldsen lives there.'

'And this Else, was she from here as well?'

'No. She was his girlfriend, someone we'd met via an acquaintance. A modest girl. Very modest, I believe you could say. We hoped for a long time that having responsibility for her and the children would keep him on an even keel, because it wasn't as though he couldn't work. He was a good electrician, it was said, if he turned up. But he had this problem, which was then aggravated by … taking pills. He went to see a doctor to get some help, but this doctor … Well, he prescribed sedatives in such huge quantities that that, in its turn, created a new addiction problem.'

'Mm. Not that unusual, I'm afraid.'

'We were thinking of the children, of course.'

'We? That's still neighbours and friends, is it?'

'Yes, you could say so.'

'That's how this committee was formed, I understand.'

'Yes, it … To support Frankie and his family. Both of his parents had died, one after the other, in 1969. Luckily they experienced the arrival of the first grandchild, Siv, whom they worshipped above all else. I don't think I've ever seen such ecstatic grandparents as Nils and Henny when she was born. So sad that they witnessed only the first year of her life.'

'How did they die?'

'Of natural causes. Nils of a heart attack. Henny had a stroke, just a few months later. Some thought she died of grief, but it was a stroke, nothing more and nothing less.'

'And then things became more difficult for Frank and Else, I suppose?'

'Yes, I don't think we should underestimate the significance Nils and Henny had for the young parents. You know, Frankie was a mere nineteen when Siv was born, Else was eighteen. And the year Nils and Henny died … that was when he was called up to do military service.'

'Right.' I made some notes on my pad. 'To sum up then. He meets Else, and she becomes pregnant, I guess. Then they marry and move into his parents' house. Siv is born in 1968, the following year his parents die, and he is called up. He comes back in 1970, is that correct?'

'Yes, sounds right.'

'And the same year Margrethe is born. Two years later KG is born. Karl Gunnar. How were these years, the 70s?'

'Well, I can't tell you from first-hand experience. Even though we lived in the same area we didn't really see much of each other. You know what it's like, you nod to familiar faces, and Frankie was, as I said, a few years younger than me. But I could see that he looked a bit … run-down. Else too. Pale and unsmiling. The children … well, I don't have such a vivid memory of them. I saw Else pushing them in a pram when they were small, and sometimes I saw them in the playground by Jacob Aalls gate.' He put on a melancholy smile. 'On wonderful, sunny Sunday mornings I saw the whole family. I can remember thinking: so things turned out well for Frankie after all.'

'Although they didn't.'

He chewed a bit on what I had said before answering. 'No. I suppose they didn't, in a way.'

'What did he die of?'

'Frankie? He fell down the stairs at home and broke his neck. Inebriated, of course.'

'There wasn't an investigation?'

'Regarding the cause of death? No. He had drunk himself senseless and in fact was in a coma when he fell.'

'OK. Back to the family situation then. I have made a note telling me that social services were alerted around 1978.'

'Yes, and that was when we decided to stick our oar in, those of us who had known Frankie since he was a boy. There's a saying we have here: Once a Minde boy, always a Minde boy.'

'Right …'

'More coffee, Veum?'

'Yes, please.'

He poured, and I took another coconut macaroon.

'I would like to stress one thing though. What we did was for purely idealistic reasons. It was to help the children. It was to support the family. After all, family is the nucleus that the entire society is built around. Isn't it?'

'Many believe that.'

'Family, school, church. You might think it strange that I say this, seeing as I live alone.'

I shrugged. 'I live alone as well, by and large.'

'Indeed?' For a moment he looked at me with interest, then he was back to his story. 'Well, this is life's destiny, not something over which you have any control. I never met the right one. Such was my life.'

'Not even at the Ritz?'

He gave a sudden smile. 'No, Veum. Not even there. And I can tell you … I know of at least two marriages that had their beginnings there. Erm … It was the health visitor at Fridalen who first voiced her concerns. Social services paid them a visit and action was mooted. To move them away from home.'

'Was there any particular reason given?'

'In Margrethe's case, and she was the one who prompted the health visitor's concern, there was talk of malnutrition, ADHD and generally poor adjustment to school and her surroundings. As for Karl Gunnar, that was primarily ADHD and perhaps inappropriate nutrition. There was nothing wrong with Siv. So there was a choice: leave Siv at home but move the others out. Split up the children! Can you imagine anything more painful?'

'It's a problem, of course, but on occasion it can in fact be necessary.'

'On occasion, yes. Well, perhaps. But we – those of us on the committee – decided to take a hand, as I said. We went to social services and said we were willing to look after the family. Said that with God's help and the parish's support and joint commitment we would look after them. Help them with the children, in every way possible. Ensure they received enough food, got up in the morning, did their homework and offer them a range of leisure activities. For as long as was necessary. Our main intention, of course, was to be what Nils and Henny had been for Frankie and Else when they were newly-weds, a support network for every day. And we got the support. Perhaps not at the lower levels of the social services, but we had management on our side, and we agreed to give it a go at any rate.'

'And how did it go?'

'It went well, didn't it?' As I didn't answer, he added: 'For quite a while anyway.'

'Tell me how it worked.'

'It worked as I said. We shared tasks. Someone always checked that they got up and were given breakfast. Alf and Wenche were living in the house anyway, and Wenche taught at Fridalen School. They often accompanied her to school. We others helped in any way we could. Lill dropped by every so often and helped with cooking. She didn't go out to work. Furthermore, Carsten and Lill had a cabin in Gulen where they took the children walking. Carsten, Alf and I tried to get Frankie to join us in other contexts. Carsten and Alf were hunters. They took him hunting many times, but Frankie's physique was nothing to boast about, so it was never a great success. It's hard work, as you know. The hunt itself is one thing, but later they transport the animals to the cars, skin them and cut them up. They have each got a freezer in the cellar where they keep all the venison in different shapes and sizes for meals throughout the year. I don't go in for hunting myself, but we had a man's group in the parish, a discussion group. I invited Frankie along a few times.'

'No success there, either?'

'Well, no, now you say so … he had a difficult temperament, Frankie did. You could see it in his eyes. Forever wandering. He could never look you straight in the eye. As though there were something he didn't want to tell you, something that was a source of embarrassment. And perhaps that was not so strange. He was ashamed of his whole life, I suppose. Of needing help for something as simple as taking care of his own children.'

'It's not always that simple.'

'No, no, perhaps it isn't.'

'But perhaps you and the committee didn't score such a great success, either, in light of the results?'

His eyes flashed. 'You can gloat, Veum! You as so many others. I know that people were talking behind our backs. Telling one another: this will never work. And when it didn't … Oh, yes, here in this region where Jante Law has never gone out of fashion: Don't think you're anyone special, don't think you're better than us … There was a lot of *Schadenfreude* when suddenly … when the catastrophe struck.'

'And by the catastrophe you mean …?'

He raised the coffee cup with a trembling hand to his mouth and took a hefty swig. He was searching for the words. 'I … it … you know.'

'Are you thinking about what happened at Gimle?'

He nodded and set his cup down so hard the plate rattled. 'Yes, Veum. I am thinking of Gimle.'

16

MARKUS RØDBERG COLLECTED HIMSELF. He took a coconut macaroon, leaned back in the chair and sighed. 'It was a tragedy. I can remember the moment I was told … I could scarcely believe my ears.'

'Do you know anything about the background to it?'

He slowly shook his head. 'The background? This and that. We were pretty pleased with results as far as Karl Gunnar was concerned. We had got him through middle school and he stayed on after sixteen, both schools in Gimle. But then this situation arose. This supply teacher.'

'It was a supply teacher?'

'Yes, for PE. Someone who had barely left school himself. Had done his military service and then enrolled at the school to do supply. But he was one of … them.'

'One of … them?'

He blushed. 'Yes. I don't know what you call them. A paedo, a homo, a … molester. It came out during the trial. There was no doubt that it happened in … self-defence. Karl Gunnar was groped, and he hit back. But alas he was holding a heavy object when he struck. A much too heavy object.'

'A dumbbell, I was told.'

'A … yes, that sort of thing … a weight. The kind you do muscle training with.'

I nodded.

'But this was a bolt from the blue, Veum. This had nothing

to do with what home he came from or the work the committee had done. This was a terrible personal tragedy.'

'How did he take it himself? Karl Gunnar, I mean.'

'He battened down the hatches. Completely. Wouldn't talk to anyone. Not about that. The detectives had to drag it out of him, and I think it was that – his not wanting to speak – that led to him getting the sentence he did. If he had opened up about what had happened he would have been given a lighter sentence.'

'He's on his way out again now.'

'At last! After how many years?'

'Was on his way out, I should say. He didn't return from his last weekend leave. He hasn't contacted you in recent days, has he?'

'Me, no. Why would he?'

'Well … did you stay in touch with him afterwards?'

He nodded. 'We visited him, Carsten, Alf and I, in prison. But he wasn't very forthcoming, and gradually it got to a point where we stopped visiting him. Now it must be three or four years since I last went.'

'How did his parents take this?'

'With apathy, as good as. They were shocked, that goes without saying. As shocked as we all were. I remember Frankie's outburst in the courtroom. He shouted at the prosecutor: I would have killed the bastard myself if I'd have got hold of him! I would've killed him … He was so angry it took two officers to quieten him down. Else, as always, said nothing. I can hardly remember her doing anything more than mumble something or other. Thanks for the help, that sort of thing. Very distant, Veum. Very distant.'

'Perhaps this was what the social services had noticed during the home visit. That she was not a motivating mother, she didn't give her children either resistance or … the opposite.'

'Are you blaming us?' he said accusingly. 'Us? Who supported the family. But I've told you … How could we have checked what was going on in school? We couldn't at Gimle. It was a different matter at Fridalen. We had Wenche and *frøken* Vefring there. I tried several times to get him to join a youth club I was running, but it was no use. It obviously wasn't what he wanted.'

'Did what actually happened between Karl Gunnar and this supply teacher ever come out?'

'No more than they managed to force out of him at the end. But … he was examined by a doctor. There had been nothing … physical. It must have been an approach that produced this catastrophic result. Catastrophic for all sides. For the young man, for Karl Gunnar … and for the whole family.'

I nodded and sat flicking through my notes. 'The other children. How did they fare?'

'Everything went fine with Siv. Always. She completed her education, got a job with an insurance company and they trained her.'

'But she had managed well … even before social services made their report.'

'Yes, I … We don't take sole credit for her turning out so well. She had a good base. One year with Nils and Henny around her. She was a clever girl, Siv was. Never any problems with her. She matured early.'

'Yes, some say she assumed the mother's responsibilities towards her siblings.'

'That may be right. She was a grand support for us on the committee at any rate, not least with regard to everyday organisation. As she grew up, that is. She was only ten when the committee was set up, you have to remember.'

'And Margrethe?'

He moistened his lips. With saddened intonation he said: 'Little Margrethe ...' It was as if he had to choose his words judiciously before he continued, and the first ones were hesitant. 'In many ways my impression of her ... was that she was the most ... difficult of them all. At least there was some go in Karl Gunnar. He could put up a fight ... er ...' He sent me a mortified look. 'By that I wasn't referring to ... I was talking about him as a boy. He was perhaps the one who was most like his father, when Frankie was a boy. But Margrethe ... perhaps she had inherited her mother's genes. She was a bit lacking in energy, right from birth.'

'Yes, malnutrition was diagnosed.'

'Indeed, but I think it was because she lacked a scrap of initiative. I think she's one of those who could die in front of the bread bin. She was passive, unmotivated, in fact, well, a lot like her mother.'

'And how did she get on at school?'

'Not too well, I'm afraid. Neither Wenche nor *frøken* Vefring could do much there. She simply didn't have any talent in that direction.'

'So what talents did she have?'

'Well ... after school we tried to shunt her towards something practical. Perhaps an apprenticeship as a hairdresser. No. Care assistant. Nothing at all. She couldn't even sit by the till in a supermarket. The cash desk was too complicated for her. She was a loser, Veum, I'm afraid. I have to tell it as it is. I have to be honest.'

'You know where she ended up, don't you?'

He looked at me glumly. 'Yes.' Made a vague gesture with his small, well-manicured hand. 'She's out there – in Nordnes, isn't she?'

I nodded without saying a word.

We sat for a while like this. I didn't know if I had any more questions. Then I said: 'Carsten Mobekk was found dead yesterday, killed by an unknown person. Karl Gunnar is on the loose. Is it conceivable … that Karl Gunnar may have a score to settle with Carsten Mobekk?'

'What could it be? Carsten, like all of us, did only what he could to help him and his sisters. No, Veum, that is too far-fetched!'

'The others on the committee … Wenche Torvaldsen is dead. What about *frøken* Vefring?'

He gave a weary smile. 'She's alive. But she must be over eighty now. She was the oldest of us at the time the committee formed. At least twenty years older than many of us. Sometimes she behaved as if she were our mother!'

'Really?'

'Yes, she wanted to be in charge and have the final say and did not always agree with everything we did.'

'Such as when?'

'Well, I can't give you any examples. But in general terms. If you ask me she was a bit gaga at the end.'

'You aren't in touch any more?'

'No. Not since the committee was wound up.'

'When was that in fact?'

'Well, five, six, perhaps seven years ago. In a way, our job had been done.'

'With varying degrees of success.'

'That's for others to judge.'

'Have you ever wondered how things would have been if social services had got their way that time, in 1978? Whether Karl Gunnar and Margrethe might have been better off?'

His eyes darkened. 'What use is it crying over spilt milk? What's done is done, as they say.'

'Well …' I got to my feet. 'I'll say my farewells. Thank you for the coffee and biscuits.' At the door I turned. 'Have you got a car, Rødberg?'

He studied me with surprise. 'Certainly not! I don't even have a licence.'

'Right. What about Mobekk and Torvaldsen?'

'Yes, of course. They both have cars.'

'Has either of them got a black car?'

'A black …? I have no idea. I know nothing at all about cars.'

'Not even colours?'

'They change cars so often it's impossible to keep up. Why on earth are you interested?'

'Well,' I shrugged, and smiled. 'I was only wondering.'

A couple of minutes later I was in my car and starting up; I didn't have far to go. Past the old tram turnaround, up to the crossing by Wergeland and thence to Bendixens vei. Passing Falsens vei, I noticed that uniformed police officers were performing what looked remarkably like a door-to-door search. I could, of course, have offered them my assistance, but I held back. I had the feeling my offer would not have been received with warmth.

17

FROM HER FLAT IN BENDIXENS VEI HULDA Vefring had a view over Årstad Sports Club training ground in Rautjern and the small parkland area around it. In the clubhouse on the other side of the pitch there was a children's nursery, and as I got out of the car I heard the gleeful screams of children playing. It often occurred to me when I was outside on jobs, which not infrequently were tied up with death and misery, that the backcloth was often an everyday event: children playing, a distant siren, building works, an aeroplane passing overhead. Everyday life that I had to interrupt with a message not nearly as popular as that of the famous messenger of antiquity from Marathon.

From Hulda Vefring's living room window the training ground resembled a gigantic flying carpet, ready to take off for brighter times. The shale was grey, the grass around it winter green and the treetops bare. Summer was still a long way off. There were no passengers on board.

Hulda Vefring had scrutinised me with a sharp, schoolmarm's gaze as I introduced myself at the door, but I had passed the inspection, and she let me in without further ado. She was a slender, thin woman with a trophy-shaped head; her hair was white, cropped and clung smoothly to her scalp. Easy to cut, practical to maintain.

The flat gave the same impression: clean and tidy. The furniture was simple and functional, nothing very old-fashioned.

Most of it seemed to date from the 1970s, as though she had performed a cull when she joined the ranks of pensioners. There was not even a trace of the abundance of potted plants that women of her generation often tended with care. The arrangement of flowers was meticulous: a few orchids in simple vases, a bonsai tree on a nest of tables in one corner, a small cyclamen on a mantelpiece.

'So Margrethe has disappeared, you say?'

'Yes.'

'How long?'

'Since before the weekend.'

She looked at me with concern. Her nose was sharp with a rounded arch, her eyes bright blue, her complexion a fine network of neatly etched wrinkles. 'I see.'

'And her brother has disappeared, too.'

Angry ridges appeared between her eyebrows. 'What? Anything else? What about Siv?'

'No, Siv's fine. I spoke to her myself as recently as yesterday.'

'Hm.' She seemed displeased. I had the feeling my grade had dropped at least one level in the last minute. 'And why are you visiting me?'

'Well, I'm collecting background information. I've just come from seeing Markus Rødberg.'

'Mm.' She pursed her lips in a way that spoke volumes. 'You're a private investigator, you said?'

'Yes.'

'Is it possible to live on that?'

'So far it has been.'

'Hm.' There was still no enthusiasm to be detected in her eyes. 'Tell me then. What is it you want from me?'

I noticed that there was little point addressing *frøken* Vefring in the informal form and I concentrated on using the most polite intonation I could muster. 'I understand you were a member of this committee formed to assist the Monsen family with everyday living.'

'Yes, that's correct. I … Well, a colleague of mine, *fru* Torvaldsen asked me if I might give some assistance. After all, Siv was in my class. Wenche – *fru* Torvaldsen, that is – had grown up in the area. In fact, she was my pupil when I started at Fridalen. In my very first class.'

'People here seem to be loyal to the districts where they grow up.'

'Yes, indeed. Well, Wenche came from Langhaugen in fact, so moving to Minde was a step down. But on the other hand … Well, we do stick together. We're like a little town within a town.'

'What was your impression of the Monsen family?'

'I'd had Frank at school as well. In the first and second classes before they had male teachers. A class of boys. One of the last.'

'He was a bit … restless, I've been told.'

'A bit? Ha! He was a fidget from the very first morning. But unfortunately for him … the uphill road was long and hard, and by the time we set up the committee there was already something resigned about him, a lost soul.'

'Lost soul?'

'Yes, now please do not analyse everything I say, *herr* Veum! I am not myself a believer of the convinced breed. I take one day at a time and keep eternity on hold. What I meant was there was something dejected about him. He was unable to cope with everyday life, and it has to be said, he did not receive much support from his wife. A more anonymous individual I have never met.' Then she added, 'Barely at school,' whatever she meant by that.

'And the children?'

'I knew Siv best. She was a decent girl. Good at school, tidy in everything. Always did her homework and never missed a day, as far as I can remember.'

'So there was nothing wrong with her health?'

'Nothing at all. This was not the case with Margrethe, however. But she must have inherited some of her mother's qualities. There didn't seem to be an ounce of initiative in her tiny carcass. She was thin and bony, suffered from a lack of vitamins, couldn't concentrate in class, in short ... That was when the health nurse and social services stepped in.'

'But all of you on the committee undertook the responsibility to look after her and her siblings?'

'Yes, we did. But Wenche, Carsten Mobekk and Markus Rødberg were the ones on the committee who took the initiative.'

'Have you heard what happened to Carsten Mobekk?'

'No, I ...' Her eyes widened until an expression of disbelief spread across her face. 'Was Carsten Mobekk the man who ... down in Falsens vei?'

I nodded.

'Well, that was what I was thinking when I read about it this morning ... hoping it wasn't someone I knew. So it was. You know ... I've taught most of the children in this district – well, until I retired. They're all grown up now. Even my last batch must be way over twenty. But ... I have a feeling I know them, all of them. So when something like this happens ... how strange that it should be Mobekk.' She shook her head. 'Well, I never went to their homes. As a rule the meetings were held at *herr* Rødberg's, and sometimes here. How is Lill taking it?'

'She's in shock, of course.'

Again she pursed her lips, in the same way as when I first mentioned Markus Rødberg. It was like an unconscious reaction, and it reflected – as I interpreted it – a form of disapproval.

'I don't suppose the police think … this has anything to do with the disappearance of Karl Gunnar and Margrethe, do they?'

I hesitated for a second. 'There's no reason to assume that for the time being. But … now we're talking about him, Karl Gunnar, what impression did you have of him as a boy?'

She gave this question some thought. 'He was a … survivor. We meet types like him all the time. However difficult the circumstances they grow up in, some float to the surface. Like small corks on the river of life.'

'Like small … that's a poetic image, *frøken* Vefring.'

She put on a dry smile.

'However, sometimes the current can be too strong, even for small corks, can it not?'

'Indeed,' she replied succinctly. 'And I'm afraid we all know how things went for Karl Gunnar.'

'Yes. Do you know anything about the case?'

'No more than was in the newspapers, and what people said.'

'And what did people say?'

'Well … that it was molestation. Or an attempt. There is nothing else to say about the case. It was a terrible tragedy, for all parties concerned.'

'Could you imagine any reason why he would react in such a violent manner?'

'No, but boys of his age … they can be highly unpredictable and have a very short fuse if they're teased.'

'I'm sure you're right.' I paused before continuing. 'I have to ask you this, since you knew the children so well. Now that both Margrethe and Karl Gunnar have disappeared. Do you know anywhere they might go? Childhood friends, any other connections?'

She slowly shook her head. 'No, no one apart from Siv. I would imagine they got in touch with her.'

'She says they didn't.'

'Well ... Then I'm afraid I can't help you any further. I have to confess that after the committee finished their work seven or eight years ago I haven't had much contact ... neither with the children nor with the other committee members.'

'Why not?'

Her mouth narrowed again. 'I don't know how proud we can be of the outcome.'

'So perhaps you concluded that it would have been better to let social services handle the case as they wanted, back in 1978?'

She nodded briefly. 'I can't rule out that possibility, *herr* Veum.' She got up as a sign the session was over. 'Shall we say that's all?'

I got up, too. 'Almost all.'

She sent me a sharp look. 'Almost?'

'*Frøken* Vefring ... I have a feeling you're holding something back.'

Her cheeks flushed. 'Holding something back? What are you suggesting?'

'I'm used to interpreting signals, and I think I caught some disapproval when we touched on ... some of the other committee members.'

Her eyes flashed. 'And so what? Having worked together in close union it would hardly be surprising if there had been some conflicts.'

'Would you mind specifying what these conflicts were?'

'They won't have had anything to do with Margrethe's and Karl Gunnar's disappearances!'

'Perhaps you should let me be the judge of that?'

'Something happened.' Her facial expression told me that this was not something she was happy to talk about. 'Don't ask me what. But at some point between 1989 and 1990 ... some ill feeling arose between several of the other members. I had the impression something had happened between Rødberg, on the one hand, and the Torvaldsen and Mobekk couples, on the other. Which no one wanted to talk about, but it hung in the air ... like a toxic atmosphere at every single meeting we held. It was almost a relief when the Karl Gunnar business happened and we had something else on our minds.'

'Did you ever try to confront the others with this ill feeling? It must have made your work harder?'

'Let me confide in you, *herr* Veum. In my work I've always had to deal with conflict. To deal with people who don't like each other, talking behind others' backs and savouring the malice this brings. I've grown quite a thick skin, I can tell you. Furthermore, I knew this work was coming to an end. When the Karl Gunnar business was finished, in a way our task was completed as well. There was no longer any need for us.'

'I see. Well, in that case I'd like to thank you for taking the time to speak to me.'

'Time is what I have most of, *herr* Veum,' she said sardonically. 'Although from a statistical point of view I have little left.'

She escorted me to the door. Then a thought seemed to strike her. 'There was one thing by the way ...'

'Yes?'

'You asked about childhood friends. Karl Gunnar had a best

friend. They were inseparable all the way through school. They got up to quite a few pranks. It would be worthwhile checking to see if they were still such good friends.'

'Yes? Do you remember the name of this friend?'

'Do I remember? I remember the names of all my pupils, *herr* Veum. All of them.'

'Impressive. And the name was …?'

'He grew up in Falsens vei as well. In one of the Vestbo blocks. Good family. Father taught Norwegian. Lektor Dalby.'

'I see!'

'The boy's name was Rolf Terje Dalby.'

18

I FOUND A PARKING SPOT at the far end of Strandgaten. Back in the office, I checked the answer machine and the computer, but no one had tried to get into contact with me since Cathrine Leivestad earlier in the day.

I resorted to the natural method, opened the telephone directory and looked for Rolf Terje Dalby. I couldn't find him. A quick call to Karin Bjørge and I had his address. A house in Rosenbergsgaten.

'At least that's the last official one,' she added.

'Thank you.'

'Nothing to thank me for this time, either,' she said and rang off.

I dialled the number of my old friend, Paul Finckel, the journalist.

'Varg? I can see it's you.'

'You've got a rear-view mirror on your phone, have you?'

'It can be useful now and again. What are you after this time?'

I still wasn't sure if it was sarcasm, depression or a common hangover that coloured his life these days. 'The Gimle case. Can you remember it?'

He cranked the cerebral handle a few times before answering. 'Yes. The PE teacher killed by an aggressive pupil or something like that. Never much of a case. Too open and shut for that. 1988 or 1989.'

'1989. You couldn't dig up some archive material, could you, and meet me for a beer?'

'Yes to the former. With all the usual provisos. No to the latter. Doc's instructions.'

'What?'

'Been told to stop drinking.'

Then I knew. It was depression. 'Wow ...'

'You don't need to envy me, Varg.'

'I don't.'

Despondent, he said: 'But we can meet for a cup of tea tomorrow morning some time. Can't make it before.'

'Half past eleven at Holberg. Is that OK?'

'If I live that long,' said Paul Finckel, and he rang off.

I was tempted to call Atle Helleve to find out how far they had got in the course of the day, but realised it would be best to keep my distance. I didn't have that much to offer, anyway. Not until I had checked the home of Rolf Terje Dalby. I made that point number one in my plan of action, locked the office door and left.

It was a shade past four o'clock, but already dark as I entered Rosenbergsgaten from Sverres gate, right behind the large cinema building. The house where Dalby lived was a classical grey house with a chimney, built in the late 1800s, judiciously modernised and redecorated not long ago. Unlike in the ever-increasing number of city centre blocks the ground entrance door was unlocked. I stepped in and checked the names on the letter boxes. I found *Dalby* on one of them. To be on the safe side, I checked the others. No names I recognised there.

I ascended the semi-dark staircase, illuminated by over-sized lamp globes on each floor. I reached the top without finding his name on any of the doors.

I went back down and spotted a door at the back of the hall. I wandered over, leaned forward and squinted in the darkness. On a bit of cardboard fastened to the door with two pins was written *Rolf T Dalby*.

I rested my head against the door and listened. It was a solid, wooden door with no glass of any kind. No sounds.

I cast around. No bell.

I had been in blocks like this before. On the opposite side of the hall there was a door leading to the cellar. It was locked, but not so much of a problem that I couldn't open it inside a minute with the help of a hairpin I always kept in my pocket for such purposes. Inherited from Beate; that was how long I had been carrying it around.

From the cellar a door led to the back yard where a fire escape wound up the house. The doors to the fire escape looked about as secure as the cellar door.

I wouldn't have to climb far, no more than one floor. I scanned the yard. There was a light in several windows, and I heard children's voices, the sounds of cooking, a radio on full blast. But everyone was busy. No one was in the back yard.

I mounted the iron steps. The green door that by my calculations led to Rolf Terje Dalby's modest bolthole was locked. I leaned over from the staircase and peered into what must have been the kitchen. There was no light to be seen. The flat seemed to be as good as dead. If anyone was there they were in a coma. The likeliest scenario was that no one was at home.

I had a choice to make. Even when entering the cellar I had been on the outer fringe of legality. But I could always have said that the door had been unlocked. If I entered the flat I was in breach of the law and risked being charged if caught red-handed. On the other hand, if I told the police I was hunting an escapee from Bergen District Prison …

I decided to take the risk, took out the hairpin and went to work as though I had never done anything else. It took a bit longer this time. The lock was slower, but with some extra jiggling I managed it.

I scanned the adjacent houses again. Then I pressed the handle and pushed. I stepped inside, closed the door quietly behind me and stood holding my breath. Not a sound. I was met by the stench of a messy kitchen. Filtered light descended from outside, and I glimpsed worktops piled high with unwashed plates, cups and glasses, a plastic bin full of beer bottles on the floor and some plastic bags of indefinable content in one corner.

A couple of the bags aroused my curiosity. SuperBrugsen was printed on the outside. Had he brought them from Margrethe's flat, or had he been on the Danish ferry as well?

I peered inside. The contents appeared to be relatively fresh. A milk carton squeezed flat still had two days to run. The crust of bread was dry, but not green with mould.

Was there perhaps an additional explanation? Had he been the one standing on the quay welcoming someone off the Danish ferry carrying … food? Or what?

The door to the next room, which turned out to be a sitting room-cum-wardrobe-cum-bedroom was ajar. I prodded it open, just to confirm that it was empty. The impression of wretched bedsit existence was reinforced. If this was where Rolf Terje Dalby resided I could well understand that he preferred to live elsewhere. It wasn't a place he could invite escapee school friends, either.

Now that I was there I conducted a fleeting, superficial

search of the room, pulled out dresser drawers, looked behind furniture and in the cheerless toilet, which had a little window facing the back yard as well.

I found two objects of interest. In one of the dresser drawers there was a colour photograph, standard album format, of two young girls I would have guessed to be fourteen or fifteen years old. Their clothes and hairstyle suggested it had been taken some time in the 1980s. Both were smiling at the photographer. Even though she was about fifteen years younger I recognised Siv Monsen as one of them. I flipped over the photograph, but there was nothing written on the back.

In the same drawer I found a large yellowish-brown C4 envelope. In it were a number of press cuttings, and after taking them out I saw that all of them were about the Gimle case. None showed a photograph of Karl Gunnar Monsen, but there were sketches of him drawn by the courtroom artist, although they would have been of no use to identify the man.

There was one photograph of the victim, marked as private. A young man with cropped hair and a round face, wearing a checked shirt open at the neck. Øyvind Malthus was the name. A somewhat rare surname, but not so rare that I had not met someone with the very same only two days before.

19

MALTHUS INVEST had its offices in Markeveien, half a block from the law courts. It was therefore a short walk if they had any legal business outstanding. The door at street level was locked.

It was almost half past five when I rang the number from outside the arched façade that had once belonged to Bergen Telecommunications, in later years Telenor. I let my gaze wander up the building. There was light in some of the third-floor windows where, according to the sign in the entrance, Malthus Invest had its offices.

'Yes?' The voice on the telephone was brusque, but I had no difficulty recognising the bundle of charm that was Kjell.

'Veum here.'

'What!' It sounded as if he could not believe his own ears. 'Didn't I give you explicit instructions, Veum?'

'This is with reference to the Gimle case.'

His disbelief seemed to have risen a notch. 'What?'

'The Gimle case. Surely you remember it? Can I come up?'

'Come up?'

'I'm standing on the pavement across the street.'

He appeared in the window above and looked down. 'What the hell do you think you're doing?'

'Invest, isn't that what you call your business? What if I wanted to invest some money? Could you give me some useful tips?'

'The most useful tip I could give you, Veum, would be to keep well away from my hunting grounds, and I mean well away.'

'So far away that there was no chance of a chat, do you mean?'

He rang off without any further comment and moved from the window. I stood there for a while. But nothing happened. No one came out. No one called my mobile phone. People passed by, for the most part on foot, some got in and out of their cars, but everyone was in a hurry, it seemed.

So I called it a day. Ambled down to Børs Café and had a reasonable meal, with water, not beer, which made the regulars look at me as if I were something the doorman had hauled in from the street and chucked in a corner. After a cup of coffee I went out into Nordnes to get my car. I circled the blocks between Nykirken Church and the Customs House twice, but could not see Hege or Tanya anywhere. Then I left the red-light district and drove to Møhlenpris. The discovery of the SuperBrugsen bags, first in Margrethe's flat, then at Rolf Terje Dalby's bedsit, had given me a yen to chat with someone who had just been to Denmark, if I was to believe Little Lasse.

I went to at least a couple of houses in Konsul Børs gate before I found the right one. His name was not beside any of the bells but on a letter box in the hall: *L.Mikalsen.* I followed the instructions I had been given by Lasse and climbed as high as I could go. As in many older buildings in this part of town, the loft was also used for accommodation. Here it was divided into at least four bedsits, and on one of them was the same name, written in felt pen on a yellow Post-it and stuck to the door with tape.

I knocked discreetly and waited.

No one opened, but listening at the door I had a clear sense that there was movement inside.

I knocked a bit harder. 'Hello? Lars Mikalsen? This is Veum. Varg Veum. I'd like to have a chat.'

No answer, nevertheless I still had a strong sense someone was at home.

'I can pay you for whatever time it takes! The alternative is I tell the cops all I know. And then it's not certain you'll get out as fast as ...'

The door clicked. It swung open and a face that had been subjected to a severe beating came into view. He glanced at me, then at the stairs, as if to reassure himself that I was alone, before returning his attention to me. 'What d'you want?'

'A missing persons case. Can I come in?'

He weighed me up. Then nodded briefly, turned and motioned me to follow.

The room had been built beneath the slanting roof. In the lowest part there was a bed, a dresser and a bookcase. I hoped he wasn't in too much of a hurry when he got up in the morning. In which case he would bang his head on the ceiling. In the middle of the floor there was a shabby coffee table and along one wall a no less shabby sofa. On the opposite wall there was a shabby wall unit that housed a small TV, a hi-fi system and an assortment of books and journals. I noticed a few of the titles. There was everything from the history of philosophy to psychology and social science textbooks. Several current affairs books and a not insubstantial number of thumbed literary books, predominantly paperbacks with creased spines.

Lars Mikalsen was in his late twenties with longish hair, a couple of days' stubble on his chin and eyes that were so gummed up it was a job to see the colour of them through the slits. He was barefoot and clad in a grey T-shirt and blue jeans. I noticed him dragging one leg and clasping his shoulder from time to time. There was no doubt that whoever had given him the thrashing had left their calling sign. His face was crooked and swollen, clearly marked by the punches. Nonetheless I had a vague sensation that I had seen him somewhere before.

'Have we met before?'

He did the best he could to focus on my face. 'Not as far as I can remember.'

'Who gave you the pasting?'

He flinched and snapped: 'What did you say your name was?'

'Veum. I'm a private investigator.'

'Private … and what the hell has brought you here? A missing persons case, did you say?'

'Correct. My task is to find a young woman who's gone missing. Margrethe Monsen. Some people call her Maggi.'

A tic convulsed his face. 'What makes you think I've got anything to do with it?'

'Do you know her?'

'Not that well. I know who she is.' Before I could say another word he added: 'We have mutual acquaintances.'

'Oh yes? Who's that then?'

He sent me a vacant look. 'No one that's any concern of yours.'

'So you know how she makes her living, do you?'

He shrugged. 'Course. She's not exactly my girlfriend, though.'

'No?'

'No. What the hell do you want, I said!' His mood shifted, from sulky depressive to aggressive. And he still hadn't invited me to take a seat.

I took stock. 'You've just been to Denmark, I hear.'

'I hear!' he repeated with disdain. 'And so what?'

'Listen, Lars,' I said, approaching him. 'I don't run around punching people. So you can relax. But I can get pretty irritated too, especially when I meet people who beat about the bush. I would recommend you answer my questions and otherwise keep your mouth shut. Is that OK with you?'

His eyes evaded mine, as far as I could tell, and he was a lot meeker when he said: 'You mentioned something about … paying.'

'Do you need money?'

'I should have been doing a round in the park.'

I nodded. Then I thrust my hand in my inside pocket, pulled out my wallet and took out a couple of five-hundred notes. 'Twins,' I said, holding up the notes. 'Once we've finished talking.'

He stared at them intently and nodded.

'Are you ready to answer some questions?'

He shrugged. 'Depends on what you intend to ask.'

'About what's already been in the papers. I quote from memory: Man Assaulted in Skuteviken. Unwilling to Report Assault. It's not far from Skolten to Skuteviken, and rumour has it you came in on the Danish ferry, loaded with H, but were met by someone on the quay. Who took you for a drive. And relieved you of your baggage.'

A shiver ran through him, but he said nothing.

'One and a half million in street value, word has it. For which you are responsible.'

He licked his swollen lips and nodded, as far as he was able.

I leaned forward. 'Who met you on the quay, Lars?'

He shook his head. 'I've told everything to …' He raised

his hand halfway up to his face. 'I didn't know them. Total strangers.'

'Really?'

'Two guys. Strong. They said Ma … said they'd been sent.'

'Ma … as in Malthus?'

Another shudder went through him. 'I didn't say that!'

'No, but that was how I interpreted it.'

The expression across his face spoke of desperation, and I hastened to add: 'But I won't use this against you. I'll take your reaction as confirmation and make a mental note.'

As he didn't protest I felt even more secure. 'Two strong guys, you say. And they took you for a drive?'

His gaze flitted about and ended up on the floor, roughly where my shoes were. I struggled to hear what he said as he mumbled: 'They said they'd been told to fetch me, but then they turned towards Skuteviken, and the one sitting beside me pressed a gun into my ribs and told me to lean forward and keep my gob shut. They didn't drive far, straight to the open ground between two warehouses. There they grabbed my case, took … what I had in the bags, and then they beat me up.'

'Why when they already had the booty?'

'They said … this was only a foretaste. If I told the police – or anyone else – about what had happened they would give me an even tougher going-over next time. In fact I wasn't going to tell anyone anyway, but as I staggered along the street this taxi driver stopped and picked me up, and I was so black and blue that I was unable to protest until I was at A&E and the doctor called the cops. I never bloody asked for any attention!'

'You were questioned by the police, but refused to say who did this.'

'I don't know who they were! They were from Østland, total strangers to me, and I told Ma … even Rolf and …'

'We can use their full names, Lars. Kjell Malthus and Rolf Terje Dalby. I know who you're talking about.'

'Nonetheless, they beat me up as well.'

'Malthus? I thought he was the general manager of this show.'

If possible, his eyes narrowed even further. 'He can be a brutal bastard. I warn you. Keep well away from him if he has a score to settle with you!'

Another useful pointer to bear in mind. 'And what did you tell them?'

'Same as I told you. About the two from Østland.'

'And no one has a clue who they are? It must be someone trying to muscle their way into the market. If not, they're freebooters out for rich pickings. In which case they hit the jackpot this time. One and a half million in street value …'

He shifted his gaze upwards until it stopped at around my chin. 'But what's this got to do with Maggi?'

'I'm asking myself the same question. Without trespassing onto your territory … could you give me a tip about how you transported these goods? Unless I'm very much mistaken you were at SuperBrugsen and went shopping first?'

For a second or two he looked almost impressed. 'How …?' As I didn't expand, he continued: 'I've used this trick several times. I go to the meat counter in SuperBrugsen. Afterwards I pop into a pub and go to the loo. There, I repack, chuck a fair bit of the meat away, making sure there is enough left to confuse the sniffer dogs, slip the plastic bags containing the drugs in the middle and carry it on board with the cans of beer, tins and other groceries from SuperBrugsen. It's worked well to date. But then I've been lucky going through customs as well. But how the hell did you …?'

'Let's say I've come across quite a few SuperBrugsen bags of late. They have told me a story I'm not sure you'd like to hear.'

'Not connected with Maggi?'

'Why do you ask?'

'That was why you came here, wasn't it? Because you were looking for her?' As I didn't answer he went on: 'I can tell you that if Maggi's behind this she's in deep shit if she gets caught.'

'If Maggi's behind this … You said yourself there were two bruisers from Østland.'

'Yes? But …' He was searching for words. 'Someone must have told them I was on my way, mustn't they?'

'Did Maggi know about it?'

He looked puzzled. 'No … not as far as I know.'

'It could equally well have been the dealers in Denmark, couldn't it?'

'Stabbing a regular customer in the back? You can't make me believe that.'

'So who could it have been?'

'I've got no idea!' All of a sudden he looked almost unhappy. 'Everyone beats me up. The two who came to meet me, Malthus and Rolf. The police take me in for questioning, and now you come here pestering me. But I don't know anything! I don't have an earthly …'

I sat watching him. Then I leaned forward. 'Listen to me, Lars. Someone I spoke to described you as a kind of … eternal student. I can see from your books that you're well read. How the hell did you get into this business?'

He crouched over with his elbows on his knees and his long

hair rumpled and unkempt. Then he squinted up at me, as if from far back in his life, the time when he had been a different person with quite a different career ahead of him. Despondently, he rubbed his face and glanced at the bookcase beside him. Then he shrugged and began to talk.

'Things did not go well. You're right. I took psychology as my foundation subject. But there was a waiting list to go any further. So I took social studies to fill the gap. But still I didn't get to do my main course. So I started doing history, but without much motivation. And you know where the university is.' He tossed his head towards the slanted window above us. 'The closest neighbour is Nygård Park. There were quite a few of us who went there for a spliff. Got to know the crowd. Moved onto stronger stuff, and it was not long before we were hooked, myself ... and lots more. It all had to be financed, and if you didn't want to sell your ass or do break-ins there was only one thing that was any good. Become another link in the chain. For many years I've turned over enough for my own consumption, and then came the offer of bigger earnings, if I was willing to risk the Denmark trip.'

'And you've done that ... how many times now?'

He wavered. 'Many. And nothing has ever happened until now.' Again he looked unhappy. 'Just when, at long last, things were beginning to go OK.'

'Go OK?'

He smiled sadly. 'I had a girlfriend. This was the last job I was going to do. My part of the profit would have gone towards moving abroad, perhaps to a rehab centre in the Danish countryside. And then this bloody happens. Now I'm sitting here and who the hell will have me now, do you think?'

'If she's a decent girlfriend surely she won't blame you for what has happened, will she? Oh no ...' A notion struck me. 'It's not Maggi, is it?'

He sneered at me. 'Can you imagine that? No, it's not Maggi! It's a decent girl. Someone who would finally get me back on an even keel. The one I had been waiting for all my life.'

I had my own thoughts on this. He was not yet thirty years old, and some of us had been waiting a good deal longer than that.

'And what's her name?'

In a burst of passion he said: 'Not even if you beat me up, like the others did, will you find out! I'm still living in hope that everything will be alright.'

'Tell me ... have you told her what you were doing?'

'I had to justify why I was leaving, didn't I. To explain that this was the last job, and I was stopping for her.'

'I'm sure she'll forgive you.'

'And what use will it be? I'm sitting here, to all intents and purposes, one and a half million kroner in debt. And the debt becomes due sooner than you imagine. If you can't pay, the interest soars from one day to the next. What the hell can I do?' Again the look of naked desperation on his face. 'Can you tell me that, eh?'

I sat looking at him. 'There is no simple solution, but ... are you willing to go to court with any of this?'

He frantically massaged his brow. 'Court? Are you out of your mind? First of all I would get a hefty sentence myself, and then I would drag the others down with me. I would be dead before the month was out, even if I was locked up in solitary on Bjørnøya Island!'

'Would you rather rot in an attic room in Møhlenpris?'

He looked around him. 'At least I'm alive here! For as long it lasts. Think about that, whatever your bloody name is.'

'Veum.' I passed him my business card. 'Here you are. Should you change your mind about spilling the beans. If you ask me, it's the one chance you've got.'

He read the card with slow, meticulous care, then nodded. Whether that was because he had managed to read what was there or whether it meant he might contact me I would perhaps never know.

'You said … poor Maggi if she was the one who gave you away. How bad would the outcome be for her? Is it conceivable that they would kill her?'

He looked at me darkly. 'It's not impossible. Look what they did to me. They're desperate to get the drugs back.'

'KG, do you know him?'

'KG? He's in prison, isn't he?'

I nodded. 'Maggi's brother. But I suppose you knew.'

'What about him?'

'He's disappeared as well. Escaped, they say.'

'Really?!' The friendly attitude was about to evaporate. Anger was taking control again.

'Would he be able to protect her?'

'Against those guys. Not a snowball's chance in hell. But what's that got to do with me?'

'Well, nothing except that you said you knew Maggi.'

'So why do you ask such bloody stupid questions?'

'Let's put it like this. It's my job to ask questions. Not all of them are equally popular, but very few of them are unfounded.'

He glowered at me. Then he shook his head, as if to emphasise that there was no understanding me, my opinions or what I wanted from him. His eyes focused on the two banknotes I still held in my hand. He nodded in their direction. 'You promised me …'

I looked down. 'Yes, I might have done at that. Buggered if I know whether you deserve them, but … OK. Here you are.'

I gave them both to him. He looked as if he needed them, or what he could get for them. Nothing to punch the air about, perhaps, but enough to get him through the night and all its problems, a situation which for that matter he shared with most of us, in one way or another.

For me, though, it was not night yet. First of all I had to go to Landås to try another shot in the dark.

20

ACCORDING TO MY INFORMATION, Siv Monsen lived in Kristofer Jansons vei, which winds its way between Natlandsveien and Slettebakken. Together with the parallel street Adolph Bergs vei it constituted the area known, way back in the 1960s, as Chicago, not entirely without justification.

The number I had found in the directory was for one of the typical star buildings, the blocks that had been designed in a kind of star formation, with three wings leading off a central entrance. There were three of them up towards Natlandsveien and six in Kristofer Jansons vei. Siv Monsen lived in one of the middle ones, and I found an unmarked parking spot by the small common on the opposite side of the street.

The front door was open. I went in the entrance and took the stairs up until I saw Siv Monsen's name on one of three doors on the second floor. I rang the doorbell and stood waiting.

'Veum?' Her face above the security chain in the narrow crack between door and frame was pale. Her short hair was wet and untidy, as though she had just washed it, and she had a towel hanging round her neck. She was wearing faded jeans and a loose checked shirt with long sleeves. 'What do you want?'

I motioned towards the security chain. 'Someone you're frightened of?'

'No ... force of habit.'

'Are you going to let me in?'

'What do you want, I asked?'

'I'm still looking for your sister, and your brother hasn't shown up, either.'

'Yes, but …' She rolled her eyes and made a show of sighing; however, she did close the door again so that she could unhitch the chain and let me in. 'I haven't got an awful lot of time.'

I followed her into the hall. 'This won't take long.'

'You can hang it there.' She pointed to a wardrobe to the left of the hall. 'The sitting room's in here.'

I hung up my coat and followed her.

She had two views, one down towards Lake Tveitevannet and another where a door led to a balcony, west, over the Birkeveien intersection. The room was furnished with simple taste. The walls were white, the furniture modern with a combination of chromium-plated steel tubes and cushions. There was a large glass coffee table, and in the middle a bunch of winter-grown tulips in a slim crystal vase. Along the wall was a plain shelving system. Holding predominantly teaching material for banking and insurance. A couple of gaudy novels were the extent of the literature section. The TV and the hi-fi, however, looked to be top quality and well above the lowest price range, judging by the brands.

She looked at her watch. 'I'm afraid I haven't got any time to offer you anything, but … take a seat.'

I obeyed and chose one of the chairs by the glass table. She remained on her feet as if to stress how pressed she was.

I indicated one of the other chairs with an upturned palm. 'Won't you …'

With an impatient gesture she sat down, on the edge of the chair. 'I can't see how I could have any more to tell you. I told you everything I know yesterday.'

'Sure of that?'

'Course I'm sure!'

'In the meantime, however, Carsten Mobekk has been found murdered in his flat in Falsens vei.'

She eyed me, ashen. 'So it was him? Well, I thought it was his house. In the newspaper.'

'You knew Mobekk, didn't you?'

'What do you mean by that?'

'He was on the committee that was supposed to help you when you were growing up.'

Her eyes did not deviate for an instant, but they seemed to be veiled by a shiny membrane. 'The committee? Who's ...?' She broke off.

'No, you didn't tell me a thing, did you, when we spoke yesterday. Not a single thing.'

'These are all private matters, Veum. I don't understand what you're digging for. Margrethe and Kalle have gone missing, you say, but what has that got to do with anyone else?'

'Haven't the police been in touch?'

'The police? Why should they?'

'If for nothing else because both your brother and your sister have disappeared. Your brother used to give your address as his place of abode when he had a pass, and you were in regular contact with Margrethe, so ... You'll get a visit from them, that's for definite.' I cast an eye over the room. 'Neither of them has been here recently, have they? Margrethe or Kalle, I mean.'

'Does it look like it?'

'No, it looks ... I assume you don't want to show me the other rooms ...'

'You can bet your life I don't.'

'When the police come they'll ask you.'

'Then I'll show them. The police are different after all … from your kind.'

I made a mental note of that. 'But this committee, let's return to that.'

'And why should we?'

'You didn't have an easy upbringing, I've been told.'

She measured me with her eyes, showing no willingness to answer.

'But you get good references from the committee and those who taught you at school.'

Her voice trembled as she said: 'I have to say you've got around a bit since we last met! What sort of investigations are these?'

I leaned forward a smidgeon. 'What I'm doing is searching for your sister, Siv. Others are sure to be searching for your brother. There has been a shocking death. Things are coming out of the woodwork, as it were. Some claim it was you who held the façade together to the outside world, that it was you who made sure your brother and sister got up in the morning and went to school, had packed lunches, did their homework …'

'So what did we need the committee for then, eh?' she said with barely concealed sarcasm.

'You were too young for that kind of responsibility, Siv! You were ten years old when social services received the first report expressing concern.'

She pinched her lips, as if holding back all she wanted to say.

'I can't remember if I told you yesterday, Siv, but I worked for social services at one point. I've done a few home visits. Very often social services get some support when they raise a matter. This is the first time I've ever heard of anyone forming a committee to help. Close family, yes. Grandparents, uncles, aunts. There are many safety nets of that kind. But a committee of neighbours with parish council support ...' I tried to give this a positive spin. 'That says volumes about the enormous concern there was for you all, doesn't it.'

She sent me defiant, silent glares, like a small child refusing to obey.

'Yet things still didn't go well. At least, not for your brother and sister.'

Again she looked at her watch, but said nothing. She stirred uneasily.

'Why were you the only one to attend your father's funeral, Siv?'

She gasped. 'What the ... who told you that?'

'I spoke to your mother.'

Her mouth twisted with bitterness. 'I see.'

'That was in 1993, and since then not one of you has visited her, she said.'

'No.'

'Quite dramatic, don't you think? Have you broken all ties with her?'

She glanced across at me. 'What business is that of yours? Has this got anything to do with your assignment?' As I didn't answer she added: 'Will it help you to find Margrethe?'

'Not in any direct way.'

'Well! Have we finished now?'

'Just a couple more questions. Have you any idea where she could be hiding? Are there any old girlfriends? Any places where you spent your summer holidays?'

'Summer holidays?' She snorted. 'At holiday camps or in

the street at home. Sometimes we had to go to Torvaldsen's cabin, that was the closest it got. The photo you showed me yesterday.'

'Right, and *fru* Torvaldsen helped you with your homework, didn't she?'

She shrugged. 'Maybe she did. I don't remember.'

'You might have repressed it.'

Another twist of the mouth.

'Have you repressed a lot? Can you remember the details surrounding what happened to your brother … at Gimle?'

'Details? Nothing apart from what was in the papers. He never told us anything. And when it had happened, *it*, then he ended up on remand and later in the clink.'

'I suppose you must have visited him though?'

'Ye-es …'

'And later he stayed here, on weekend passes?'

'A few times over the last couple of years. He wasn't exactly on leave every weekend.'

'But you must have spoken about …'

'No, we did not. We never spoke about it. Never!'

'Karl Gunnar had a childhood friend, I've been told. Rolf Terje Dalby.'

For the first time this evening she showed me the shadow of a smile. 'Rolf Terje, yes. That was weird. He hadn't had such a good home life, himself.'

'Really?'

'His father was at school, and Rolf Terje still went round spouting a load of strange expressions we didn't understand a word of.' She imitated him. '*Cattle dies, kith dies* … Ugh, ugh!'

'*The Håvamål.*'

'The what?'

'Good advice from old Norse times, in a manner of speaking. And later?'

'Later?'

'Did you see him in later years, after you moved from Minde?'

'Rolf Terje? Not that I can recall.'

'He's got a photo of you at home.'

'A photo! Rolf Terje?'

'Taken some time in the 1980s from what I saw. You and another girl in the sun in Minde.'

She made a show of rolling her shoulders. 'Funny. Must have been Anne-Lise, I suppose.'

'Anne-Lise?'

'She was in my class at the time.'

'But you had no idea he had that photo of you?'

'No, I told you!'

'OK, OK. He was secretly in love with you. Perhaps he kept it, as a souvenir.'

'Perhaps! He was five years younger than me, so ... Have we finished now?'

'Almost. What I wanted to ask was ... did Karl Gunnar and Rolf Terje stay in touch? Could Rolf Terje have helped Karl Gunnar go underground?'

'And how would I know? I haven't seen him for ages, as I said.'

'He's kept in touch with Margrethe.'

'Has he?' Her expression betrayed uncertainty.

'He's one of those men who ... protects her, if I can put it like that.'

The doorbell rang. She jumped up: 'I told you, didn't I! I had no time for this!' She grabbed the towel and feverishly dried her hair as though I had prevented her from finishing.

I got up. 'OK, OK. Of course. Please don't let me disturb you.'

She scowled at me and headed for the front door, slinging the towel in a room as she went by and trying to smooth her hair. I was putting on my jacket when she opened the door. A half-strangled cry escaped her lips, as though she was just as surprised as me to see the person standing in the doorway.

For a moment we stood staring at each other. He seemed no less surprised. 'Varg?'

'Nils? A little collegial visit of an evening?'

'A collegial conversation,' he mumbled, apparently the first thing that occurred to him, without succeeding in making it sound very convincing.

'Veum's on his way out,' said Siv Monsen, blushing.

'Uhuh,' Nils Åkre mumbled, no less embarrassed. 'We'll catch up another time,' he said to me as he passed.

'Have fun,' I said, as she closed the door hard behind me. But I didn't hear her slide the security chain. She had nothing to be frightened of any more.

21

I HAD HIM ON THE TELEPHONE before I was in the car. He spoke quickly in a low voice, and it was my hunch she was in another room fixing her hair or changing her clothes. Or perhaps she was as God made her, for all I knew.

'Varg … we must have a chat.'

'I'm ready anytime you like. At your office or …?'

'Not this time. Can I come to yours, before office hours?'

'Before your office hours or mine?'

'I'll be at yours for eight,' he gabbled. Suddenly his voice was raised. 'No, I don't have any time right now. If we could talk tomorrow we can take it from there. Alright? Bye.'

Then he rang off. She was obviously back in the room, dressed or undressed.

I sat in the car peering up at what I had worked out had to be her windows. No curtains drawn, no lights turned off. Not yet.

Then I twisted the key and drove back down to the centre. I was in Kong Oscars gate when my mobile rang again. I drove straight to the crossroads by Nygaten and pulled in by Bergen Cathedral School before answering. 'Yes?'

'Varg Veum?' It was a woman's voice, and it took me a couple of seconds to recognise Inspector Annemette Bergesen.

'Yes?'

'Where are you?'

'In Kong Oscars gate, a stone's throw from the police station.'

'Yes, but that's not where I am. Are you driving?'

'I'm sitting behind the steering wheel and I'm stinking sober, if I can put it like that.'

'I wonder if you could come to Tollbodhopen?'

I had an unpleasant feeling in my gut. 'Tell me more.'

'We've found a body in the sea. A young woman.'

The feeling rose to my throat region, and I found it difficult to swallow. 'But why ring me?'

'We checked her purse for ID and found your card, among other things.'

'What colour's her hair?'

'Just get over here and we'll take it from there.'

It was an unpleasant drive. To the best of my memory, I had given my card to Hege and Tanya. Passing through C. Sundts gate, I noticed the street was conspicuously empty of working girls. At Tollbodhopen I saw an ambulance and two police vehicles, as well as a throng of spectators. I parked my car by the kerb in front of the large, white customs building with the hipped roof.

In the car park to the west a large crowd of people had gathered. As I approached I scanned the ranks but it was difficult to make out those I was looking for in the darkness. The police had cordoned off the area where they had found the body by the sea. I elbowed my way roughly through the milling masses. At the front I was stopped by an officer, but when I said I had been summoned by Inspector Bergesen I was allowed through. Behind me camera flashes went off. The press was on the spot, as always. Not for nothing did they have police radios on their office desks.

The woman had been dragged up onto the quay. There was a defibrillator on the ground beside her, but it was too late for that. Much too late.

Annemette Bergesen met my eyes as I arrived, but I looked past her and down. Her hair was red, even though it was soaked in seawater. Her skin was pale blue, her eyes unnaturally wide open, and there were dark marks around her neck. Even in death I seemed to be able to hear her northern Norwegian tones.

Annemette Bergesen looked at me. 'Do you recognise her?'

I nodded. 'Her name's Tanya. I don't know her other names. Russian. I talked to her a couple of days ago about a case I'm investigating. A young woman who's missing, from the same milieu.'

'Can you confirm she's a prostitute?'

'Yes.' I hesitated. 'Who found her?'

She looked round. 'The man over there. With the dog. He was out taking it for a walk.'

A man in a blue coat with an old-fashioned peaked cap on his head and a red setter on a lead was speaking to one of the police officers.

'Where was she found?'

'Down there.' She pointed to the big rocks by Tollbod Quay, and I shuddered. The sea washed in from Byfjorden, black and cold. Not a nice place to be found.

'Any idea how long she might have been there?'

'Not yet. When did you see her last?'

'Monday evening.'

She made a note on her pad. 'We shall of course have to question the others, but for the moment we have to wait for the report from Forensics.'

'The marks on her neck ...'

'Yes.'

'When I spoke to her she told me she had been subjected to

an assault by two very brutal punters before the weekend. For your information.'

'Did she have those marks then? When you spoke to her, I mean.'

'No.'

'She didn't say anything that could identify the customers, I suppose?'

'No, but her so-called protectors are Kjell Malthus and Rolf Terje Dalby. I wanted to speak to them.'

She nodded and took notes.

'Do you need me any more?'

She considered the question. 'In fact we don't. Drop by early tomorrow so that we can question you formally.'

I smirked. 'As a suspect?'

'As a witness, Veum. For the moment.'

I nodded in confirmation. Then I took a few steps closer to Tanya and stood studying her. I had little or no idea of her background, but for reasons unknown she had chosen to make her living roaming the streets as a prostitute in Bergen, a coastal town with several hundred years of history of such activity. But once, not a very long time ago, in an overcrowded metropolis or in a frozen rural district, she had been someone's little daughter, a small girl who played with her tatty dolls, if she had any, a schoolgirl who had taught herself to read, heard about Brezhnev and Kosygin and other famous people, had her first lover, if she hadn't been raped by a brutal stepfather, a precocious boy or a seaman on leave; one small person on her way into life, later across the border in the neighbouring country in which she stayed long enough to acquire the local dialect before moving south to the town where all too abruptly she would end her days, without anyone knowing where she came from or who she was.

'Well, well …' Sad at heart, I took my final leave of Tanya No Surname, nodded to Annemette and plodded wearily back to my car.

A storm of flashes went off, but I dismissed the journalists flocking round me with 'No comment. No comment, I said!'

They snorted with irritation, but were forced to accept that I had nothing to say to them. Then I caught sight of a figure peeling off from the flock of spectators and following me to the car. It was Hege.

She came up close to me. I saw the trails of tears in the streaks of mascara running down her cheeks. She clasped my lapels and stared me in the eye.

'Good to see you,' I said. 'For a while there I was frightened it was you.'

'Was she killed? Was she beaten up?'

'Looks like it. She didn't die from natural causes at any rate.'

She gasped as she inhaled. She looked around, desperation in her eyes. 'And Maggi? Have you found out anything about her?'

'Nothing. At least nothing that can tell me where she is.'

She forced a blink with both eyes and tossed her head towards Tollbodhopen. 'I'm afraid they're going to find her like that as well.'

I was about to say something, but she spoke first. 'Take me with you!'

'With me … you mean …?'

'I'm scared, Veum. Scared to death. Next time it could be me.'

'Why?'

'Had I known this, I wouldn't have told you!'

I looked at her. 'Of course I can. I can drive you home. Where …?'

'Home! Do you know where I live? In a bloody hospice, full to the brim with dopeheads and … people like me.' After a brief pause she added: 'Will you take the responsibility for them finding me tomorrow … like Tanya?'

'No.' I opened the door with the remote control. 'Get in.'

She sat at the front. I sat behind the wheel. Before starting up I turned towards her. 'But I will say one thing, Hege. This is the first time I have taken a girl home from this area. I hope you won't make me regret it.'

'I promise not to tell your mother.'

'My mother died a long time ago.'

'The policewoman over there.'

'Hm.' I made no comment, just turned the ignition key and set off.

'I can give you a night you'll never forget.'

'Didn't you say you'd dated Thomas?'

'That's why.'

'Then thanks, but no thanks. A good night's sleep is what we both need, I'm afraid.'

'Aren't you going to offer me a drink first?'

'Think I can manage that …'

Then we said very little until I parked in Øvre Blekevei and I led her as discreetly as possible to Telthussmauet. If we had met any neighbours on the way my reputation would have been in tatters for good, for all the difference that would have made. But we didn't bump into anyone, and she sent me a grateful look as I unlocked the front door.

22

WE DOWNED A BOTTLE of red wine between us. When it was empty she asked whether I had another one.

'I'm afraid not. But I have a bottle of aquavit open.'

She shrugged. 'Whatever. So long as it works.'

She sat down on the sofa, I sat on a chair. She seemed to have made herself at home. For myself I was still a bit uneasy with the situation. Had the cards played out differently she could have been my daughter-in-law.

I got to my feet, found two spirits glasses and poured from the bottle of Simers.

Her black skirt was short. Her red blouse was décolleté enough to give you problems knowing where to look. She had tousled her black hair, but fear lay smouldering in her eyes, as black as the sea at Tollbodhopen.

She had told me that she had spoken to several of the other girls. No one could remember having seen Tanya being picked up. No one could remember having seen her at all that day. And who said it was a punter who had picked her up? It could have been anyone.

I asked her if it was Kjell Malthus and Rolf Terje Dalby she had on her mind, but as far as they were concerned she was not very forthcoming. She had been totally unaware that Rolf Terje and Maggi had grown up together, or that he had been her brother's best friend.

I had referred to what Tanya had told me, that Maggi had

said she wasn't going to be there long, she would soon be on her travels. She had looked at me with astonishment and asked me: 'Why the hell did she say that to Tanya, and not to me?' I had explained it was tied up with the trick she refused. When I told her about the two guys who had beaten up Tanya, she said: 'That was what I told you when I hired you! Do you think …? Perhaps it was them who came back? Were they the ones who killed Tanya? Did it just go too far this time?'

We got no closer to the answer.

Over the rim of the aquavit glass I asked: 'What got you into this mess, Hege?'

'What do you think? Nine out of ten girls are victims of child abuse. Drugs come with the territory …' She swallowed hard, and the follow-up lived long in the memory. 'As for me I was raped by three classmates when I was at school. And I didn't have anyone I could talk to.'

This burned right through me like an electric shock. 'Not even …?'

She laughed when she saw my expression, but it was a cheerless laugh. 'No, not even Thomas. It was over between us when this happened. The little there had been …' Her smile softened. 'He was sweet, actually …' Then her eyes darkened again. 'One of them was my best friend. Or so I thought.'

'A girl?'

'Yes, she held me down. But that was the worst bit, anyway. Her being part of it. Afterwards she said it was because I had made a move on her boyfriend.'

'And this boyfriend, was he one of the attackers?'

'No. But I was in love with him. So, in a way, she was right. It was my own fault.'

'It's never your fault when that sort of thing happens, Hege.'

'Never?'

'Never.'

'But Maggi ...?'

'Yes? Did she tell you ... a similar story?'

'No, but she ... not in so many words. It was a hellish winter night, ten degrees below and not a single bloody punter out in a car. We went up to hers and sat drinking. I told her – the same as I've told you, but perhaps in more detail, and she said ... Yes, I understand how you feel, Hege. I know exactly what it feels like.'

'Exactly what it feels ... Did she say anything else? Who, when, how?'

'No, she didn't say any more. It ended up with us lying in each other's arms and crying. And the next morning we spewed in unison.' She smiled cynically. 'At one in everything.' Then she held out her empty glass. 'Another?'

I poured slowly. 'Perhaps it's time to go to bed?'

She gave a wry smile. 'Have you changed your mind?'

'My bedroom's in there. You're here.' I pointed to the sofa. 'I'll find you some bedlinen.'

I went into the bedroom and fetched some clean sheets and a padded quilt from a wardrobe. When I entered the living room again, she had removed her blouse. Her lingerie was black, but her upper body was pale and a bit flabby.

I threw the linen on the bed while she slid down the zip on the side of her skirt, let it fall and blew a kind of trumpet fanfare.

'Relax, Hege. I've see naked women before.'

'So you're not a homo then? That's not your problem?' she blurted with an aggression I had not expected. 'Or is it because I am who I am? There have been far too many on top of me? And you'll become a customer like all the others?'

'No, it's not that. On the contrary. In fact, you're my customer. You pay for my services, and it would be immoral of me to … exploit the situation.' The moment I said it I knew what the counter-argument would be.

'Exploit the situation! Don't make me laugh! As if I haven't been …' With a swing of the arm she unhooked her bra at the back and slung it into the air. She peeled off her panties and threw them towards me. They didn't quite reach. 'I haven't had a trick all day. I'm showered and fresh, as fresh as any girl on the game!'

She thrust her hands behind her neck, spread her legs and strutted her stuff. There was a feverish glow in her eyes, and the artificial smile she put on for me would have disintegrated at the slightest touch.

I tried to hold her gaze. In a dry, sober voice I said: 'I'll go and get ready in the bathroom first, Hege. I'll put out an extra toothbrush and hang up a towel for you.'

'I'll put out an extra toothbrush!' she mimicked. 'You're not going to wipe my arse for me as well, are you?'

'Let me know if there's anything you need. And put on your clothes. The show's over. The audience's gone home.'

I turned and left. In the bathroom I washed with cold water, thoroughly. Raising my head and looking at myself in the mirror, I glimpsed a shadow of the same feverish glow I had seen in her. I finished and cleaned up for her, but when I went in she had crawled under the quilt and turned her back on the room.

'Good night,' I said.

She nodded in silence.

'I have to get up at seven for a meeting at eight, but you can lie in for as long as you like, just close the door after you when you leave.'

She rolled over and looked at me with raised eyebrows. I knew I was taking a risk, but on the other hand both the TV and hi-fi were such old models that she wouldn't get much for them on the open market. Besides, the TV was bigger than bankers' bonuses. She nodded. 'Thank you … I'm sorry I was … so stupid. You're almost as sweet as Thomas.'

'Almost,' I said.

She smirked. 'Good night.'

I closed the door behind me and lay for a while listening to the sounds of the night: a cat out a-courting in Fjellgaten, an owl flying low over Skansen, a driver changing down with revs too high on the Øvre Blekevei hill. The whole time I was distressed by the image of Tanya lying on the quay by the Customs House, pale, dead, without even the minimum accompanying customs declaration.

Then I must have fallen asleep. I woke with her standing beside my bed. Her voice was thin, reedy. 'Varg? I can't sleep. Can I come into your bed?'

Half delirious and incapable of resistance, I folded the duvet to one side. 'OK then, but to sleep, alright.'

She snuggled up to my back and put her arms around me. 'I kept thinking about Tanya,' she said.

'I did, too. But try to sleep now.'

'I've got some condoms in my handbag.'

'Jesus Christ!' In one agile leap I was over her and onto the floor. 'I'll take the sofa. Sleep tight.' Once a scout, always a scout. Someone should have awarded me a medal.

At that she gave in. Perhaps when it came down to it what she had been after was my bed.

The next morning she was fast asleep when I inched the door open to say that I was off. I shrugged and crossed my fingers that she would take no more than the aquavit bottle as she left.

At eight I had a meeting with Nils Åkre at my office. If nothing else, at least I felt I had a kind of moral advantage over him now.

23

IT WAS CLOSER TO HALF PAST when he turned up. On the other hand, I'd had the time to brew some coffee in the meanwhile.

'Heavy night, Nils?'

He sent me an annoyed look. 'Don't you go thinking ...' But he broke off, accepted the offer of coffee and sat staring stiffly out of the window, where the sun still had a bit to do before it struggled over Mount Ulriken.

Then he turned to me with a gloomy countenance. 'How long have we known each other, Varg?'

'More than twenty years. I remember contacting you when I first started in this business, and that was in 1975.'

'I've given you lots of jobs over the years, haven't I?'

'If that's an intro to saying it's all over now, save your breath, Nils. I've never been a moralist. What folk do in their free time and with whom they do it has never been any concern of mine. And I've never met your wife.'

His face creased. 'You don't understand. Siv and I are not in a relationship.'

'No?' I observed him over the top of the coffee cup. It was not a pleasant sight. Lack of sleep lay like a grey membrane over his massive face. He had been unfortunate with his morning shave, and his hair looked thinner than it was wont to do. 'Well, some time ago you said you hardly knew her, if I haven't mis-remembered.'

'Everyone can have one lapse, can't they?'

I did something between shrugging and showing with a nod that I understood what he meant.

'I'd had a bit too much to drink. I mean … when it happened. And I was fascinated by that cold distance of hers. Always felt like that. Wondered what you needed to do to break the ice.'

'And you found out?'

He sent me another annoyed look as though I had disturbed his line of thought. 'She'd been drinking too. It was after the annual … Christmas dinner.'

'Original.'

'Oh, I know! Spare me your usual comments, Varg. Sometimes I get so bloody sick of them.'

I didn't answer. I hugged the ropes in case he began to wind-mill flailing fists.

'We were standing in the taxi queue, and when at last it was our turn we took the same taxi. We arrived at where she lived, and she said she would pay, but I said: "No, no, Siv. I'll take care of it." Then she looked up and asked: "What about another glass of wine?"' He eyed me defiantly. 'Would you have turned down the offer perhaps?'

I could have told him about what I had turned down over the previous day, but I saved that for another occasion. Once again I shrugged, so as not to provoke him further.

He had finished his coffee, and angrily snatched the coffee pot and poured himself a refill, right to the brim. 'Shit, Varg! It was the very devil's own dance!'

'Some think he has a finger in most things we do.'

Resigned, he raised the cup to his mouth without bothering about the coffee slopping over the side and dripping onto his lap. His gaze was distant and very close at the same time. For a second or two I wondered whether he was on something, but I rejected that idea. Not Nils Åkre, our insurance man for more than two decades.

'It's been like a nightmare for me ever since that unfortunate December night. As though I were ... as though ... it goes against everything I believe in, Varg. Everything I stand for.'

I nodded with complete understanding. 'Perhaps it would help ...'

'If I unburdened myself?' he interrupted, not without a hint of sarcasm.

'For example.'

'OK. Listen to my charming little fairy tale then!'

I settled down to do precisely that. To listen.

'The taxi driver sent me a knowing wink as I paid, and I gave him an extra tip to stop him opening his gob. I went up with her and was given a glass of wine ... and a bit more.'

Another pause as his eyes flitted in and out, back and forth in time.

'I'll tell you something, Varg. That woman has got major problems.'

'She ... changed her mind, did she?'

'Changed her mind?! Did she hell! You don't bloody think I raped her, do you ... or something similar? I told you I got ... what I wanted.' He corrected himself without delay: 'What she had to offer.'

'I see. So what were the problems?'

'Women nowadays are not very shy, are they.'

'I'm not sure that I'm an expert on women nowadays ...'

'Ho ho ho!' A touch of the good old easy-going Nils Åkre returned. 'Don't make me laugh, Varg. You a single man and all that.'

'Sort of living apart together, I think some say.'

'Oh, yeah, but enough of that. Siv wasn't like that.'

'Like what?'

He sighed and his eyes went distant again. 'We finished our glasses, and then we messed around and kissed a bit. I began to fiddle with her dress. It was a wonderful dress, black with silver glitz in the material, but quite special. The neck was cut quite high up, with long sleeves, as though … as though she wanted to show as little skin as possible.'

'Well …'

'But then … she suddenly pulled away. "Wait! Let's go into the bedroom" … I didn't mind of course, the way the situation had developed, but … when we went in she closed the door and insisted we kept the light off. The black blinds were down, and for a second or two I thought, oh shit! The woman's mad! She's going to kill me. But then I felt her hand on … yes, between my legs, and it wasn't long before we lay on the bed and … went for it.'

'Right. That sounds disturbingly normal, Nils.'

'Yes, but she didn't get undressed.'

'She would have had to if you … went for it, as you put it, surely?'

'Yes, but no more than necessary. She kept her dress on, just pulled it over her thighs and … her tights down … but she kept her panties on, I almost had to force my way in … from the side.'

'Well, well … embarrassment of the first meeting. Has it been that long since you were young, Nils?'

'First meeting … we're not bloody seventeen years old any more, Varg. This is two adults getting down to business of their own free volition and without any form of persuasion or force.'

'Fine. But I still don't understand how this can be as serious as you suggest. I mean ... Perhaps that's how she likes it. I've heard of worse pleasures than doing it fully dressed.'

'Jesus, Varg. Can't you hear what I'm saying? The woman's got problems. Major problems. The story doesn't finish there.'

'Carry on then!'

He looked at me, nettled. 'As you know, Varg, I have a solid physique.'

'No one can take that from you. All the teacakes in Fyllings-dalen ... there are better diets.'

'It was as if the devil was inside me. I wanted her naked! I lay on top of her with all my weight and pulled her dress up until it was trussed round her neck, pulled it over her face, stuck her arms in the air and forced her evening dress off. Then I tore off her underwear, and as if that wasn't enough, I searched for the lamp on the bedside table, found the switch and turned on the light. She jerked back against the bed head, as naked as a baby, trying in vain to cover herself ...'

'And you still maintain you didn't rape her?' I mumbled.

He was barely listening. 'But it wasn't her breasts she was trying to cover. Nor her muff. It was her arms.'

'Arms! Not needle marks?'

'Needle marks? No, scars. Both arms were covered with scars. Long, swollen scars. Some of them with fresh scabs; others were old and healed.'

'But ...?'

'She's been self-harming, Varg! She's been cutting herself for years!'

'Herself?'

'She ... admitted it herself. She said: "You should go, Nils. Forget this evening. Forget what you saw. This is my dark secret, and now you know it you can never come back."'

Shaken, I sat in my chair as chaotic images flickered past my skull. 'But you did ... the last time was yesterday.'

'The last ... yesterday! That was the first time I had been there since then.'

'So why did you go there yesterday?'

He smacked the coffee cup down hard and stood up. 'It was a fiasco, of course. Had I known you would be there ...'

'And what difference did that make?'

'The reason I went was that you had been talking to her as part of your assignment. I went there to tell her whatever she told you she must not under any circumstances mention this.'

'And what was so dangerous about it?'

'You should be old enough to understand, Varg. This will complicate our relationship for years to come.'

'Had you rung her beforehand to say you were coming?'

'Why do you ask?'

'She had washed her hair and she didn't like me being there. I had the feeling she was expecting someone.'

'It wasn't me at any rate. I hadn't rung to ... forewarn her. I went on the spur of the moment.' He checked his watch. 'But I have to go. I have a meeting at ten. And now you know, Varg. Now two of us know. I hope you can understand that Siv Monsen is a woman with major problems. Approach her with caution. Great caution.'

I nodded, got up and escorted him to the door. 'Don't delete my telephone number, Nils. This will stay between us.'

He nodded back. 'Nothing will be as before, but let's try.'

We shook hands in a formal manner, and then he was gone. I slumped down onto the chair behind the desk and sat looking out of the window.

The sun had risen above the mountain now. But it was pale

and ill humoured. It seemed to be already regretting its appearance. And I felt quite secure. It wasn't going to shine on us for long on this January day.

24

ANNEMETTE BERGESEN LOOKED STRESSED. She finished what she was doing on her laptop, shoved some high piles of paper to the side, fetched something that looked, from my side of the desk, like an autopsy report, flicked through it swiftly and put it down with an impatient gesture before, at length, fixing me with her eyes and saying: 'Right, Veum.'

I felt exactly as if I had been summoned to the headmaster for a serious offence during my wild schooldays at Bergen Cathedral School. 'Don't blame me. You're the one who asked me to come here.'

'Obviously a hasty decision. But let's get down to brass tacks, Veum. What can you tell me about Tanya Allilujeva Karoliussen, which according to our investigations is the official name of the dead woman?'

'Tanya Allilu … Karoliussen. Married in Norway?'

'Separated. Former permanent address given as Kirkenes. Now living in a basement flat in Løvstakksiden. Rogagaten. But I was doing the asking, wasn't I?'

'Yes, but I don't have a lot to say. I was given her name in connection with a case I have.' In brief outline, I told her about Margrethe Monsen, my results so far and my short meeting with Tanya Karoliussen on Monday night. I rounded off by referring to her trip in the car Margrethe had refused to enter, and gave her the same number I had tried to check at the Vehicle Licensing Agency: SP-523 …

'No more than the first three numbers?'

'I'm afraid not, no. The car was thought to be black, though.'

'No make of car?'

'No.'

She made a note anyhow. 'I'll see what we can find out.'

'As far as I'm informed, both this Margrethe and Tanya had the same – what do you call them? – business manager?'

'Pimp, do you mean?'

'I thought that kind of thing was illegal.'

'It isn't.'

'They call themselves Malthus Invest anyway.'

She didn't look unduly surprised. 'Indeed.'

'And they don't just invest in girls, if I may say so.'

'Don't they?'

'The man who was beaten up in Skuteviken last weekend. Lars Mikalsen. Rumours in the town say he was a courier for Malthus & Co.'

I had her interest now. 'A drugs courier?'

'Yep.'

'But as far as I've been told, he refused to lodge a complaint.'

'Don't you think that's strange, all things taken into account?'

'No, justice is brutal in those circles. How did you find out about it?'

I tilted my head. 'One has one's connections. Those of us who do not have any police authority to bang on the table.'

'Do you think he will tell us any more now?'

'Not unless you give him special treatment, under the table, as it were, and that is not exactly *comme il faut* any more, is it.'

She sent me an old-fashioned look. 'It never has been, Veum.'

'Yeah, yeah. There are black sheep in most pens.'

'Back to the case. Is this in any way connected with the murder of Tanya Karoliussen?'

'You've established that she was murdered, have you?'

She nodded. 'She was strangled. And ...'

'Yes?'

'The sole bright spot at the moment. We found remnants of skin under her nails. If we're lucky we'll find the killer's DNA there. But that particular point is no business of yours. What I was about to say was ... Have you anything else to tell me?'

'Have you spoken to Helleve?'

'Yes, I promised to ...' She lifted the telephone receiver, dialled an internal number and got through. 'Atle? I've got Veum here. Fine.' She cradled the receiver and nodded. 'He's on his way.'

Thirty seconds later Atle Helleve was in the doorway. He shook his head. 'Two bodies, Varg? A busy week for the private investigator, eh?'

'Hey, hey, hey. Let's maintain a certain degree of accuracy, shall we. Someone else found the first body. I happened to be in the vicinity, that's all. As for the other, Inspector Bergesen here phoned me up.'

'Because the girl had your business card on her,' interjected Annemette Bergesen, not letting the grass grow under her feet.

'And we've resolved that matter, haven't we?'

She turned to Helleve. 'Nonetheless, he has a lead on the attack in Skuteviken that Bjarne was dealing with. You know, last weekend.'

Helleve pushed a chair back and sat down. 'Really? Tell me more. What's the connection?'

I gave him the same account I had given Annemette Bergesen a few minutes before. He didn't make notes, but I observed the information sticking like a layer of silicon to the inside of his skull. Whether it filled all the cracks I was not so sure.

When I reached the bit about Malthus he sent an eloquent glance to his female colleague. 'Malthus. We've never been able to get anything on him, have we.'

She returned his glance. 'Kjell Malthus is a lawyer. He knows all the tricks of the trade.'

'Let's haul Lars Mikalsen in for questioning again.'

'Agreed. I'll tell Bjarne.' She scribbled on her pad.

He turned back to me. 'But it has nothing, in my view, to do with what went on in Falsens vei.'

'Except that the now-deceased Carsten Mobekk and his wife Lill were, in the past, members of a self-established committee to support the Monsen family during Margrethe's childhood years. An extremely peripheral connection, in other words. By the way, did you realise that their father, Frank Monsen, died as the result of a fall in 1993?'

'A fall?'

'He fell down the stairs when drunk. That was the conclusion. Yet another suspicious fall in the same district.'

'That's a few years ago now, and I still don't see a direct connection. You were at the crime scene yourself. It was evident that someone had been searching for something in Mobekk's office.'

'Yes, was there anything missing though? Items of value? Papers?'

'Impossible to say. *Fru* Mobekk had no knowledge of what was in his papers. The only object she is certain she cannot find is a candlestick.'

'A candlestick!'

'Heirloom. Heavy as hell.'

'The murder weapon perhaps?'

'Not impossible. But anyway it's gone, so for the moment we'll have to register it as … missing.'

'Is there a motive for the murder?'

Helleve replied with an ironic smile. 'Nothing we've unearthed as yet. We're looking for leads or motives in his background. Entrepreneurial activities can be shifting sands, and there could be good reasons for him selling up long before he had to. But we haven't reached any final conclusion yet, and it's improbable we'll share it with you.'

'Why did he sell up?'

'No obvious reason. Solid company, as far as we know. But, as I said, we'll keep checking.'

'But … what about KG Monsen? Have you followed up that lead?'

'Not yet. I thought it was his sister you were looking for?'

'It is. But it's quite a coincidence that both have disappeared. Don't you think? Margrethe had even told one of the other women … well.' I looked at Annemette Bergesen. 'It was Tanya. … that she would soon be off. And there's a definite link between KG and Margrethe.'

Helleve studied me pensively. 'I can agree on that, Varg. There are some thin threads here, leading from one case to another. But so far all too thin.'

'What about fingerprints? There were a lot of glasses inside. At the crime scene in Falsens vei, I mean. Anything new on them?'

'No, Varg. And Margrethe Monsen wasn't on our files, I'm afraid to say. But I can give you one tiny snippet of information. During the investigation we came across a stolen car in one of the streets up there. Reported stolen in Åsane some time last Friday. As a matter of form we checked it for fingerprints, and we had a stroke of luck. KG's prints were on the wheel, gear lever and the driver's door handle.'

'What! But that must have put you on the trail, mustn't it? On his trail, I mean.'

'Yes, it did. We've stepped up the search. We don't have her prints, as I said.'

'I can help you there though.' I took out my wallet, opened a zip and held out the key Hege had lent me. 'This is to the flat she had in Strandgaten. Owned, as it happens, by Malthus Invest. There should be no shortage of prints inside.'

He accepted the key with a reflective expression. 'OK. Thank you. Perhaps we'll find her there as well?'

'I would be surprised. She wasn't there the other day at any rate. But if you do, please let me know.'

'You know what that would mean though, Varg, don't you? It would mean Margrethe Monsen would no longer be your case.'

'Oh, yes, she would! I have to continue my investigations as my employer asked.'

'And your employer would be…?'

'I don't think I am obliged to tell you.'

'Her mother? Her sister? We can ask them ourselves.'

'A girlfriend.'

'From the same ranks perhaps?'

'Not impossible.'

'Might she have something to tell us about Tanya?' Annemette Bergesen interrupted. 'In which case it's important we know.'

'I don't think so. But I'll ask her next time we speak. Shall I ask her to contact you direct?'

'Yes, do that.'

I turned to Atle Helleve. 'Are you going to go public with the search soon?'

'For KG? We'll have to, I suppose. For the moment, we're keeping it internal. Every single patrol car in town has a photo of him on the dashboard. Yesterday we did a door-to-door search in the district up there. Today we're doing the same elsewhere. Nygård Park, Torgallmenningen, you know ... wherever people are on the move.'

'C. Sundts gate,' Annemette Bergesen added.

'Yes, we'll give you a copy as well,' Helleve said.

'What about electronic leads?' I said. 'They must have mobile phones, KG and his sister.'

He gave a paternal nod. 'Yes, they did have, and we've pinged them. Since last Saturday there's been nil activity.'

'Saturday? That was the last time either of them used their phone?'

'It was definitely the last time KG rang. We checked him first.'

'And where did he ring from?'

'A base station in Bergen centre. Not very helpful, as such.'

'But ...'

'Yes?'

'Since then it's been quiet?'

'As quiet as the grave, as the cliché goes.'

'But they can't just have vanished into thin bloody air!' I said.

'No?' Helleve watched me, deep in thought. 'No, I don't suppose they can, can they.'

25

I WOULD HAVE BEEN PREPARED TO SWEAR I would never end up sitting in Holbergstuen supping tea with Paul Finckel. But there we were, and he didn't look too good.

'It's my liver, Varg. The doctor's told me in no uncertain terms. Spring water and tea, that's what I drink these days.'

'Well, I have to drive later on, so I'll keep you company.'

The tea was thin, and Paul Finckel thinner. But then he had made a habit of pumping himself up and down like a rutting toad from one period to another during his life. We each ordered a salad with the tea and behaved by and large like Spinsters Anonymous on a day out: Go wild and don't spare the Thousand Island dressing. The waitress served us with resigned tolerance. She had probably worked out that tips tended to depend on the choice of menu and there was nothing to be had from us.

'And what about you?' he asked, almost hopefully. 'What's up with you?'

'Me? Nothing? Bit of rheumatism in the wound when there are big fluctuations in the temperature, but it's around ten degrees summer or winter in town, so ... it's fine.'

He took an envelope from his briefcase. 'And now you're investigating the Gimle case?'

'Well, investigating may be overstating it, but the case cropped up in connection with another one.' I swiftly put him in the picture, not forgetting Frank Monsen, Carsten Mobekk or Tanya Karoliussen along the way.

'Three deaths, Varg? Bit over the top, even for you, isn't it?'

'The first was an accident. Looks like it at least. KG Monsen is linked to the killing of Mobekk. Thus far.'

'But has it got anything to do with the Gimle case?'

'Not as such. But KG is involved, of course.'

'Right.' He opened the envelope and pulled out some photocopies. 'There were quite a few articles written about the case when it was news. Opinions were divided as to how severe the sentence should be. Most people thought that being exposed to undesired sexual approaches can be such a dramatic experience that a violent reaction is absolutely understandable. The defendant's young age was the centre of a lot of speculation. All things considered, I believe he got the sentence he deserved.'

He pushed the photocopies over to me. I flicked through them briskly. The first ones were news stories of the murder itself, along with photographs of the arrest, with the young boy's face blurred, and others showing him being led into the magistrate's court with a jacket over his head. Later there were full-page spreads of the trial, with photographs of the prosecutor and the defence counsel and shadowy sketches of KG. Perhaps because of his young age he was never named, not even after his sentence had been passed. "The Boy (16)" was the description that was used throughout. The murder victim, Øyvind Malthus, was mentioned by name in one of the first reports, a couple of days after the murder had occurred. It was the same spread I had found in Rolf Terje Dalby's bedsit. In later articles and during the trial he was referred to as "The Supply Teacher (24)".

The waitress came with our salads, and we pounced on them like starving rabbits. The pale pink dressing dripped onto Paul Finckel's chin, and he gazed longingly at the juicy steaks that were being served two tables away. It was a dog's life, no two ways about it.

Between lettuce leaves he mumbled: 'But … there was one aspect that never came out in court, I was told by a colleague of mine.'

'Mm?'

'The victim, Øyvind Malthus, had been on the police's radar before.'

'For sexual molestation?'

'No. Narc. But the police had never been able to get anything on him.'

'Neither him nor his brother.'

There was a glint in his eye. 'So you know him?'

'Malthus Invest,' I said. 'With several mobile investments in C. Sundts gate.'

'Exactly.'

'Furthermore, there are rumours circulating that the guy who was beaten up in Skuteviken last weekend was a drug mule for Malthus. Lars Mikalsen. Name mean anything to you?'

'Nope. Have we written anything about this?'

'Just a note. None of this is official, but what you've told me about Øyvind Malthus puts everything into an interesting perspective. Do you know anything else about what happened at that time? About the drugs connection, I mean.'

'No, I didn't follow this case in person, so everything is second-hand.'

'What do you know about him? And here I'm thinking of Kjell Malthus.'

He sopped up the remains of the salad with a piece of baguette and chewed slowly. With a grimace he washed it down with the thin tea. 'Not so much. He's known for keeping his cards close to his chest. But his papers are in order. Trained lawyer with experience as a broker before starting out on his own a few years ago.'

'And do you know what he invests in?'

His face was expressive. 'A moveable feast, Varg. Everything from barrels of oil to prostitution. Probably not averse to some drugs, so long as the earnings are good enough. I've heard speculation verging in that direction, but never anything specific.'

'Right.' I held up the photocopies. 'Can I keep these?'

'Be my guest.'

'In that case I can see only one solution. To visit the lion in his den.'

'The lion?'

'Kjell Malthus himself.' I nodded towards his empty plate. 'Full?'

He pulled a face, and we asked for the bill. We'd had more festive sittings, there was no doubt about that.

26

THIS TIME, DURING BUSINESS HOURS, the front door was open. I took the stairs up to the third floor, where a plain gilt sign beside a grey door announced that this was the residence of Malthus Invest.

I knocked and entered. The room was furnished in minimalist fashion. No plants, no pictures on the walls, a huge calendar of the current year, basta. On a small table to the left lay a couple of financial newspapers, the latest edition of *Kapital* and today's *Bergens Avis*. For an investment company the room was unusually devoid of people. But at least they employed a secretary.

She was a Mediterranean beauty of the kind that would have made even the girl from Ipanema pale beside her. Golden brown complexion, with long, undulating hair as black as ebony, she looked as if she had been cut out of an advert for exotic travel destinations, and the tight-fitting yellow dress did nothing to dull the impression. But when she opened her mouth I knew that she had not been employed for her Norwegian language skills.

'Ja? What you like?'

I flashed my nicest smile. 'Kjell Malthus. Is he in?'

Her eyes were dark and lustrous. 'Who I can announce?'

'You can announce Varg Veum. Say it's important.'

'Varg Veum?' She had difficulty repeating it.

'That's right.'

She got up from her place behind the desk and sashayed to a door at the back of the room, knocked, waited for an answer and opened. It was not long before she came back out, with Kjell Malthus in her wake.

'Didn't I tell you to keep well away, Veum?' he barked, and the woman in the yellow dress regarded him with alarm.

'We have important things to discuss, Malthus. Do you want to do that in front of your secretary or shall we do it in your office?'

'Maria?' He glanced at his secretary. 'There's not much she hasn't heard. Isn't that true?'

'Was never more true word,' she gleamed.

'However, on the other hand, there are more useful things she can do with her time.'

'Yes, the clients are queueing outside. I could hardly elbow my way through.'

He sent me a chill glare. 'We're first and foremost a Net-based company, Veum.'

'So what's Maria doing here then? Making coffee and filing her nails?'

'She brightens the place up, don't you think?'

Another gleaming smile.

'Does it cost much to hire her? At night, for example?'

His eyes hardened. 'Watch your lip or you'll be leaving head first.'

'And who's going to do that? You?' Fair enough, he was taller than me, and a good bit broader, but he would not have things all his own way.

He motioned towards his office door. 'Come on.' He turned to Maria. 'No telephone calls. Just take messages.'

He closed the door hard behind us and with a brief nod

indicated a reasonably comfortable-looking client's chair. The office was furnished in the same minimalist way as the ante-room. No artwork on the walls here, either. Not so much as a calendar. The desk with the black glass top was clean and tidy, and the only feature that suggested this was a business was the laptop on the left and the two telephones on the right, both cordless, one a mobile.

'So this is the control room of your worldwide empire, is it?'

'Shut up, I said.'

'How many employees have you got? Apart from Maria and Rolf Terje, I mean?'

'Enough.'

'Most on contract, eh? Highly informal contracts?'

'Veum.' He placed both palms down on the table, with his arms positioned in such a way that he looked even broader, in theory ready to launch himself forward, and it was precisely that impression he wanted to convey. His voice was low and intense. 'Cut the crap and get to the point.'

'That is not quite so simple. You still haven't heard from Margrethe Monsen?'

'My relationship with ... *frøken* Monsen is exclusively land-lord to tenant. As long as she pays her rent everything is fine by me.'

I curled my lips into a smile. 'I hear what you say. What about Tanya? Did you have the same deal with her?'

'Tanya? I don't know any Tanya.'

'Don't you? *Fru* Karoliussen from Kirkenes? In which case, you have missed the opportunity. She was found dead in the sea by the Customs House last night.'

'Oh, her ...'

'So you had heard about it?'

He sent me a blank look.

'Two out of the picture within a week. How does that affect the budget?'

'The budget? What the fuck are you talking about?'

'It's bad publicity, anyway. For someone who offers protection, I mean. But I suppose the biggest loss was when Lars Mikalsen was met off the Danish ferry last weekend and had his luggage pinched, wasn't it?'

'Veum, listen here …'

'No, Malthus, you listen here. KG Monsen. Name mean anything to you?'

Now he no longer made any effort to hide it. His expression was implacably hostile.

'The Gimle case, right?'

'Your brother was killed because he molested one of his pupils. Is it in the family? Homosexuality, I mean?'

He jumped up from behind the desk. 'Øyvind was not a fucking poof!'

'No? But you are?'

'Veum …' His face was a deep red, and the blood vessels on his forehead swollen. This was something experience had taught me. If you want to get one of these macho guys excited, the surest way was to call them homosexual.

'So why was he killed then? Was it a fight for territory? Had KG gone solo and moved into Øyvind's market? Was it a situation that got out of hand with a fatal outcome for your brother? Control of the school market has always been important in this industry. Everyone knows that. That's where the clients of the future are groomed,' I said, then tried to put as much contempt as I could into the next two words: 'Malthus Invest.'

'I'm not …'

'Yes, you are. It's just that no one has got anything on you yet. But your time will come, Malthus. It's waiting for you round the corner.'

He slumped back into the chair. A storm was raging inside his skull. 'Veum … Øyvind was my little brother. I had promised my parents I would look after him. When he was killed everything seemed to collapse around my bloody ears.'

'So we're agreed then.' I muted my tone. 'He was not a homosexual. This was a drugs showdown.'

He didn't move behind the desk. His glare was still as hostile, but there was something vulnerable and human in his features that had not been there before.

'You must have wanted to take revenge. For the murder of your brother, I mean.'

'He got his punishment.'

'Margrethe's brother.'

I let the words hang in the air between us. There didn't appear to be any reaction, apart from the subdued glare.

As he didn't speak I added: 'Who has vanished without trace, like his sister.'

Still no reaction.

'No one vanishes without trace nowadays, Malthus.'

'Don't be so sure about that!'

'Should I regard that as a threat?'

'You can regard it as whatever you fucking want.' He rose from behind the desk. 'Anything else?'

I got to my feet, to maintain some kind of control over the situation. 'You may not consider these people to have any worth, Malthus. A woman from Russia, down on her luck in her new homeland. A woman with a skewed take-off from Minde – and her brother. For you they may be no more than incomings and outgoings in the annual accounts. Sources of earnings, expendable items.'

'And what's the bloody point of that? If I can earn money with these girls, as you claim, is it logical that I would get rid of them?'

'No. That's why I'm asking you: what's going on? Is there a street war? Is someone muscling their way into your part of the market as well?'

'What do you mean?'

'Who robbed Lars Mikalsen, for example? An outsider perhaps?'

His eyes narrowed. 'Veum, I'm warning you ...'

'Relax, Malthus. I know the package was meant for you. And I'll promise you one thing. As soon as I can prove the facts, the walk from Strandkaien to the police station will be very short.'

'Strandkaien?'

'That's where I have my office.'

'Handy to know. Very handy to know, Veum.' For some reason, every statement he made sounded like a threat.

'If I don't find them, Margrethe or KG, soon, don't rule out a second visit. Also handy to know, eh?'

He glowered at me, but confined himself to indicating the door with one hand, to show which direction he wanted me to go.

I bowed and took the hint. In reception I winked at Maria. She was as charming as when I arrived. But I assume that is how it is in most investment companies. Red carpet on the way in, account in the red on the way out.

27

IT WAS TIME FOR AN EXPEDITION to Minde. On my way to Skansen to pick up my car I dropped by my flat.

'Hello?' I called out loudly as I unlocked the front door.

I was not rewarded with an answer, and walking around I was soon able to confirm that she had gone. She had even made the bed and rinsed the glasses before leaving. As far as I could see, nothing was missing. So, the end of the world wouldn't be this year, either.

I opened the top drawer of the dresser in the bedroom and took out the small photo album I had found in Margrethe's flat. I quickly thumbed through to the photo of the cabin, with the three children and the five adults. Even though they were a great deal younger here I still had no difficulty recognising Lill Mobekk, Alf Torvaldsen and Markus Rødberg in the picture. The other woman was most likely Wenche Torvaldsen. The third man was Carsten Mobekk.

I thumbed back through the album and stopped by the photographs I suspected must have been taken in Børs Café. I recognised him at once. One of them sitting with a raised beer glass and toasting the photographer was Lars Mikalsen. In one of the pictures he was sitting with his arms around Margrethe's shoulders and saying something to her. I studied the other faces, though without any luck. I may well have seen a couple of them during my visits to the self-same café, and that of course might have been why I had felt I had also seen Lars

Mikalsen before, but this made me wonder whether I should have another chat with him before the police – or anyone else – beat me to it.

Before leaving I tapped in Hege's number on my mobile. No answer. Not that it necessarily meant anything, but it did give me a tiny feeling of unease in my stomach. In Øvre Blekevei I got behind the wheel of my new Corolla. I drove past Skansen fire station, through Proms gate and Brattlien towards Leitet and Kalfarlien, keeping the town centre – situated in a hollow and enveloped in January mist – to my right, a quilt of old and new, a jigsaw puzzle that had never been finished because the last piece was always missing, a medieval town waiting for the great infarct, once all the arteries had been blocked. It was safer to hug the hillsides in an elongated arc towards Årstad and Minde.

I parked in more or less the same spot as last time, by the playground in Jacob Aalls vei. As I turned into Falsens vei, I saw Lill Mobekk coming out of the garden gate in front of her house, wearing the same olive-green coat she wore when she arrived two days ago. We met by the gate to the remnants of the Torvaldsen and Monsen families, one person on each floor.

We stopped, and she looked at me with puzzlement. 'Yes?' I could see that she was struggling to recognise me.

'I'm Veum. I was here on Thursday when your husband … was found.'

'Oh, yes. Now I remember you.' She scrunched up her face in a blink, as if to hold back the tears. 'Thank you for helping.'

'It was no more than … How are you?'

She shook her head. 'I'm still in shock. I'm not sure I've taken in what happened. I'm glad I have … Alf.' She looked at the house in front of us. 'He's offered to help me with all the practical details. He and Carsten were best friends for so many years.'

'Yes, so I understand. I'm going to see *fru* Monsen. You know her as well, don't you?'

'Yes, of course. Known her for years.'

She walked ahead of me to the house.

'Ring Torvaldsen's bell,' I said. 'That seems to be the most effective way.'

Without another word, we waited. When the door opened Torvaldsen sent Lill Mobekk a bright smile, which faded the second he spotted me. 'Veum? What ...?'

'I'm going to see *fru* Monsen again.'

'Right. Any news on Margrethe?'

'I'm afraid not.'

'Margrethe?' Lill Mobekk queried.

'Yes, she's gone missing,' Torvaldsen answered, then added pointedly: 'Her and ... Karl Gunnar.'

'Really?' I watched her receive the information with unease.

'The day before yesterday you omitted to mention,' I said to Torvaldsen, 'that you, your wife, *fru* Mobekk here and her husband were on a sort of a committee set up to take care of the Monsen family, the children first and foremost.'

'No, I did not. Why would I? I mean ... Who are you? A kind of private investigator, I was told.'

'I cannot deny that.'

Lill Mobekk faced me again. 'A ... detective?'

I nodded. 'Yes. If you should ever need one, then ...'

'Alright, alright,' Torvaldsen said. 'I think we'll leave this case to the police. Are you coming, Lill?'

'Yes.' He held the door open for her. 'Thank you.'

I followed them into the stairwell, unbidden. 'I'll do the same as last time,' I said, motioning upwards.

Neither answered. Torvaldsen let Lill Mobekk into his flat, then closed the door firmly behind him. I went up to the first floor and knocked on the door.

Else Monsen hadn't changed her outfit since Tuesday, and the cigarette butt in the corner of her mouth seemed to be a permanent fixture. Her gaze was just as dead, just as lifeless, as she regarded me from the doorway.

'Hello,' I said with a gentle smile. 'I was here a couple of days ago. Veum.'

She looked at me expectantly, although she didn't make a move to invite me in.

'I was wondering whether I could have a couple of words with you.'

She stepped aside to let me through, but without uttering a sound. I entered the hall and allowed her to lead the way to the same dismal sitting room as on my previous visit. The parish journal and the magazines lay untouched in the same positions. The portable radio and the TV were as lifeless as before. The ashtray was, if possible, even fuller. The tiny cigarette ends formed a white sugary mound in the middle of the coffee table, a burial mound over dead hours.

She placed another stone on the mound, took another cigarette from a freshly opened pack and lit it without a look in my direction. I coughed, as if to draw to her attention that I was still present. She raised her eyes to my chest, but no higher.

'*Fru* Monsen … I asked you the other day whether you'd heard from any of your children. Have any of them contacted you since then?'

'Since when?' she asked my shirt front.

'Tuesday, two days ago,' I sighed.

After a long rumination she concluded the answer was no. 'Tell me … Don't you have any photos of your children?'

'As adults? No.'

'Not even as children?'

She turned round at her own pace and her gaze traversed the bare walls, as if there should have been something there, but it had been removed. 'We did have some.'

'And where are they now?'

She struggled to her feet and shuffled out of the room, the smoke trailing behind her like a bridal veil. I sat and waited. After a couple of minutes she returned with a small cardboard box in her hands. She set the box down on the table and pushed it in my direction without a comment.

I opened the top flaps and peered inside. It was a little box of surprises: a small jewellery casket, some old newspapers, among which I recognised an article about the Gimle case, a few picture postcards of other parts of the country, some documents including the children's birth certificates and a handful of framed photographs.

I picked them up one by one. Else Monsen concentrated on the cigarette, but I noticed her casting sharp glances in my direction each time I picked up a photo, as if to make sure I wouldn't run off with any of them.

Several were photographs of babies. For someone who had not seen any of them before, it was difficult to distinguish one from the other.

I assumed three were confirmation photos, judging by the clothes and age. I recognised Siv without a problem and Margrethe from the small photo album. Karl Gunnar stood erect in a smart, dark jacket with a white shirt, pink tie and hair in the typical mullet cut of the 80s.

Their expressions varied. Siv was the only person smiling, a rather stiff smile probably at the exhortation of the photographer more than from any inner conviction. Margrethe and Karl Gunnar had distant looks on their faces, as though they were not fully present, neither then nor now.

'Good-looking kids,' I said.

She gave a minimal nod and took a huge drag on her cigarette.

'I understand you were given some assistance by a committee for a while?'

Her mouth tightened a fraction, but still she had nothing to say.

'Why was that?'

'... The parish thought they could help us. We were ... my husband wasn't a well man.'

'No? What was wrong with him?'

'... It was ... his nerves. They had troubled him all his life. He could ... Now and then he wasn't quite himself.'

'I see. He died in an accident, didn't he?'

'... Yeah.' She glanced at the door, as if fearing someone would come in and deny it. 'He fell down the stairs. Out there.'

'In a drunken state, wasn't he?'

She nodded. 'Yes, probably. I didn't see it happen myself.'

'You weren't at home?'

'Yes, I was, but ... I was in here. I thought he was going to the loo.'

'Perhaps both of you had been drinking?'

'... Yes, I suppose we had.'

'And then he fell?'

'Yes.'

'Did you find him?'

'No, *fru* Torvaldsen did. People underneath. All of a sudden she was outside ringing the bell, and afterwards it was just a mess.'

'Just a mess?'

'Yes. Ambulance and police and priest and all at the same time.'

'Police?'

'Yes, but nothing else happened. Frank had fallen down the stairs, under his own steam, so to speak.'

'Were any of the children at home?'

'No, no. They'd moved out. There was just Frank and me here at that time.'

'Margrethe still gives this address as her fixed abode.'

'Oh?' She regarded me with puzzlement. 'But it's ... she moved out ages ago.'

'Docs post still come for her? Here, I mean.'

'Post?' She looked as if she did not understand the word. 'Bills. And advertising brochures. Loads of ads.'

'For Margrethe too?'

'For Margrethe? No, for me!' She heaved a deep sigh, flicked ash and put the cigarette between her lips again without missing much more than one drag.

'Well ... but when your husband died ... you said ... Siv was the only one to go to the funeral, didn't you?'

'Yes, I suppose she was.'

'You're not sure?'

'Yes, I am ...'

Cigarette smoke hung like a cloud of mist over her part of the room. I held out the photo of Karl Gunnar. 'Could I borrow this one?'

She hesitated. 'Just that one?'

'Yes, I've met Siv, and I've got better photos of Margrethe.'

For the first time I detected some emotion in her voice. 'I want it back again though!'

'Yeah, yeah, no problem. If you'd had a photo of him as an adult I ...'

'That's the only one I've got.'

'I promise you, *fru* Monsen, you'll get it back.'

'What are you going to do with it?'

'Tell me, have the police been here?'

' ... Yes, there was a woman.'

'Mm, but you know that Margrethe and Karl Gunnar are missing? The whole police force is out looking for them. That is, for Karl Gunnar. He's escaped from prison. Margrethe has disappeared.'

'Disappeared? Margrethe? She hasn't been here for years and years.'

'No.' I was unable to refrain from releasing a little sigh. 'You don't have any idea where she could have gone? There's no ... family?'

' ... All we had was the committee.'

'You mean I should talk to them?'

She shrugged. 'It's too late. Everything's too late.'

She had finished the cigarette. She stubbed it out firmly against the edge of the ashtray, pushed into the heap, got another one from the packet and lit it, all automatic actions, as though she were standing by an assembly line and thinking about something else.

I decided that the cigarette would have to live and die without any attempts on my part to save it from the fate for which it was destined. I took my leave, went down to Torvaldsen's and rang the bell.

28

TORVALDSEN ANSWERED HIMSELF. He did not look very thrilled. 'Veum? What's this about now? Couldn't you get in upstairs?'

'Yes, I did. I spoke to *fru* Monsen. I'd very much like to have a word with you as well.'

'With me? What about, if I might venture to ask?'

'Changed circumstances.'

'Changed circumstances? At this particular moment I'm busy.'

'Yes, so I understood. But it concerns *fru* Mobekk, too. The whole committee.'

'Hm, the … Well, alright. You'd better come in.'

He stepped aside and ushered me in. I smelled the faint but enticing aroma of coffee. As I followed him into the sitting room the aroma became stronger.

They were no longer alone. Markus Rødberg had joined the gathering. He rose to his feet as I entered. Lill Mobekk remained seated, with a cup raised to her mouth, as if caught in a freeze-frame.

'Hm, the whole committee is assembled,' I said airily, before correcting myself: 'Well, not quite. *Frøken* Vefring's missing.'

Rødberg held out his hand. 'Nice to see you again, Veum.'

'Is she coming as well?'

'Who?'

'*Frøken* Vefring.'

Rødberg looked at the others, confused. 'I can't imagine she will be.'

Torvaldsen came alongside me. 'You'll have to find yourself a chair, Veum, and I'll get you a cup, if you want one.'

'Yes, please.'

I sat down in the free chair by the coffee table and took stock. The impression here was so far from the one on the floor above you could scarcely credit it was the same house. The furniture was comfortable, practical and stylish, without appearing ostentatious. The walls were covered with bookshelves and pictures, many of which were in enormous gilt frames. There was a rug with a Persian pattern on the floor, and the TV set in the corner was a solid Finnish brand from the early 1980s, one of the best around. A radio cabinet containing a record player, a CD player and a selection of LPs and CDs was positioned along one wall, and facing the rear window there was a dark brown dining table with six chairs.

Lill Mobekk completed the movement she had begun, swallowed the sip of coffee and carefully set the cup down, as though afraid it would break. She was dressed in black: blouse and smart trousers. Around her neck she had a simple pearl necklace, with no other jewellery apart from her wedding ring.

Torvaldsen came in from the kitchen. After putting a cup and plate on the table he served coffee from a tall, white flask and pushed the cup towards me.

The suite was brown with red upholstery. Lill Mobekk was sitting on the sofa.

Torvaldsen occupied the free chair at the end of the table. 'Markus has told us about your visit, Veum. We understand that you're here regarding Margrethe and Karl Gunnar. Both have vanished apparently.'

'Without trace so far.' I didn't mention anything about the fingerprints in the stolen car. That was up to the police to inform them, to the extent that it was deemed necessary.

'Well … How can we help you?' He threw out his arms.

'In fact I was thinking of asking you to tell me a bit about Frank Monsen's death.'

All three of them looked at me in surprise. Torvaldsen answered: 'But what has that … got to do with all this?'

'It was your wife who found him, wasn't it?'

'Who said that?'

I pointed to the ceiling. 'His wife.'

'Well, I can't see how that has anything to do with anything at all. It was a tragic accident. The man fell down the stairs drunk and broke his neck. The conclusion to a sorry life. Both Wenche and I were out when it happened, but Wenche came home first and it was she who found him. By the time I arrived, straight afterwards, she had already rung for an ambulance, but it was too late.'

'He was dead when your wife found him?'

'I don't know. He was unconscious, but then he had so much alcohol in his blood he was way beyond normal communication.'

'And you never suspected it could be more than an accident?'

Lill Mobekk drew in her breath sharply, but said nothing. Markus Rødberg glanced at her with concern.

'No. Could be more? You don't mean that … Else?'

'For example.'

'Ridiculous, Veum. In that case she would have done it years before. She had good reason.'

'Yes?'

'Yes.' He pursed his lips and scanned the assembly with a stern look, as though to warn them not to object.

'Leading us to the second item, which might be worth dwelling on.'

'And that would be ...?'

Again I pointed to the ceiling as though I were a preacher in a Christian Youth Club, indicating every so often the way to lofty celestial chambers. 'Conditions at home. With the Monsen family.'

'Conditions at ...?'

'You work for public services, don't you, Torvaldsen?'

'I'm a manager at the county council, yes.'

'Off today?'

'Time in lieu.'

'But you understand *Nynorsk* and *Bokmål?* What were conditions like upstairs?'

Rødberg coughed. 'I told you the other day, Veum.'

I turned to face him. 'Yes, you did.'

I looked at Lill Mobekk. 'You all have a right to speak on this matter.'

At length I directed my attention back towards Torvaldsen. 'After all, you lived in the same house. You must have noticed if there was anything unusual.'

'The unusual feature about the Monsen family,' Torvaldsen said, 'was that neither of the parents was capable of performing their duties ... in full. They needed external help.'

'A dysfunctional family, as it's called in technical terminology.'

'Indeed. I can hear you've got the jargon.'

'In fact I am a trained social worker with five years' practice from ... well ... Has it ever struck you that if social services had got their way back in 1978 the whole of the Monsen family might have been better off, from Frank through to Karl Gunnar?'

Torvaldsen looked as if he had a bad taste in his mouth. 'Better off?'

'Yes, I don't suppose you can say that the results suggest a resounding success, can you? Frank Monsen continued to drink and lost his life while drunk. Else is a shadow of a human, barely on the level of her own ashtray. KG, Karl Gunnar, was in prison for murder until almost a week ago. Margrethe ... well, you all know where she ended up, don't you.'

Everyone nodded in confirmation, with varying degrees of regret in their eyes.

'And Siv ... she appears to have coped well, but ...'

'Appears?' queried Markus Rødberg.

'Yes. The façade seems fine, but does anyone know what lies smouldering beneath, just below the surface?'

'Now you're speaking in riddles, Veum,' Torvaldsen snapped.

'The point is this. One of the children is a prostitute, one reacted with such violence to a sexual approach that he became a murderer, the third ... well, let's keep her out of this until later. But my experience from years in social services ...'

Torvaldsen interrupted me and sent the other two an eloquent look. 'There we have it! Now that cat's out of the bag. So that's where your sympathies lie, Veum, with the social services. Now I understand better.'

I raised my voice. 'All my experience tells me that there are clear signs here of sexual abuse at a young age, and most often this happens within the four walls of home. Did any of you ever have a suspicion that something like that may have been going on?' For the third time I pointed heavenwards.

They exchanged looks. It was difficult to interpret them, but I had an unpleasant feeling that this did not come as a huge surprise to any of them.

Rødberg spoke up. 'I told you the other day, Veum. This was a task we embraced for one hundred per cent philanthropic reasons. If we'd had the slightest inkling that something of that nature was on the cards we would never have opposed the social services' expression of concern. I beg God for forgiveness that this went awry, but in this event it was without our knowledge or intention.'

'This went awry?'

'The outcome. What we are left with today. The lives of these unfortunates.'

'Torvaldsen?'

'Markus is right. We took this task on together, although with different backgrounds. I don't have the religious affiliation that Markus has. Furthermore, Wenche was the driving force here. She knew the children from school, of course. She and Hulda Vefring were utterly committed, along with Markus and Carsten, who both knew Frank Monsen from childhood.'

'Carsten and Frank were in the same *folkeskole* class,' Lill Mobekk said. 'Carsten tried to help his childhood friend as best he could. Got him a job as an electrician, to cut a long story short …' She burst into tears.

'Lill …' Markus Rødberg laid a consoling hand on her shoulder.

There was a flash of obvious annoyance in Torvaldsen's eyes, but this time it was not directed at me. Was there already a tug of war going on between the two men for the recently bereaved widow's favour – or to see who could show the greatest sympathy?

Tearfully, she said: 'I'm sorry … This is too much. Excuse me a moment.' Her shoulders shaking, she went into the hall, and we heard the door to what I assumed to be the bathroom being opened and then closed behind her.

Torvaldsen sent me an accusatory look. 'See what you've done, Veum! This is not the right day to drag all of this up, for Christ's sake!'

'My apologies, Torvaldsen, but I have a job to do as well. And I don't have any days off in lieu, if I may say so.'

He glared at me. Then he leaned forward and lowered his voice. 'Now that Lill's out … Markus told me you had suggested that Karl Gunnar may have … attacked Carsten. Were you being serious?'

'So that's why you got together today? To assess whether more of you might be in danger?'

'Danger? What the hell are you talking about? Karl Gunnar had no reason to kill Carsten! And you saw yourself the state of his office. Someone had been searching for something. My theory is that it was either a standard burglary … or else it was connected with the work he was doing.'

'There were no signs of a burglary. He must have let the perpetrator in himself.'

'So … a business connection! Perhaps he was threatened with a weapon, what do I know? There are lots of rotten eggs in the industry where he works.'

'Yes, you must know all about that, being in public administration.' Out of the blue, I asked: 'So why isn't *frøken* Vefring here?'

'Hulda? Why should she be?'

'The whole committee's here. Those still alive, so to speak. Except her.'

Torvaldsen sent me a long-suffering look. 'This is no committee meeting, Veum!'

'No? What is it then?' Now it was my turn to lean forward. 'Let me tell you something, Torvaldsen. I spoke to *frøken* Vefring yesterday, after I'd been to Rødberg. She said that at the end of the 80s there had been an atmosphere on the committee. Between Rødberg on the one hand and the two couples on the other ...'

I glanced at Rødberg, and there was no denying the triumphant expression on his face for Torvaldsen, a classic Bergensian *I-told-you-so* look. When I turned back to Torvaldsen the bitterness in his eyes had grown into massive loathing.

'The old biddy! So she couldn't keep her bloody mouth shut again.'

'What she said was right, then?'

'What's right, Veum, is that this has got bugger-all to do with you. Well ...' He looked at Rødberg, as if to encourage him to chime in. 'What happened was ... There was a minor dispute, but it was about ... religion. Markus was the contact with the priest and the parish. The rest of us were more ... personally committed. As individuals. In other words, there was a minor disagreement about faith, wasn't there, Markus.'

Markus Rødberg reciprocated his stare, gasped for breath and moved his lips silently as though searching for the right words.

The door in the hall opened. Torvaldsen found the words: 'But let's not talk about this any more. Not now.'

'No?' I queried.

'No,' he said firmly.

Markus Rødberg's face had undergone a deep flush, as if he was sitting and holding his breath.

Lill Mobekk came to the door. Her eyes were shiny and tinged with red, and her voice trembled as she said: 'I'm sorry. It just came over me. I couldn't help it.'

Then she became aware of the tense atmosphere in the room. She glanced from me to Torvaldsen and in the end to Rødberg. 'What have you …? Has something happened?'

Both Rødberg and Torvaldsen got up and moved towards her.

'No, no, no,' Torvaldsen said.

Rødberg coughed. 'It was Veum who … But he's leaving.'

Torvaldsen stopped, halfway towards Lill Mobekk. Then he turned to me. 'Yes. He's on his way out. Talking time is over.'

I rose from my chair. 'For this round maybe.' I turned to Rødberg. 'But we have more to talk about, all of us. Of that I am convinced.'

Rødberg nodded, almost on autopilot.

'I find that hard to imagine,' Torvaldsen reacted, in a loud voice, as if to strangle any signs of compliance. With a lingering stare he watched Lill Mobekk as she passed, before Rødberg led her to the sofa and pushed a chair aside so that she could slip through. Again I had the feeling I was witnessing a strange duel, and the next thought struck me: Wonder if she's a wealthy widow? How much had Carsten Mobekk left her?

'Allow me to accompany you out, Veum,' Torvaldsen said against his will, unhappy with the idea of leaving the other two alone inside.

'I can find my own way out, thank you,' I said, to relieve him of the dilemma.

But he stuck to his guns and escorted me out.

By the front door, I stopped. 'What happened that year, Torvaldsen? The winter of 1988–89, according to *frøken* Vefring?'

'Nothing happened. *Frøken* Vefring imagined all sorts of things. She was beginning to go soft in the head.'

'What sort of things? She didn't seem soft in the head when I spoke to her.'

'Veum! I'm warning you …'

'About what?'

He gave me a look of desperation. Then pushed me through the door, with very little resistance on my part.

'I'll find out soon enough,' I said, to give him another little something to think about.

He shot me a final withering glance. Then slammed the door.

I strolled towards the gate. On the frozen lawn lay the dark green petals of autumn's last roses. They reminded me of hearts. Fallen, stunted hearts, on the road to death and decay.

29

FROM MINDE I DROVE TO MØHLENPRIS. I found a place to park in Professor Hansteens gate and walked from there up to the house in Konsul Børs gate. I slogged up all the floors to Lars Mikalsen's tiny shoebox in the loft, but no matter how hard I knocked no one came to answer this time.

Forewarned by previous experience, I felt the door. It was locked. Perhaps he had already been taken in by the police for further questioning. The alternative was a less attractive thought.

I went back down to the car. From Møhlenpris I turned up towards Puddelfjord Bridge and drove through Fyllingsdalen tunnel. I parked in such a way that I could keep an eye on the entrance to the insurance company. Then I rang Siv Monsen's number.

She was quick to answer. 'Yes? Siv Monsen.'

'Veum here.'

The reaction did not come quite as quick. 'I see.'

'Will you be at work much longer?'

'What do you mean? I have ...'

'I'm sitting in my car outside. I was wondering if I could drive you home.'

'How presumptuous.'

'I think we may have a bit to discuss. It might be practical for both of us if we did it in the car.'

'Right! Where are you?'

'In the car park on the left, first row.'

'It'll take me at least half an hour to finish what I'm doing.'

'That's OK. I'm used to waiting.'

I made myself comfortable, searched the radio for a station that had anything more than inane music and recycled news, but ended up with one of my CDs instead, Miles Davis's immortal *A Kind of Blue*. That was close to how I felt, a bit blue.

In the middle of Coltrane's solo on *Freddie Freeloader* my mobile rang. It was Atle Helleve. 'I'm afraid we'll have to keep the key to Margrethe Monsen's flat for a while longer, Varg.'

'OK. Did you find anything?'

'Yes. If it's her prints on a tumbler and in several other places we've got a match with one we found on a wine glass at Mobekk's.'

'Great! That's a big step forward.'

'Definitely.'

'So she's been to the crime scene at any rate, if not when the murder was committed, then at least some time while *fru* Mobekk was out.'

'That's one obvious conclusion we can draw,' he said, not without some sarcasm in his voice. 'And if that weren't enough, we found her prints on the door handle of the stolen car up there as well.'

'Great! A picture's beginning to emerge, isn't it?'

'At least we can see the outlines of one, yes.'

'I assume then there'll be a full-scale search for her as well?'

'Absolutely. So you can go on holiday. We'll find her before you do, I suppose.'

'Have you picked up Lars Mikalsen?'

'Bjarne's on his way there now.'

'Then I hope he has more luck than I did.'

'What do you mean?'

'I was there about half an hour ago, and no one answered the door.'

'And what were you …?' He broke off. 'Well, alright! This is an impossible task. I suppose we knew that already.'

'What is?'

'Getting you to stay out of the way, Varg. Have you made any progress?'

'Not with respect to the disappearance, no.'

'So what are you doing now?'

'Sitting in a car park in Fyllingsdalen, waiting for their sister, Siv.'

'Well … get in touch if anything comes up.'

'May I venture a thank-you for doing the same?'

'You may, but I doubt it'll help.'

With that, the conversation was over, and I continued to listen to Miles & Co while keeping an eye on the entrance to the insurance company.

It was closer to three quarters of an hour before she appeared. I had just begun to wonder whether she had left by the rear exit when she came out, peered round and walked in my direction. I opened the car door to show her where to come, although that didn't seem to make her jump with joy. The distaste on her face was easy to read as she bent forward and looked in. 'What is it now then?'

'Wouldn't you like to sit down?'

'Have you found her?'

'No. Not yet.' I indicated the front seat with an open palm. 'I'll drive you home, as I said.'

'Well, alright.' She got in without enthusiasm. Only when

I had reversed out of the marked bay and put the car in first gear did she fasten the seat belt. 'The quickest route is via Bønestoppen.'

'Do you drive yourself?'

'I haven't got a car.'

I lowered the music and bore left at the first roundabout. 'So other people give you a lift, do they?'

She snorted quietly, as a sign that it was none of my business.

Three roundabouts later we began the ascent to Bønestoppen. 'Your father's death was dramatic,' I said as we passed the social housing by Lillehatten.

'Dramatic?'

'Yes. Losing his life in the way he did must class as … not very usual anyway. I suppose you know that, being in the branch you are.'

'He didn't have any life insurance, if that's what you're wondering.'

'So no one gained financially from his death, in other words?'

I could feel her eyes on my face. 'What are you implying, Veum?'

'I'm not implying anything at all. You were the one who didn't think there was anything dramatic about falling down the stairs at home and breaking your neck with fatal consequences.'

'I didn't say … I said you were over-dramatising. It was an unlucky accident. He and Mum had been drinking, and well … you know the rest.'

'There was a lot of drinking in your childhood, wasn't there,' I said quietly.

'Yes, there was!' She inhaled in a sharp gasp. 'It's not for no reason that we've … None of us has very happy childhood memories.'

'Your brother reacted with such force when he was subjected to what might have been a sexual approach. Such force that I wonder whether … he might have experienced something similar before.' I weighed my words carefully before adding: 'At home, for example.'

We were at the top of the hill now. As we began to descend towards Bønes we passed a yellow bus at a stop. Without any warning she undid her seat belt and grabbed the door handle. 'Let me out! I'll catch the bus.'

I drew in to the side, braked and held her arm. 'Siv! Take it easy. I didn't mean to …'

Her face was crimson. 'Let me go! I'll shout for help!'

'Listen to me.'

'Help!' she howled, and struggled to get free. 'Heeeelp!'

I let go of her arm, and her jacket sleeve was up. I caught a glimpse of the scars Nils had told me about. Then she twisted away, prised open the door and jumped onto the pavement while waving at the bus driver in desperation.

I yanked on the handbrake, killed the engine and jumped out on my side. 'Siv!'

The bus driver was crouched over the steering wheel staring at Siv. As I reached her and grabbed at her arm, he opened the door.

She hissed at me: 'Let go!'

Some frightened passengers on the pavement side of the bus watched with wide eyes. A man got up in the central aisle as the driver shouted to us: 'What the hell's going on?'

'Let me on!' Siv shouted.

The man in the aisle was by the driver now. 'Do you need some assistance, *frøken*?'

'Yes! This man. He's harassing me.'

The passenger was no heavyweight and in his mid-sixties. He hesitated to alight and join us. The driver, on the other hand, was a great deal stronger. Now he got to his feet. 'Let her go, or I'll call the police!'

'No!' Siv shouted.

'Please do,' I said. 'Ask for Hamre or Helleve and give them my regards. Veum's my name.'

'Don't!' said Siv.

They looked from her to me, bewildered. I let her go, but she didn't move. 'The choice is yours, Siv,' I said in a low voice. 'The police or me.'

Tears appeared in her eyes, and her lips quivered. 'Can't I just catch the bus?'

I swallowed. 'Let me drive you home. That'll be the simplest anyway. I promise … I won't ask any more questions if you don't want to tell me anything. No one can force you. Not me at any rate.'

The driver slumped back down behind the wheel. 'What's it going to be, *frøken*?'

She made herself look up at him. 'It's fine. You can go.'

'OK, but first of all Prince Charming will have to get his bloody car out of the way!'

The passenger was sending me stern looks, as if telling me to watch out or he'd …

I responded with a glare to make him think twice, and his eyes wandered to the side. Then I gently led Siv back to the car, held the door open for her and waited until she was in before walking round to my side, while the bus driver made a show of sitting on the horn and whistling angrily.

I ignored him, got behind the wheel and started up. I waited until Siv had put on her seat belt before signalling to move out and drove at an unhurried pace down the hill with the bus half a metre behind me to the next stop, where some impatient prospective passengers were looking at their watches as we passed.

In deafening silence we drove to Landås. Not a word was said. It was so quiet that after a while it cannot have been solely unpleasant for me. When we stopped in front of the star-shaped houses in Kristofer Jansens vei, she remained in her seat staring into the middle distance, not showing any signs of wanting to get out.

I glanced at her. In a cautious voice, I said: 'I couldn't help seeing the scars on your arm.'

She flushed and pursed her lips. She gulped, and I could see she was fighting with herself. Then the dam burst. A strangled sob forced itself up her throat, tears flooded out, she hid her face in her hands, leaned forward against the dashboard and wept without restraint.

I let her cry. After a while I bent over and stroked her shoulders and back. She leaned even further forward, into as close as you could get to a foetal position in a car seat.

Crying fits like this are like rainfall in a gale. It sweeps across the landscape, the sky darkens, and there is a sudden deluge with a power that seems supernatural. When it is over, the clouds drift by, patches of blue sky appear above and – on good days – a ray of sunshine.

Siv Monsen's crying stopped, too. But there wasn't much sun as she lifted her head, took out a pack of tissues from her bag and dried her tears. Her face was pale and blotchy, and there was an air of infinite vulnerability about her lips. It was an expression I had seen before in far too many children. The reflection of a lost childhood.

'It was Dad,' she whispered. 'But only when he had been drinking. Always when he had been drinking. Then he came up to us in the loft.'

The words came, slow and halting. This was not something she was used to talking about, to strangers. 'At first it was me. Later it was Margrethe, too. He never switched on the light. It always happened in the dark. We heard him come in. For many years I knew he was coming to me. After he began with Margrethe as well, it was almost worse. When I heard the sound of his shuffling steps in the loft it was as if I couldn't breathe. Then he was standing in the doorway. I could see his silhouette against the outside light. He would close the door behind him, and I would hear him groping his way in the night. Who would he choose … her or me? Next … I would feel him lift the duvet … his hands on my body. Or I would hear him creeping towards Margrethe, and that was almost even worse, because I could hear everything that went on, and I was so ashamed! Ashamed that I was so relieved it wasn't me, but her. I would lie listening to his coarse breathing, smelling the stench of alcohol, feeling so nauseous that I could have vomited. But I didn't dare move, could not say a word. Afterwards … I found it impossible to sleep without the light on.'

'And this persisted for many years, did it?'

'Right up until I left home! With Margrethe not long after, I suppose.'

'But Karl Gunnar …'

For the first time she looked straight at me. 'No, never. He wasn't interested in him at all. But of course he lay there in the dark listening to everything as well.'

'You never tried to talk with someone about this?'

'No. Who?'

'A teacher. A health visitor at school. This committee that was set up.'

She shook her head. 'It was impossible. Margrethe and I didn't even talk about it.'

'But there were signs. When the health visitor reacted to Margrethe's condition. Were you never asked about ... anything?'

'Never. *Fru* Torvaldsen and *fru* Vefring ... they said everything would be fine when they started taking care of us.'

'But it wasn't?'

'No.' After a pause she added: 'There was perhaps more order in terms of homework and eating and so on. But not the rest. Things just carried on.'

'It's not always easy to detect ... for outsiders.'

She didn't answer that, and I went on: 'What about your mother? Didn't she understand what was happening?'

'She must have done! She wasn't a complete idiot, I suppose. But she probably thought that in that way ... she was free. Why do you think we never visit her?'

'She still seems very weighed down by it all. Was she ever ... were you ever hit?'

'Margrethe and I weren't. Karl Gunnar was, a few times. But that was when he came from school with a teacher's note – there were other incidents.'

I sighed. It was not an unusual picture that she was drawing, not for someone with my background. The most important difference was that now, despite everything, someone was daring to come forward with their experiences. Until a few decades ago it was hushed up. No one talked about this, from the most Christian of homes to the most radical. But it had to be admitted: there was more of this behind closed doors in religious communities. In other circles they found satisfaction for their drives in a more acceptable way.

'But you all got away in the end.'

'Got away! Kalle had to go to prison to escape. That might be why he killed the boy. To escape.'

'Do you mean that?'

'What do I know? And Margrethe … you know where she's ended up. She must have thought that's how it was meant to be. Wasn't used to anything else. When she was old enough she knew how to exploit it. There were advantages, she could buy herself things, be out longer, if not …'

'If not …'

'… she threatened to tell someone. To go to the police.'

'How old was she when she moved out?'

'Eighteen. Autumn, 1988.'

'1988? Why then?'

'Why not? She couldn't stand it any longer, either.'

'But she never told the authorities that she'd moved.'

'Oh? Well, I suppose she didn't take that very seriously. She didn't get much more than her tax code in the post, and I'm sure she could manage without that.'

'Not an easy childhood for any of you, I can see.'

She slapped the dashboard. 'Do you know who I blame most? Not my father. He was just a pathetic bastard. Not my mother. She was a zero. But the sodding committee. These self-righteous neighbours who were so proud of all the things they were going to do – and then they weren't any better! I can never forgive them. Once I went to him, Rødberg, and asked for help. But all he did was hush it up. He said that I shouldn't, that it was a one-off, that I had to forgive. And then he wanted us to pray together. Pray to God for forgiveness of all our sins.

I could have spewed. I ran out, out of his house and back home to ... hell!'

'A one-off?'

'Yes.'

'But surely you told him ...?'

'Yes!' she interrupted. Then she held her head. 'Ohhh! This is driving me mad!' When she turned to me again it was with a sombre, distressed expression. 'What's happened to them, Veum? Where are they?'

'Margrethe and Karl Gunnar?'

She nodded. 'They were here ...' She gazed up at the star-shaped building. 'Friday night.'

A second or two passed before what she had said sank in. 'What! Here?'

'Yes.'

'Why didn't you tell me before?'

She shrugged. 'Kalle was going to spend the night with me, as usual, but this time he had Margrethe with him as well. Something had happened. I don't know what. She was very, very upset. The next day they said they were moving on, they had a plan. But I didn't believe them. I thought they were dreaming. But they did anyway. All of a sudden they were gone, and you and the police came to the door asking after them. Could ... could they be safe somewhere ... abroad?'

'Do you think so?'

She slowly shook her head.

'They would have contacted you, wouldn't they?'

'Yes, they would.'

I brooded. 'Listen, Siv ... there's something I have to tell you that very few people know. About what happened to Carsten Mobekk. The police have found Margrethe's prints at the crime scene. On a wine glass. And in one of the streets up there, in a stolen car, both of their prints.'

She looked at me, with such vacant eyes that for an instant I feared she had not understood what I had said.

'You said yourself that the people you blamed most were those on the committee. Perhaps Margrethe and your brother felt the same?'

'But ... No, I refuse to believe that. Margrethe?'

'Or both of them?'

'And so?'

I splayed my palms. 'It might have happened in a moment of passion. They could have been so frightened by what they had done that they just fled – as far as they could.'

'Where then? They didn't have anywhere to hide!'

'Nowhere?'

'No!'

For a while we sat in silence. At length I vaguely indicated her arm. 'When did you start self-harming?'

Again her face darkened. 'Don't remember.'

'Was it ... to punish yourself?'

She shrugged. 'I don't know. It was something I did. There was no one else I could ... be bad to.'

'But you know it's unfounded. There's no reason whatsoever to punish yourself for the abuse others have committed.'

'I know that, yes. But it's not so easy to ... Sometimes I just have to do it! It's like a kind of ... high. Something has poisoned me, for ever.'

'Yes, I know. Have you tried to get any treatment for it? Talked to a psychologist? What about the company doctor?'

'He's taken an oath of confidentiality!'

'But perhaps he recommended you to have treatment, as well?'

'Yes, he did. But … I thought I could cope without. I'm used to … coping alone. The last six months have been better after I …'

'After you …?'

'Got a … boyfriend.'

'Not … Nils Åkre?'

She shook her head. 'No, no, no. My goodness, he's a colleague.' She looked up at the apartment block. 'But now I think I have to …'

'Perhaps that was who you were expecting the other evening when first I, then Nils came … and disturbed you.'

She tossed her head. 'Maybe. I have to go, I said!'

'One last question, Siv. After you moved out … did you see … did you ever meet your father again?'

Her lips tightened into a fierce grimace. 'I went to his funeral, and I would have liked to dance on his grave! No, Veum. I never saw him again, and I would … If I had been able to, I would have killed him myself!'

'Do you think someone else … did precisely that?'

'Did … what? Killed him?'

'Yes.'

'Who could have done it?'

'I suppose your mother was the closest.'

'She could never have done it.'

'Your brother or sister?'

'Kalle was inside. And Margrethe? She'd also moved out before his death. None of us was at home even!'

'Who did he go to, do you think, when his needs were too great? Back to your mother? Could it have been too much for her?'

'I don't know! I know nothing about this. The day I moved

out I drew a line under the life I had lived to that point. Since then I've tried to start afresh, live a new life … without such occurrences. Since the funeral I haven't even seen her, my own mother!' She opened the door and set a foot on the tarmac. 'But now I have to go.'

She got out of the car. I leaned over and tried to catch her eye. 'Thank you for telling me all this, Siv. I don't know if it will help me to trace Margrethe, but at least it gives me a better background for understanding her. Understanding all three of you.' *Your mother as well,* I might have added. But I didn't. I don't think she would have understood that. I barely did myself.

She gave a brief nod, closed the door behind her and walked towards the entrance of the star-shaped building.

I sat watching her.

A shooting star … Why did I always think about shooting stars? A streak of light in a dark sky. Then it's gone for ever, and the sky is as black as before.

30

BEFORE STARTING THE CAR I rang Helleve and asked whether they had made contact with Lars Mikalsen.

He sounded irritable. 'No, Varg. Have you got anything to offer?'

My stomach knotted. 'Did you get inside?'

'Yes, Varg. We got into the flat. And, no, Varg. He wasn't there. Another disappearance?'

'I certainly hope not.'

'Was there anything else?' He sounded more unfriendly than usual.

'No. I assume ...'

'Yes, Varg. We've got a full-scale search for him under way. We'll pick him up inside a couple of hours. Was there anything else? No? Have a nice evening, Varg, and please ... no more bodies. Deal?'

'Deal,' I said, and we rang off. But I was not at all sure that I could keep my end of the bargain. I had a feeling that danger was afoot for several people in this case. One and a half million in street value was not what one might call small change. And I was beginning to have an ever clearer idea of who had robbed Lars Mikalsen for that sum of money.

From Kristofer Jansons vei I drove home to make myself something to eat. I took the fish from the freezer box, opened a can of chopped tomatoes and sliced the leeks. While I was waiting for the potatoes to boil I dialled Hege Jensen's number again. This time she answered.

'Yes. Hege here.' Her enunciation was unclear, her voice reedy and trembling.

I felt my throat constrict. 'Veum here. How are you?'

'… Fine.'

'Where are you?'

She mumbled something I didn't catch.

'What was that? I didn't hear.'

'… in a safe place. They're looking after me.'

'What? Where? Who's looking after you?'

I heard a voice in the background. She turned away from the telephone and said something. I heard some indefinable sounds from the mobile until a new voice answered. 'Hello? Veum? Weren't you told to keep away?' It was Rolf Terje Dalby.

'Several times. But now the situation …'

'Shut up. We know it was Hege who gave you the job. We're not very happy, neither with you nor her. One of our girls has disappeared, another's dead.'

'Our girls? Can I quote you on that next time I talk to the police?'

'You, Veum, should keep a very low profile. Otherwise it'll be you they find floating in the sea next time!'

'I'm inundated with good quotes here. To hell with it, I think I'll contact them right now.'

'Don't do anything hasty now, Veum! I'm warning you … for the last time.'

I heard Hege say something in the background.

'By the way, Hege says hello and the job's off. You'll get what she owes you, and you can stop the search.'

'Is that so? Could I have that from her own mouth?'

Again there was an exchange of views in the background, more fumbling with the mobile, and then Hege was back. 'He's right. There's nothing else to concern yourself with. There'll only be … a lot of trouble.'

'Hege … I understand that you're under pressure now. Where are you? At his house?'

'Yes, I … but I'm not under any pressure.'

'You're stoned. They've pumped you full of drugs, and now you're saying what you have to, aren't you.'

'I am not … stoned.'

'No, I've seldom heard anyone admit it. But I can hear it in your voice. I know where he lives. I'll be there within a quarter of an hour.'

'No! Don't …'

I rang off, switched off all the rings on the stove, covered the fish with a plate and hurried out. I took the car, even though I could have got there almost as fast with a quick walk. But if I wanted to bring her back – which was my intention – it sounded as if we would need a means of transport.

In Rosenbergsgaten I parked by the kerb, went to the front of the block and straight to his door. There was no bell outside. I pounded on the door. 'Dalby! If you don't open I'll ring the police! … Do you hear me?'

I stood listening. I couldn't hear anything inside.

'Dalby! I know you're in there. Come on! Open up!'

Now I could hear something. Her faint voice reached the door. 'Don't! You're breaking my arm!'

I cast around. Then with the space there was I took a run-up and kicked the lock hard. The door quivered, and I felt the recoil as a dull pain in my calf. But the door held firm.

From upstairs I heard a woman's voice, accompanied by a child's screaming: 'What's going on down there? We'll ring the police if it doesn't stop!'

I put my mouth to the door crack. 'Dalby! Last chance! I've got my mobile in my hand. Now I'm ringing the police …'

Hege screamed – a long piercing shriek.

'Dalby! I'm ringing now!'

I put my hand in my inside pocket. Then the door opened. Without waiting I placed my foot against it, kicked it inwards and barged my way through.

Within seconds I had an overview of the situation.

Rolf Terje Dalby had lost his balance when I kicked the door in, but now he was spoiling for a fight. In his right hand he held the same knife as when I last saw him, and he stood with legs akimbo, arms out from his body and the knife pointing upwards. His alert eyes watched me.

Hege lay on the ground, her arm bent to the side in an unnatural position. She was whimpering and moaning, and her eyes roamed the room, unseeing. 'You broke my arm!' she groaned. 'You broke my arm!'

Fury rose in me like a tidal wave, but I stood where I was. I didn't like the knife.

'Dalby … Wise up now. Don't add to the crimes you'll already have to answer for. Greetings to you by the way.'

'Greetings? Who from? Father Christmas?'

'From KG Monsen.'

'From KG? He's escaped from prison for fuck's sake! The whole town's after him. When we get hold of him …'

'Yes, what then? You grew up together.'

'So? Get the hell out of here! We haven't got anything to talk about.'

I made a gesture towards Hege. 'Not without her. She has to go to A&E, surely you can see that, can't you?'

'She's not going any-fucking-where! She has to work!'

'To work? With her arm in a sling?'

He brandished the knife. 'I'm warning you!'

I moved a couple of steps forward, without taking my eyes off him. 'Hege? Can you stand up?'

She whimpered. 'Don't know ...' She struggled to her knees, grabbed the edge of a chair, managed to stand up.

Dalby hissed at her. 'Hege! Don't you dare! We'll break every bone in your body!'

I sidled round in an arc to her, bent down and grabbed her under the arm, not taking my eyes off him for a second. 'Don't listen to him. Come on ...'

She was heavier to lift than I had expected. For a moment I looked down to see how she was doing. That was when he made his bid.

The attack was swift and brutal. I saw the blade coming, but utter fear gave me unexpected strength. I dragged Hege up from the floor, at such speed that she growled with pain, pushed her to the side, twisted round and avoided the knife by a whisker.

For an instant, Dalby was off balance. Without mercy I brought my knee up into his groin, snatched his arm and smacked his wrist against the table so hard that he dropped the knife, then I forced him into a half nelson, pushed him down onto the floor and buried my knee in his spine.

I could hear my own breathing, as heavy as a two-stroke uphill. Dalby gasped for air with a whistling, bronchitic wheeze. He pressed his free hand down to his groin as he writhed in pain. Hege stood leaning against the table staring at us with narrow eyes and tiny pupils.

I looked at her. 'Can you walk unaided?'

A shudder went through her and her eyes wandered. 'I can try.'

'Ohhh!' Dalby groaned aloud and fought to get free.

I pushed his arm even further up. 'One broken arm's enough, don't you think?'

He mumbled something into the floor.

'What did you say? I didn't hear.'

He turned his face to the side. 'You're finished, Veum. Your days are numbered in this town.'

'And who's counting them? Kjell Boy?'

'*Witless man lies awake all night, thinking hither and thither.*'

'Which means?'

'You sound as stupid as you look, you prick!'

'But I know all about what you and Malthus are up to. I know exactly what you were waiting for last Saturday, and what you're so desperate to get your hands on now. I think I even know where it is.'

'What!' He tried to turn his head right round.

'Give my regards to Malthus and tell him if he wants his package back, ring me.'

'You're bluffing!'

'Try me!'

'You're bluffing!' he repeated.

Hege had at last plucked up the courage. She staggered from the table to the door, grabbing the inside handle and stood swaying. 'Shall we ... go?'

'Hege!' Dalby yelled. 'Kjell's gonna kill you! I can promise you that!'

I forced his head hard against the floor. 'Shut up, you blockhead.'

'*Witless man,*' he started, driven by an inner demon.

'Shut up, I said!'

'... *safest silent,*' his mouth chafed against the filthy wooden floor.

'Perhaps you should listen to Odin's words of wisdom yourself, Rolfy son. Now you just listen to me. From today onwards Hege is under my protection. Do you hear me? Tell Malthus too, and take note, both of you.'

'Varg,' Hege whined. 'My arm.'

'Yes, I'm coming.'

I stretched to the side and grasped Dalby's knife. 'I'll look after this.' Once again I pushed down the back of his head. 'And you stay here! Got that!'

'*One is never recompensed by evil men for the good one does.*'

'Your father would be proud of you.'

In one rapid leap I was on my feet and over by the door. I opened it and ushered Hege into the corridor. In the doorway I turned round.

He had got to his feet. With eyes like hot coals, he stood glowering at me.

Neither of us had any further words of wisdom to impart. I slammed the door between us and led Hege quickly and firmly to the car.

'Next stop A&E,' I said, getting behind the wheel and inserting the key.

31

AT BERGEN A&E they were used to most things. A person, obviously drugged up, with a broken arm was not the most sensational visitor they'd had in the building. Nonetheless, they treated her with decency and respect, as if she were a CEO's wife from the swish district of Fana, who had been so unfortunate as to twist her foot on the marble steps up from the swimming pool.

I sat outside and waited while she had her arm attended to. The colourful community of casualty department patients passing me would have made Noah pull up the gangplank long before departure time. Most also came in pairs. Small boys and girls who had broken arms or legs practising indoor sports were accompanied by their fathers or mothers. Two young brawlers were each escorted by a uniformed officer, one with a broken nose, the other so unruly that he was led past the queue in handcuffs. An elderly, down-at-heel woman was accompanied by another woman who might have been her daughter, but equally well could have been a home help. There was a touch of merriment when two gentlemen, somewhat inebriated and advanced in years, who could not agree on who required treatment first, had to account for what ailed them.

I was beginning to feel in need of a bit of emergency psychiatric treatment myself after waiting for an hour before Hege was led out again by a nurse with straight, blonde hair and red roses in her cheeks. I got up and went over to them.

Hege still had problems standing on her feet without help, and the nurse regarded me with concern. 'Are you a relative?'

'No.'

'She shouldn't be left alone. The doctor considered she was still under the strong influence of drugs. Where ...?' She searched for the right word.

'She was in a flat I visited as part of an investigation.'

'Oh? You're from the police, are you?'

'No. Private investigator.'

'Really?'

'Don't you hospitalise patients in situations like this?'

'There's an acute assessment unit in Haukeland for such cases.' Before I could spit out the word ambulance she had anticipated my thinking. 'I can ring them and tell them you're on your way, if you can drive her.'

'No problem. My car's outside.'

She left Hege with me. I offered her my arm, and she hung on it like a drowning woman clings to a branch by the river-bank. We stumbled towards the car. I leaned over and opened the door, a complicated manoeuvre while keeping her upright at the same time, and coaxed her into position on the front seat.

I leaned across her to fasten the seat belt. She laid her face against my shoulder and breathed into my neck. This was not a sign of affection; she was falling asleep.

I suddenly thought of Thomas and how lucky we had been, Beate and I, despite everything, we had not had this problem on our plate. I tried to imagine them, Thomas and Hege, when they were in the same class. I could remember Thomas with such clarity it hurt. Hege was more blurred, but I did have a vague memory of her, a sweet girl with a somewhat bitter smile even then, not altogether unlike the smile Siv had given me earlier in the day. But what was it that caused lives to veer off in different directions? Was it possible to predict, or was it simply woven into your destiny from a very young age? Such fragile boundaries, so easy to take the life-saving step across the precipice … or plunge down headlong into it …

I got in behind the wheel, reversed out of the car park and turned into Vestre Strømkaien. For a short while I was on the motorway from the spaghetti junction by Nygårdstangen to Danmarks plass. At the beginning of Fjøsangerveien I moved into the left lane to take Ibsens gate towards Haukeland. I arrived at the back of the main hospital building, by the entrance to the acute assessment unit, and had no sooner got out of the car than two nurses appeared and helped me to carry Hege from the car and into reception, where she was seated in a wheelchair.

I went to reception to see if there was anything else they needed from me, but they already had personal information from A&E. 'The only detail we lack is next-of-kin.'

'Mm, I don't have a name to give you there, but ring Cathrine Leivestad at the Outreach Centre. She's bound to be able to help you find the right person.'

The woman in reception nodded and made a note. 'And your name is?'

'Veum. Varg Veum.' I gave her my telephone number as well, but refrained from inviting her to dinner.

The woman smiled professionally, thanked me for my help, and then Hege was whisked off for another examination.

I departed with haste. Emergency departments have that effect on me, as though they were a kind of flesh-eating plant that sucked in everything that came within range, whether bumble bee, wasp or private investigator.

It was pitch black by the time I returned home to Telthussmauet. I put my unfinished meal in the fridge and cut myself four thick slices of bread instead, spread peanut butter on two of them, put sliced fresh tomatoes and sheep sausage on the others. With this late supper I had a glass of milk, in case I had to be up early and drive the next day. It was too late to do anything now anyway. I had a quick shower, went to bed and switched off the light before I could count to twenty.

My mobile woke me. I turned over in bed and groped across the bedside table until I found it. With the other hand I found my watch. A quarter to nine.

'Hello?'

'Is that Veum?' It was a woman's voice, young and tentative.

'Yes. How can I help?'

'Er … Have you been asking after me?'

'That depends on …' Then I was wide wake. 'Who am I talking to?'

'This is … Margrethe Monsen.'

'Margrethe! Where are you?'

'It …'

'Is your brother there, too? Karl Gunnar?'

'… Yes, we …'

'Where are you?'

'We're keeping low. There are people after us.'

'I know. But listen … Where can I meet you?'

Silence.

'Hello! Are you there?'

' …Yes, I just had to consult … my brother.'

'And what did he say?'

'You're a … private detective, aren't you? You won't arrest him, will you?'

'I'm not allowed to arrest anyone, Margrethe. His escape is not my concern. All I want is to talk to you both.'

'We're in a boathouse, up by Flesland.'

'I see. Can you give me any more precise directions?'

'My brother was driving, but … You drive past that ex-holiday camp.'

'Lønningen.'

'Yes, that must be it. And then down to the sea and up the hill until you come to a side road.' As she spoke I could hear in the background, almost as proof that she was telling the truth, the sound of a plane taking off. She raised her voice. 'There are planes overhead all the time!'

She explained where to go and where to park, and I jotted down notes on the pad I always kept by my bed for occasions such as these.

'When you've parked, continue until you come to a postbox. It's been squashed flat. From there it's only five minutes through the forest and down to the sea. You'll see some rooms at the back of the boathouse.'

'And I'll find you there?'

' … Yes.'

'Anything special about the boathouse?'

'The path leads to it, but it looks ancient. It hasn't been painted for years.'

'I'll be there as fast as I can. Don't go anywhere.'

'Where could we go?' she said with a hollow laugh and terminated the conversation.

I swung my legs onto the floor and padded into the bathroom. The one question remaining was this: should I treat myself to a hurried breakfast before leaving or just jump in the car?

The answer was a halfway house. With two bananas in my stomach, an apple in my hand and a sports bottle filled with tap water on the seat beside me I was on my way to Bergen Airport twenty minutes later, the official name for what most called Flesland airfield. But I wasn't going anywhere, not by plane at least. For that matter, I wasn't going to the airfield either, but to what was originally farming country behind it. I could feel the excitement mounting in my body with every kilometre I covered.

32

FROM BOYHOOD DAYS I remembered so well that one of the most exciting things you could do on a spring Sunday was to cycle to Flesland. There, we climbed up the rocks by the high barbed wire fence, took out packed lunches and sat down to wait. We had brown cheese and sheep sausage on our bread and a bottle, with a screw top, of homemade red juice. If we were lucky we got to see a plane land or take off. If not, we could at least see a couple of them parked by the runway before cycling the long distance back to Nordnes.

Now a road led to the original Flesland south of the airfield, from the Blomsterdalen exit. I passed the entrance to Lønningstrand campsite, where the old holiday camp had been. I had never been to a holiday camp myself. Most summer holidays we were at my grandmother's in Ryfylke, but when school began in August classmates always regaled us with dramatic adventures that had taken place in holiday camps, not to mention the strict discipline and forced feeding of porridge, which not unusually was the cause of successful, or less successful, attempts to flee the camp. Some managed to make it all the way home in fact, whether it was from Ferstad by Os or Brattholmen on the island of Sotra. The legendary escapes from Alcatraz paled in comparison. Punishment could be severe if children were caught by the authorities, unless a soft-hearted mother allowed her conscience to dictate and kept them at home for the rest of the holiday.

I followed the instructions I had received over the phone, left Fleslandsveien at what I thought was the correct place and parked where she had said. There were no other cars in the tiny area by the road. I followed the road, between tall, dark spruce trees, so sombre now in January's dim light. I found the squashed postbox in which there was not even room for a belated tax return.

I scanned the horizon. There were many houses that were lived in all year, discreetly withdrawn between the trees and bearing visible signs of a variety of security companies. A couple of them had a car parked in front. To the east a large passenger plane was about to land in Flesland. It was near enough for me to make out faces behind the windows in the fuselage.

With caution, I began to make my way down the path. It was narrow and overgrown, and no one had bothered to cut back the buckthorn in recent years. I came to a ridge, and from there the path descended in a steep slope to the sea and the tumbledown boathouse below. Again I stopped. I cast a wary eye over the grey, ramshackle structure. There were two small windows and a door at the rear, but curtains were drawn and the door was shut. Not a sign of life.

I clambered down towards the boathouse. The nearer I came, the stronger the fresh sea smell from Raune fjord. Across the island of Tyssøy I could see the typical mountain formation of Liatårnet, the highest point on Sotra, and a ferry in the fjord heading for Sunnhordland or Stavanger.

Everything was as it should be in this the busiest of all worlds. Some arrived by plane, others by express ferry. I was on my way down to a boathouse and a rendezvous with two people who had been in hiding for almost a week.

But who were they hiding from? Malthus & Co? The

police? Others? And who had told them I had been asking after them?

I felt a deep and intuitive scepticism as I approached the sea-smoothed rocks at the rear of the boathouse. I scoured the area for anything I could use as a weapon. The closest approximation I could find was a large stone. I picked it up and stood weighing it in my hand. Then I threw it away. It seemed silly.

There was no evidence of any electricity leading to the boathouse. It had to be freezing inside. I walked to the nearest window and tried to peer in, but it was impossible to see anything at all through the drawn curtains.

A gull screamed above the sea. A plane took off from Flesland. A small freighter was on its way north along the coastal route. I leaned over and knocked on the door. No reaction.

I retreated a pace and gazed up at the faded exterior. 'Hello? Anyone there?'

Only the gull answered, and now it had been joined by many more. The gulls were embroiled in a free-for-all above Raune fjord: shoals of winter herring had been seen west of Marsteinen.

'Margrethe? Karl Gunnar?'

Not a sound.

I took out my mobile phone, tapped in the number she had used and rang back. Somewhere inside the boathouse I heard a ringing tone, but no one answered. Then it stopped, and a woman's voice told me that the number I was trying to reach was busy now, but I could leave a message.

'Better go in,' I said to myself and switched off. If nothing else, at least there was a mobile phone inside.

I studied the door. It didn't seem to be locked. I tried the handle and pushed it in a fraction. It was dark inside.

Again I bent down and picked up a heavy stone. This time I didn't throw it away. I nudged the door wide open with my foot and followed quickly – in and to the side, with my back to the door. A smell of sea and gutted fish met my nostrils.

'Hello! Anyone there?'

In the dim light from outside I looked around. I was in a medium-sized room. On a table to the left there was an old fishing float, a broken crab pot and the remains of a fishing net. That was all. Two doors led out of the room, one evidently to the boathouse itself, the other to a further room.

I took out my mobile and dialled her number again. There was a ring from inside the adjacent room.

I followed it. By the door, I shouted: 'Hello! Margrethe? You can come out now.' But no one emerged.

I placed my hand on the handle, pressed it down and pushed open the door. A rabbit chop struck my arm above the wrist. Then I was dragged into the room, and before I had a chance to do anything with the stone, which fell from my hands unused, both arms were twisted around my back, I felt a knee in my spine and I fell to the floor, where my face was brutally smacked against the wooden boards, causing clouds of dust to rise.

'Hold him and I'll …'

I knew the voice, but it was not the office version he was using today. Now he was hunting prey.

My arms were forced together, and I could feel them being trussed with strong tape. When they had finished, they did the same with my feet, round the ankles. Then they turned me over. Rolf Terje Dalby raised me into a sitting position and thrust me hard into the wall. Kjell Malthus switched on a halogen torch and shone the beam into my face.

'Took you a bloody long time to come in, Veum,' Malthus grumbled.

'Were you scared perhaps?' Dalby taunted with an irksome grin.

'Close the door, Rolf.' Malthus motioned with his head. 'We don't want anyone to hear what we're doing. In case he starts screaming.'

I tried to look around, but the torch had blinded me. 'Where's … Margrethe?'

'Maggi?' Malthus mocked. 'We sent her back home. She's got to work, so to speak.'

Now it dawned on me. 'It wasn't bloody her, was it! It was one of your other girls.'

'Oh, how smart detectives are nowadays. Just a shame you didn't realise earlier.'

'And what the hell do you think you can achieve with this?'

Malthus put the torch down on a worktop and strode forward. He was wearing blue jeans, a hip-length dark jacket and sturdy black shoes. He bent over, grabbed me by the jacket and lifted me up the wall until my face was at chest height. We were so close I could smell the heavy aroma of the sweetish aftershave he used, and my eyes met his in a way that made it difficult to have contact.

'Now listen here, Veum. We're after something that belongs to us.'

I smirked. 'I know. Worth one and a half million, I've been told.'

His eyes narrowed, and he pushed his knuckles up under my chin. 'You're well informed, I see.'

'The whole town knows, Malthus. You were robbed of one and a half million when someone welcomed your mule on

Skoltegrunn Quay last Saturday. Apparently two bully boys from Østland.'

'The blabbermouth!' He half-turned to Dalby. 'I told him to keep his trap shut! But does anyone listen to me?'

'Poor you,' I mumbled. 'But right now he's talking to the police. That could be worse.'

He devoted his full attention to me again. 'What? The cops? Have they hauled him in again?'

'At my request. Everything you do hangs on one very thin thread, Malthus, from drug trafficking to the women on C.Sundts gate.'

'And by the way, what the fuck have you done with Hege? Eh?'

'So you admit it now, do you? She was in your stable, like Maggi and Tanya. One gone missing, one dead. You're bad news for your tenants, Malthus …'

He bared his teeth in a callous smile. 'What I admit or do not admit is neither here nor there any more, Veum. You won't be leaving this boathouse alive anyway.'

'Oh, no?' I felt my desperation growing. 'A great many people know where I am!'

'Where the fuck's Hege, I asked you!'

'Have you done any ringing round? The first call could go to Haukeland Hospital.'

'Hospital? What's she doing there?'

'She was drugged up to the eyeballs, and that charmer there …' I nodded to Dalby. 'He'd been so kind as to break her arm.'

'What!' Malthus half twisted round. 'Rolf?'

'I told you, for fuck's sake. She didn't obey. I told her I would have to punish her …'

'Yes, but shit. A broken arm and she's out of circulation as well.'

'So you circulate your tenants, do you?' I said.

He forced his fist up under my chin. 'And I told you to shut it!'

'*On foreign ground keep your head and hold your tongue,*' Dalby said behind him.

'And you, too!' Malthus barked, dropping me on the floor with a bang. And he drew himself up to his full height.

' ... *and it will befall you no ill,*' Dalby completed sulkily, as if it was impossible to stop the tape once it had started.

'Sometimes I think I'm surrounded by idiots,' Malthus said.

'In itself ...' I started but was forced to break off by a vicious kick in the chest. 'Ooof!'

'Shut it!'

There was a charged, angry atmosphere in the dark room illuminated only by the sharp light of the torch. Malthus and Dalby stood scowling at each other. I sat against the wall in some discomfort, with legs and arms bound with the strong tape and a dull pain in my chest where his foot had struck me.

Malthus held his arm out in the beam and looked at his watch. 'I have to go.'

'Oh?' Dalby queried.

'I have an appointment I can't ...'

'But, shit, Kjell! What am I supposed to do with ...?'

'Tommy has to go to the doctor's. Kristine's at work. I have to pick him up from the nursery.'

'Now I'm getting a lump in my throat,' I mumbled.

'As for him,' Dalby concluded, with a nod in my direction.

Malthus turned to me with a surly expression 'Pack him up in a sack, wait till it's dark and chuck him in the sea. Make sure he doesn't surface!'

'Malthus!' I shouted. 'Loads of people know where I am! You'll never get away with this!'

He swivelled round towards me, looking as if he was going to give me another kicking. 'Loads of people? Who for example?'

'I'll …'

As if in answer to his question my mobile rang. He bent forward, took it from my inside pocket, slung it on the floor and stamped on it so hard it would never give another ring tone.

The subsequent silence was deadly.

'What about … What about if I know who did a runner with the package?'

He regarded me with derision in his eyes. 'Don't you think we know? Why the fuck do you think we've moved heaven and earth to get our hands on them? Maggi and KG. They went behind our backs, and they'll burn slowly in hell when I find them. Trust me!'

'And how did they manage that?'

'Maggi and Lars knew each other. He must have been sloppy.'

'So you think she and KG have upped sticks with the whole lot? To Oslo?'

'Or somewhere else. Haugesund, Stavanger, how should I bloody know?'

'I can help you to find them.'

'Yes, we can see how good you are at that.' He looked around and imitated my voice: '*Hello! Anyone there?* Forget it. You're done for, Veum. You've done your last job, and you failed.' He looked at Dalby. 'If he tries anything, smash his jaw. Use the knife, if necessary.'

Dalby glanced dismally from Malthus to me, without answering.

'Run out of words of wisdom, Dalby?' I muttered.

'Do you understand?' Malthus checked.

Dalby gave a sullen nod. Malthus sniffed and went on his way without a backward glance. But he made sure he closed the door behind him. With a click.

33

I WAS STILL SITTING with my back against the wall. I tried to move, to get into a more comfortable position.

Ill at ease, Dalby watched me. 'Don't you try anything!'

After Malthus had gone he paced up and down. He took out the flick knife and kept opening and closing it, again and again, endlessly. Now and then he glanced in my direction, as though he was looking forward to sticking it in me.

'What was that supposed to be? I can barely move.'

'One is never recompensed by evil men for the good one does.'

I followed him with my eyes. He was a weirdo. I tried to imagine him in his younger years, a small screwball going round quoting Odin's wisdoms at all times of the day. He must have been the perfect victim for bullying.

'You and KG were best mates, I understand.'

'When we were kids, yes!' he snarled. 'I haven't seen him since he was sent to the slammer.'

'But he came out on weekend passes, didn't he?'

'I haven't seen him, I told you! Are you hard of hearing?'

'Since you've decided to do away with me, surely you can answer my questions,' I said, and added, not without a faint tremolo in my voice: 'A last wish?'

'I can only bloody say it how it is! I haven't seen him, I'm telling you!'

'Well, that's that then.'

'Yes, that's that.'

'What about Siv?'

'Siv?'

'His sister. The oldest Monsen. Why have you got a photo of her in your drawer?'

His face reddened. 'Have you been snouting in my drawers? That's fucking … Did you break in?'

'You can always report me to the police.'

'Won't be necessary. Tomorrow you'll be at the bottom of the sea.'

'Were you in love with her perhaps?'

He advanced on me. 'That's none of your business! Get me? Or do you want me to chop you up into tiny chunks before I sling you into the sea?'

I felt the sweat breaking out on my forehead, but had to go on. 'Did you ever go to their house?'

'To KG's house? Never!'

I was about to say something, but he broke in. 'If anyone grew up in a living hell it was KG and his sisters.'

'Uhuh?'

'Yes. On the outside it was all supposed to look great, with *fru* Torvaldsen and the others looking after them. But there was a bit of everything going on in that family behind closed doors, I can tell you!'

'Yes, so I've been told. The father was abusing both of his daughters.'

'He wasn't bloody alone.'

'No?'

'No.' He whipped out his flick knife again. Made slashing movements with it in front of my face. 'Don't you bloody think you can talk your way out of what's in store for you!'

'Not alone, you said?'

He made a sudden lunge with the knife, catching my cheek and causing a sharp, stinging pain.

I recoiled as far back as I could. 'Rolf! Think about what you're doing!'

'I'm doing what I've been told,' he snarled.

'And who do you think will be blamed? If you carry out orders and get caught – and that's a certainty – Malthus will be free while you're behind bars. It's your word against his. All the evidence will point to you. Forensic evidence from this crime scene, for example.' I looked around. 'The potential murder weapon you have in your hand.' I nodded to the knife. 'And all the other clues you've left behind.'

'Shut up! *Wisdom and silence become the son of a king. Happy and brave to his dying day.*'

'Tell me something I don't understand, Rolf. You come from a good home.'

'What do you know about that?'

'At least you've got solid literary ballast on board. There are not many who can quote the *Håvåmål* fluently, as you do.'

'And perhaps that is the precise reason it wasn't such a good idea!'

'What do you mean?'

'My father was a terrible sadist. He was so pissed off with my results, from the first class upwards. To discipline me he forced me to learn all the verses – by heart.'

'By heart?'

All of a sudden it was as if he were no longer present in the boathouse, but somewhere else, far back in time. 'He had his office at home where he sat correcting Norwegian essays and so on. Every bloody day I had to go to him and prove that I had learned another verse by heart. I had to lay my hand on the desk, and he sat with a ruler in his hand and whenever I made a mistake he whacked me over the fingers. Not that hard at first, but he hit me harder and harder for every mistake I made. *Witless man who strays among men is safest silent.* But even keeping quiet didn't help me.'

'But your mother …'

'My mother? She was busy with her own things. She didn't know what was going on.'

'Did you have any brothers or sisters?'

'No. It was just me. Luckily.'

'And how did you get on at school?'

'Badly. All his cruelty was for no purpose. That may be why KG and I became friends. We had nothing to go home to, neither of us. So we preferred to stay out and cause trouble. We weren't much more than fourteen when we stole a car for the first time. We robbed a homo when we were fifteen. The same year we raped a girl from the area up by Lea Park and threatened her with a knife so that she wouldn't grass on us.'

'Real heroes, in other words.'

'*Better to be blind than burned on a pyre. Death helps naught,*' he mumbled, staring grimly into the distance, caught up with his own memories.

I kept my eye on him while probing the strength of the tape round my wrists. It was taut, without the slightest give. But … behind my spine I could feel something sharp and pointed, perhaps a nail hammered in from outside. Gingerly, I manoeuvred my hands into position, pressed and felt the point going through the tape.

'Tell me something,' I said to distract his attention. 'When KG killed Malthus's brother what was it really about? Was he gay or was it a quarrel about drugs?'

He grinned. 'KG and I had been hired by Øyvind to sell drugs for him. A fantastic business! We worked on commission and were big wheels. Now we didn't need to rape girls any more. They were prostrating themselves before us. Did it for free, for a lump of hash. But then ... we gave away a bit too much and it came to a confrontation. KG got so angry he smacked Øyvind in the kisser, and he snuffed it. Of course, he hadn't meant to kill him, all he wanted to do was rough him up a bit, and afterwards, when the cops came ... he couldn't say anything about selling drugs. So he made up the other business instead.'

'And no one challenged him?'

He shook his head.

'Didn't even say that they knew better?'

'No.' Again he grinned, as though he thought that particular part of the story was incredibly funny.

'You never came in the spotlight?'

'Spotlight? What do you mean?'

'You said yourself both of you were selling, but only KG ended up behind bars.'

'He was the one who clobbered him, wasn't he? I wasn't even nearby.'

'No?'

'No. Lots of people saw KG running from the gym, and when the cops came and took the dumbbell he had used to smash his head in, it had his prints on it.'

'And how did Kjell take this? After all, it was his younger brother.'

'A week later he was sitting in his car outside the school waving to me, that's how badly he took it. I got in, we went for a drive and he offered to let me continue selling drugs – on my own.'

'But ... he didn't touch on the murder or the quarrel over money?'

'No. I think he kind of believed what KG had said to the police. Øyvind had tried it on him. At any rate, this wasn't something he wanted to talk about, see?'

'I see.' I gently stretched my hands apart. The tape didn't seem to be quite as taut any more. Aloud, I said: 'So ... you did then? Took over sales, I mean.'

'Yep.'

'And since then you and Kjell Boy have been partners?'

'Partners? What the fuck do you mean?' Again the knife came perilously close to my face.

'Workmates! Colleagues! Don't be so damn touchy.' I moved on fast. 'How did Maggi and KG get to know about the package last Saturday?'

'You heard what Kjell said? Maggi and Lars knew each other.'

'And you and KG never spoke?'

'I've told you that ... several times!'

His mobile rang, with such an angry tone that we both jumped. He stepped away, pressed the green button and held the phone to his ear. 'Yes? ... Now? Right away? ... But you said ... oh shit ... Yes, I can check ... I'm sure he has. And just leave him there? Until it gets dark? ... OK. I'll come as soon as I can ... Yes ... No, sure!'

Rolf Terje Dalby concluded the conversation and put his mobile phone on the table. He glanced at me, shifted the knife from one hand to the other and wiped his palms on his trousers.

I held his gaze. I had an unpleasant sinking feeling in my stomach, and could sense my bowels wanting to evacuate. 'What was that about?'

He grinned. 'That was Kjell, and there's an emergency on. I have to take your car and keys, he said. But first …'

He inched towards me. The knife quivered.

'Rolf! Think carefully. Have you ever killed before?'

'Nothing to do with …'

'This is the greatest mistake of your life …'

'Your greatest mistake was coming here, Veum. *Use your eyes before you enter, for who knows what foes you will meet.*'

Summoning up my strength, I rubbed the tape up and down against the nail. It tore, and suddenly I had both hands free. At that moment he lunged with the knife. I twisted to the side and grabbed his arm. The tape round my ankles inhibited movement, and I had only one chance: to be more brutal than I had ever been before. I grabbed the arm holding the knife and smashed it onto the floor so hard that he dropped it. Then I snatched his hair, pulled his head forward and rammed my knees into his face with all my strength. There was a nasty crunch, he screamed with pain and blood spurted from his shattered nose.

I shoved him away, leaned over and stripped the tape off my ankles. He groped for the knife. Blood was streaming from his nose, and his eyes were watering so much he was blinded. I trod on his hand and exerted pressure until dust rose from the floorboards. Another scream.

Then I kicked his knife away, threw myself on him from behind and twisted his good arm so far up his shoulder blade that he shouted for me to stop. By way of an answer I pulled his head back and slapped him hard from side to side. At length I rammed my elbow into the back of his head and brutally forced it down to the floor.

'Don't move!' I said, standing up. My ears were rushing, and I felt dizzy. I had a quick forage around. The roll of tape they had used was on the table. I grabbed the knife on the way, fetched the tape and dashed back.

He was already struggling up. I placed my foot on his spine and pushed him back down. I brought both his arms round his back, ignoring his cries of protest, peeled the tape and bound his wrists with the same thoroughness that he had bound mine.

Afterwards I did his ankles, then dragged him to the table and taped him to one table leg, hoping that would make it harder for him to break free.

He groaned. 'Veum! You will never get out of this alive.'

'You said that earlier in the day as well, Rolf. But who's lying on the floor whimpering and who's standing and watching?'

I took his phone, dialled Atle Helleve's direct number and waited for him to answer. When he heard my voice he said: 'Varg? Have you got a new phone?'

'No, I'm ringing on behalf of one *herr* Rolf Terje Dalby. He was so kind as to lend me his. Now he's wondering whether you have an unoccupied room for him, preferably in the cellar.'

Dalby groaned something incomprehensible from his position on the floor.

I gave Atle a brief summary of what had happened and concluded: 'I'd like to report both Dalby and Malthus. For unlawful restraint and attempted murder this time round. All the other stuff will come later. We have a powerful case against them, I can guarantee you that. I can testify until the cows come home, if you wish.'

'We've got Mikalsen here for questioning, but he's not saying a peep.'

'So you did find him?'

'We picked him up where we find most of them. At a corner table in Børs Café.'

'And … the other two?'

'Not a trace, Veum. All gone quiet. The search is now being extended to Interpol.'

'Right … What are you going to do? Come and fetch him?'

'I'll send out a patrol car. Stay there and keep an eye on him until we arrive.'

'Don't be too long then.'

'And what are your plans once you're done?'

'Home and rest.'

It was a white lie, and I think he guessed. In reality I had quite different plans. But I wasn't sharing them with anyone. Not yet.

34

IT WAS AN HOUR before the police car arrived. In the meantime Dalby had been so impatient to be off that I'd had to reassure him several times: 'They're coming, Rolf. Relax! The bridal suite awaits ...'

Police Officer Hans Melvær from Sunnfjord, a young man on his way up through the system I had met on a couple of previous occasions, insisted on a preliminary statement from me, which delayed my departure further.

The short day was as good as over as I pointed my car back towards town. The sun was setting, not over Askøy as in the summer months but behind the long, dark, leonine mountain ridge of Løvstakken between the Fjøsanger and Fyllingsdalen valleys. Arriving in Minde, I turned up Jacob Aalls vei and pulled in by the playground. There were no children, it was like an omen of worsening times.

Thence I went up to Finnbergåsen. Markus Rødberg looked at me with composed resignation in his eyes, as though he had had a feeling I would show up sooner or later. I noticed him glance at the thin cut on my cheek, but being the cultured individual he was, he made no comment.

I followed him into his living room, which was as well kept and tidy as on my previous visit. This time, though, he did not offer me coffee, and I had to find my own chair. He sat down on the sofa and observed me from under heavy eyelids with hard-won composure.

'Correct me if I'm mistaken, Rødberg, but when we met at Torvaldsen's yesterday, I had the clear perception that the atmosphere was a trifle fraught. Between you. Could I be right?'

He sat with a half-smile round his mouth, and when he answered, the words came slowly and laboriously, as though he had to deliberate before he found the right one. 'No. Between us? A close friend of ours, Lill's husband, had been killed in his own home. Of course, there was a fraught atmosphere, if that's the right word.'

'And how close are you to Alf Torvaldsen?'

He blinked several times, as though removing a speck of dust from his eye. 'Well, what should I say? Carsten and I were childhood friends, of course, and Wenche Torvaldsen – who is dead now – had also grown up here. Alf came with Wenche, so to speak.'

I already had my pad in my hand and flicked through it. He watched me attentively, prepared for the worst, it seemed. 'Wenche Torvaldsen died last autumn, I understand.'

'Yes, poor thing. She had a tough time of it. Cancer was eating her up from inside. Had it not been for strong painkillers it would have been unbearable. But that also meant she was very lethargic. She didn't take part in anything for the last six months of her life.'

'When we spoke yesterday we touched on a disagreement you'd had, on the committee. Torvaldsen got very worked up, as you must have noticed, about Hulda Vefring mentioning this to me.'

He nodded slowly. 'Well, yes ... what can I say?'

'According to Torvaldsen, the argument was about differing views of faith. *Frøken* Vefring was in no doubt that you were on one side and the two couples were on the other. Could you expand a little?'

His eyes narrowed. 'I just don't understand ... What has this got to do with all the rest?'

'We'll come to that.'

He stirred, ill at ease. 'Erm. Well ... I don't quite know how to put this. I suppose it didn't really have much to do with faith. More with morality. There had been an incident which I see no reason to go into in any more detail here.'

'An incident?'

'Yes.'

'Concerning ...?'

He raised his voice a notch. 'I don't want to say anything about it, I said.'

I leaned forward. 'So let me say this to you, Rødberg. After talking to you yesterday, I met Siv. Siv Monsen. She also told me about an incident.'

He paled, and within a few seconds I could see beads of sweat forming on his brow. 'R-r-really?'

'She had visited you, she said, and told you, but you had said she should just forget it, it had been a one-off, and she should show forgiveness. Are we talking about the same incident?'

His eyes flitted round. 'I cannot be held responsible for something others have done!'

'No. I'm not accusing you.'

'And of course she gave you her version of events.'

I sent him an inscrutable look. In reality she hadn't told me about any events. The question was simply how far he was willing to go.

'Every coin has two sides, Veum!'

'No argument there. Can I hear your side?'

'It's not my side! It was Carsten and Alf who … well, she told you, of course.'

Again I played the game. 'I'd very much like to hear … the other version.'

'Carsten and Alf were hunting friends.' His lips narrowed, as though this was one part of existence he had no time at all for. 'Every now and then they met in one of their houses and had what they called hunting evenings, where they revived memories of various hunting trips and … sat drinking. They both insisted they were excessively drunk the evening it happened.'

'Mm.' I nodded as a sign he should go on.

'The girl was excessively drunk herself, and they both claim it happened with her full consent. It was not rape, which is what Siv maintained!'

'No?'

'No! You know yourself where she's ended up. Carsten said … she had even demanded money off them, afterwards.'

'We're talking autumn 1988, aren't we?'

He waved one hand with a flourish. 'Something like that.'

'And Margrethe?'

'You know yourself!'

'Was at that point …?'

'She was not a minor! She was eighteen, and no virgin, alas.'

'Nevertheless. Torvaldsen and Mobekk were her guardians. They had been responsible for her and her siblings for ten years by that point. Morally, we're talking something close to incest here, Rødberg!'

'Well …'

'She was eighteen, you say, but how old were they? In their fifties? No wonder Siv reacted. How did she find out?'

'Margrethe told her. She had confided in her … the day

after, and Siv came here. She wanted to report it, but I advised her against it. I promised I would take the matter up with them, and it would never be repeated.'

'And did you?'

He looked at me with a self-righteous air. 'Naturally! Why do you think this discordance arose? They didn't like it, as I'm sure you can appreciate.'

'But … didn't the wives get to hear of this as well?'

'Not from me at any rate. I spoke to Alf and Carsten. *Frøken* Vefring has misunderstood. What she perceived as a bad atmosphere between the married couples and me was between Alf and Carsten and me. That was how it was.'

'You never took the issue up with them afterwards?'

'Veum … after the committee was dissolved … I no longer had anything to do with them. I kept my distance, so to speak.'

I looked down at my notepad. I hadn't written any of what he had said, but I had made mental notes, which stuck. 'To sum up, Rødberg. Carsten Mobekk and Alf Torvaldsen had a party at Torvaldsen's house. Where was *fru* Torvaldsen?'

'No idea. She must have been away, otherwise they could not have … erm…'

'No, I suppose they couldn't. And Margrethe, how does she fit in the picture?'

'She'd been to a party and had lost her key or some such thing. So she rang Torvaldsen's bell, and he went to open. She could not conceal the state she was in, and he invited her in … in all innocence, he told me. But then things developed. She had seen the bottles they had and asked for a glass. They had poured one for her, and one thing led to another. According to Carsten, she had as good as offered herself. If the matter had been reported they would have stood by their account, he said.

There was no question of it being rape. She was already beyond redemption when she arrived.'

'Very drunk? In fact, that is still defined as rape, Rødberg, possibly in every other circle except your own.'

'Mine! I had nothing to do with this! My hands are clean.'

'Yes, wasn't there someone else who said that once ... in a story you of all people ought to know well.'

He raised his arms. 'It happened. Nothing came of it. Shall we draw a line under it now?'

I looked him in the eye. 'Not so strange then perhaps that Margrethe reacted in such a dramatic manner when Torvaldsen and Mobekk turned up in C. Sundts gate last Friday ...'

'What did you just say, Veum?'

'I was thinking aloud. I think I have the answer to one of the questions in this case anyway. There are a few more, though, unfortunately.'

'You'd better ask the right people then. As far as I'm concerned, I have no more to say about the matter.'

'Not even a quiet prayer?'

He looked daggers at me. Then he got up. 'I think you should go now.'

I followed suit. 'Yes, I was on my way actually.'

In the hall I turned towards him one last time. 'In the best-case scenario you'll never see me again, Rødberg. But I hope I'll be able to haunt your dreams for many years to come. And your conscience, if you've got one.'

'Go!'

'Sadly, it doesn't look like it though. As if you have one.'

'May God have mercy on your wretched soul, Veum.'

'And the same to you,' I said, as he slammed the door behind me.

35

BEFORE I WENT TO RING THE DOORBELL, I stood looking at the house from the outside. From this angle, one clear, frosty evening in January, it looked tranquil and peaceful, as if nothing bad could happen there. Light shone from a window on the first floor, at *fru* Monsen's. Several were lit in Torvaldsen's part, even though there was no suggestion that it was party time there, either.

I looked left and right along the whole row of houses. I thought: who knows what's hidden behind these façades? How many secrets, how many damaged individuals, how many children had to grow up in the shadow of their own upbringing, enduring conditions they had never asked for and could barely do anything about? On the exterior, everything looked nice and proper, but who had any idea what corruption was hidden – not only behind these walls but any such walls anywhere in the world? The sole constant, like a sickening pattern, was this: the victims were children. It was the weakest who had to suffer most. The strongest always had right on their side.

I entered through the garden gate and walked towards the house. As I was about to ring Torvaldsen's bell, the front door sprang open. Else Monsen stared at me, unkempt, hair sticking out, but for once without a fag in the corner of her mouth.

'Did you see her?'

'Did I see who?'

'Siv. She came to visit me, but then … I was in the toilet, and when I came out she was gone.'

'Siv came to visit you? For the first time in … how long?'

She looked at me, bewildered. 'How long? Ten minutes?'

'What did she want?'

'I don't know. She was just there all of a sudden. She had let herself in. And then she asked if I'd heard anything.'

'Heard anything? When?'

'Some time last weekend. Sunday.'

'Sunday?'

She nodded and stared at me with an unease in her eyes I had never seen before. 'I didn't understand what she meant.'

The unease was infectious. I gestured to ask if I could enter. She retreated into the hall. Behind her a strip of light fell onto the floor. The cellar door was ajar.

I motioned in that direction. 'The cellar door. Has it been open all the time?'

'The cellar door?' She turned stiffly.

I walked past her. With one hand I opened the door wide and peered down the narrow staircase. Light came from a single bulb in the cellar proper. 'Hello! Anyone there?'

No one answered, but I heard a faint scrabbling noise like a colony of rats fleeing or a plastic bag being blown by the wind. 'Siv!'

No answer.

I turned to Else Monsen and said with a stern look. 'Stay here! I'll go down.'

She nodded and didn't move as I started the descent.

The stairs were wooden and covered with linoleum. A cold draught met me on the very first step. The staircase twisted, and it was only when I was right at the bottom that I could see inside the cellar.

To the right was a brick wall. An open door led into another room, perhaps a laundry room. To the left were the wooden bars of the old storage stalls. None of them was locked. The first door was closed, the second open. The solitary bulb hanging from the ceiling cast light throughout the cellar, but from the stall at the rear shone a light that was much stronger and clearer. A few seconds passed before I realised it was from a chest freezer, it was open and that was where the cold air was coming from.

'Siv?' I said, once again.

She didn't answer, but through the bars I saw her sitting on a saw horse right next to the freezer.

I moved further in. Caught a fleeting glimpse of Else Monsen on her way down the stairs behind me. I raised my palm to stop her. 'No! Stay there, I said!'

The door to the stall was unlocked. She had lifted the freezer lid and half-removed two large packets wrapped in black plastic. The bags had been torn open with her nails. Through the gaps in the plastic two white faces covered in rime frost shone out at me, but I was in no doubt as to whose they were. They were together again now, all three of them. Siv, Margrethe and Karl Gunnar.

I turned to make sure that Else Monsen had stayed put. But she hadn't. She was standing right behind me, and she was not alone. Behind her came Alf Torvaldsen, and I didn't like the sight of what he was holding, a big, heavy rifle of the kind used for deer hunting. I didn't like his gaze either, as it met me above the rifle barrel. It was cold and grey and boded ill.

36

IT WAS ALMOST A STILL LIFE SCENE. Else Monsen was mute, motionless, her eyes were fixed on me. It was impossible to see whether she had realised what was in the open freezer. Behind her stood Alf Torvaldsen, rifle in hand, also staring intently at me.

I half turned round. Siv was sitting as she had done the whole time. She was staring into the distance, stiff, her eyes so vacant they could have been made of glass. Involuntarily, my gaze was drawn back to the freezer. Karl Gunnar had a deep groove in his brow, as though he had been struck by something hard. Margrethe looked as if she were asleep, with closed eyes.

When I faced Else Monsen again, she had seen them as well. Her face reflected something of what I felt, but it was rather more naked and raw. After all, they were her children in there, however long it had been since they had visited her. 'S-Siv ...' issued from her dry, cracked lips. 'What has happened?'

I shifted my gaze to Torvaldsen. 'Yes,' I heard my voice say, also frost-damaged. 'I'm sure you're the right person to tell us.'

With a sudden shove he sent Else Monsen reeling. I grabbed her to break her fall. She tore herself free, as though touching filled her with disgust. 'Don't!' she shouted, then recoiled to the wall, turned to us and stood scowling, mute.

Siv did not react to any of this. As far as I could judge, she was in a deep state of shock.

'Two bodies in a freezer, Torvaldsen? Two too many, don't you think?'

His face did not betray anything. 'None of your business, Veum. There's room for more.' As if to emphasise what he had said, he raised his weapon and pointed the barrel at my chest. His forefinger curled round the trigger.

I felt cold sweat break out. 'And what kind of toy is that?'

His smile was wintry. 'A Czech Brno, 308 calibre. The bullet'll go straight through you, Veum. I've brought down deer weighing over a hundred kilos with this, several times.'

'And where's the meat?' I asked.

He tossed his head towards the second stall. 'Else never uses hers.'

I spread my palms. 'So what are you going to do with us?' As he didn't answer I went on, in a gentler tone: 'You appreciate this has gone too far, don't you.'

'Save that intonation for others, Veum! It's you who have gone too far. Much too far. What the hell did you come down here for?'

'It wasn't me … It was Siv. She must have suspected how the pieces fitted together.'

'And how do they?' he said with biting sarcasm. 'Can Master Detective Kalle Blomkvist tell me that?'

I took half a pace forwards. He stepped back and raised the barrel to my head.

'I meant it, Veum! I'll shoot.'

'I only want …' In a moderated voice I said: 'I don't want them to hear what we're talking about. Move further back … please.'

He looked over my shoulder at the two women, both equally motionless, like dolls in a waxworks cabinet. Then he shrugged and went back a few steps, keeping his rifle raised.

I followed him. Halfway along the cellar he stopped and gestured that this was as far as he was going and no further.

'Spit it out. What's on your mind?' he snarled.

'Where do you want me to begin? The time you und Mobekk raped Margrethe? Or …'

'That wasn't bloody rape! She offered herself. Where the hell did you get that from?'

'Rødberg talked.'

'Markus! Bloody hell! He'll get to hea– '

'Oh yes? He'll get to hear about this? Is that what you wanted to say?'

'Or shall we jump to last Friday when you and Mobekk decided to take a trip to the red-light district and pick up a girl or two. It could hardly have come as a surprise when you met Margrethe there. But she didn't join you. It was someone else. Which was a matter of bitter regret afterwards.'

He pinched his lips.

'You two liked to be a bit rough with the girls, didn't you? Eh?'

'She was a whore! That kind deserves nothing else.'

'Or shall we jump to … Saturday night it must have been when you were visited by … Who was it? Just Margrethe at first, perhaps? Or did they arrive together?'

He sent me a hard look. 'This is not going to help you. Not in the slightest. I'm going to …'

His eyes narrowed, and I hastened to interject: 'Let's assume Margrethe came first. She offered herself this time as well perhaps? Or did they both arrive together? Did they have something to discuss with you? In a way, of course, they were your foster children. Yours and the committee's.'

'And what happens next?' he asked. 'In this fairy tale of yours?'

'It all culminates in a confrontation. Karl Gunnar obviously received a heavy blow to the head. I have no idea what you did to Margrethe. But both are in the freezer behind us, and you're here with a lethal weapon in your hands. That's proof enough for me, Torvaldsen.'

He didn't answer, but I saw his forefinger curled around the trigger quiver.

'When did you find out what happened to Mobekk?'

'When?' he snapped. 'You were there yourself!'

'But you must have tried to contact him after ... what happened here.'

His eyes flashed. 'I rang several times ... but he didn't pick up.'

'Naturally enough. But you didn't try anything else?'

'No, I had enough to do with ... I had thought of ringing Lill, but didn't get round to it.'

'Still it came as a shock when you ...'

'Of course it came as a shock! They didn't say anything about it when they ...' He broke off, then shrugged as though he considered it of no importance after all.

My mind was spinning in large circles, and it was hard to hold onto my thoughts. 'But ... you saw the context, I suppose. Perhaps you tied it up with your visit to the red-light district on Friday evening with Mobekk, and then ... Margrethe was dead. The other person who could identify you was Tanya.'

'Tanya?'

'The Russian woman you beat up that evening. On Tuesday you set off there again. How did you manage to get her to tag along once again?'

He smirked. 'I waved a wad of notes. Besides, I was alone this time. I said it was the other guy who had caused what happened on Friday. Anyway, she joined me.'

'And you killed her and dumped her in the sea.'

'The master detective strikes again? No, no, no. I gave her one, paid and dropped her off. I have no idea what could have happened afterwards. And what you can see there ...' he indicated the chest freezer. 'That was in self-defence. They came here to kill me. What happened to Carsten afterwards proves that. Karl Gunnar attacked me with a candlestick.'

'A candlestick?!'

'Yes. He had it with him when he arrived. But I dodged the blow, wrenched it off him and used it on him.'

'And Margrethe?'

'Same.'

'Same? I couldn't see any marks on her.'

'Back of the head.'

'You don't die from being knocked down. Don't tell me you put them in the freezer still unconscious?'

'And why not? It's a merciful death, Veum. Being frozen to death while you're ... asleep. And I could keep them there without any fear of a smell. I had thought of getting rid of them later.'

'My God, Torvaldsen! This was two young people. They had lots of life left in them.'

His face was as grey, as rock-hard as ever. He ground his jaw, and I saw the knuckles round the rifle whiten. 'And ... what sort of life?'

'They knew too much, did they? Your reputation would have been ruined for ever, in Falsens vei as well as at the council?'

'Veum ...'

Two things happened at roughly the same time. There was an angry ring on the doorbell above. Else Monsen came to life and emitted a wild scream that resounded through the narrow cellar room, a scream of sorrow and pain and some indefinable quality, animal-like, perhaps inexpressible in words.

For a second or two Torvaldsen's attention lapsed. Enough time for me to launch myself at him, grab the rifle barrel and wrest it to the side and up, with such speed that he, consciously or unconsciously, pulled the trigger. The sound was like a clap of thunder, and I heard the thud in the woodwork above us where the bullet bored its way into the ceiling and, for all I knew, came out the other side into the flat. A terrible pain filled my eardrums, and the echo of the shot reverberated with a loud piercing tone that went on and on, never seeming to end.

Else Monsen's screaming increased in volume. Torvaldsen let go of the weapon, bent forward and held both hands against his ears. On the floor above I heard ferocious knocking on the front door until it opened with a bang and someone shouted: 'Hello! What's going on?' It was Helleve.

'Down here, Atle!' I yelled. My voice seemed to come from a castrated soprano who for some reason had chosen to rehearse inside my head. 'Everything under control,' I added, standing there with the smoking rifle in my hand and looking at Alf Torvaldsen. He glowered back, still with his hands over his ears, as though this was all my fault.

37

ATLE HELLEVE AND BJARNE SOLHEIM had come to a halt at the bottom of the stairs. Without any fuss they confirmed that I had been the one to say 'Everything under control', even though 'everything' was perhaps an exaggeration and 'under control' a loose concept.

'Bjarne. Weapon,' Helleve said.

Solheim gave Torvaldsen a wide berth, held out his hand and took the rifle. He swiftly applied the safety catch and emptied the magazine. He put the shells in his jacket pocket. With great care he released the safety catch again, pulled back the bolt and took out the bullet in the chamber. Torvaldsen stared at him, unseeing.

Behind me, Else Monsen had fallen quiet. I turned in her direction. She was standing and shaking her head, as though to get rid of the sound ricocheting there as well. Siv was the only person not to have reacted to the bang. She was sitting as she had done when I arrived, lost in her own world.

Helleve came over to me. His eyes were drawn inexorably to the chest freezer, and an expression of disbelief spread across his face. 'Oh, shit!'

I nodded. 'Couldn't have put it better myself.'

'Is this Torvaldsen's work?'

'It's his freezer anyway.'

'But ...' He broke off. 'We'll have to get them moved from here, Varg.' He took out his mobile phone. Then tapped in a number. 'This is Helleve. We've found two bodies. Frozen. I need all the assistance you can muster, medical and forensic, in Falsens vei.' He gave the house number and rang off. Then slipped the phone back in his inside pocket.

'*Fru* Monsen lives on the first floor,' I said. 'Perhaps we ought to escort them there.'

'OK. Will you help me?'

'Of course.'

He turned to Solheim. 'Bjarne. Take Torvaldsen to the ground floor. He's got a lot to answer for. Wait until I come.'

Torvaldsen got up. 'It's not … how you think,' he said in a feeble voice. 'It was self-defence.'

Helleve nodded. 'We'll deal with you upstairs. Just follow Officer Solheim, then we'll go through the whole case in great detail. Now, first of all, we'll have to …' Again he stared at the two corpses in the freezer. 'This is simply unbelievable!'

Solheim and Torvaldsen were already on their way upstairs, and straight afterwards we heard their steps above our heads. It took us a great deal longer to coax Else Monsen and Siv up the same stairs. Else Monsen trudged off wearily, like an over-weight child that had just learned to walk. Siv allowed herself to be persuaded to stand up, but she was heavy in my arms as we set off, and up the stairs Helleve and I had to carry her between us.

On the first floor we deposited them in the sitting room. Helleve stayed with them while I went into the kitchen, put some water on and hunted for some tea or coffee. I found coffee in a tin and teabags in a drawer.

On my return, Helleve had sat down with them. He was trying in vain to get them to say something, but there was not a sound to be had from either of them. Siv stared ahead apathetically. Her mother stared sombrely down at the table, with a cigarette in her mouth.

'Tea or coffee?' I asked.

'Coffee,' said Else Monsen. Siv said nothing.

Helleve rose to his feet. 'Can you take care of this, Veum? I ought to …' he glanced at the door.

'Can you send me an officer when they come? I'd prefer a woman.'

'Bergesen's on her way. It was her I spoke to.'

'I wouldn't mind being present when you talk to Torvaldsen.'

He regarded me with a look brimful of scepticism. 'I don't think I can allow that, Varg.'

'I know quite a bit about this case now.'

'Did you suspect … what we found in the cellar?'

'Not at all, no! I was as shocked as … everyone else.' I walked to the kitchen door. 'Wait till I've made the coffee.' I added in a whisper: 'I don't think they should be left alone.'

'No, but get a move on.'

'I'm hurrying.'

I went back into the kitchen. The water was boiling. I brewed the coffee and rinsed three cups under the tap. When the coffee was ready I poured it, carried two cups into the sitting room and went back to fetch the last for myself.

Helleve was already on his feet. 'I still don't think so, Varg.'

'But I have important information to add.'

'We'd rather have that without the suspect being present. We'll deal with it at the station later this evening. OK?'

'Alright then,' I said, as sullen as a teenager who hasn't got his own way. 'Now answer me one thing, Atle. Why did you turn up at the moment you did?'

'The car registration finally matched. Torvaldsen drives a black Opel with a number beginning SP-523.'

'Great! Another bit of evidence. What was the upshot with Malthus?'

'He's been brought in for questioning, with Dalby. What was left of him after the treatment you gave him.'

'They started it!' I riposted, like a teenager again. 'And Mikalsen?'

'Clammed up. Claims he was on a weekend trip to Denmark after winning it in a lottery. No idea who attacked him. We don't believe him for a second, of course, but what on earth can you say? He's been around the block, and not just once.'

'But …'

'Sorry, Varg. I haven't got time for this. See you this evening, at the station.'

He left, and I was alone with the two women.

Else Monsen had set about the fresh coffee with a vengeance, as if it were the last wish of someone about to die. Now she was slurping it. Siv was unaware even of the cup. Her gaze was very, very distant, and she sat with such an immovable expression on her face it seemed to be carved in stone.

Neither of them said a word. The tiny sitting room was as silent as the antechamber of death, and in a way that was indeed where we found ourselves. The image of the two in the freezer was glued to your retina, impossible to erase.

Outside, car doors slammed. The gate opened, and I heard voices below. Not long afterwards there was a formal rap on the upstairs door. The two officers appeared in the doorway. Annemette Bergesen had brought Eva Jensen with her, and I gave a nod of consent to both. They were in the right place and perhaps even at the right time.

I stood up. Eva Jensen went towards the two women with a compassionate air. Annemette Bergesen stood where she was and whispered: 'I've been given a brief rundown of the situation. Has either of them said anything?'

'Not a word.'

'Good.' She appeared almost relieved. 'We'll take it from here. You can go.'

'Thank you.'

I cast a final glance at the two women, but I had nothing to say to them. As Annemette Bergesen had correctly said: they would take it from here.

I trudged down the stairs. Outside the Torvaldsens' front door I stood still for a moment. *Wenche and Alf Torvaldsen* the sign said, as though a very normal couple lived there. And perhaps they were as well. At least her.

All of a sudden I felt homeless. The case was solved, to all intents and purposes. The job done. Margrethe had been found. Karl Gunnar, too. But no hearts rejoiced. Not a single one.

38

IT WAS TO BE A LATE NIGHT at Bergen police station.

I met Vidar Waagenes in the corridor. Torvaldsen had asked for him as his solicitor, and it was not a bad choice. I knew him from before. He was a competent Defence Counsel, and I had even had some jobs from him. With a characteristic flick, he tossed the dark fringe from his forehead and went in to see his client. I was going through all I knew with Helleve and Solheim when Hamre also made an appearance.

'Nasty business, Atle,' Hamre said to his colleague before adding, with an oblique glance at me: 'Usually is, though, when Veum's involved.'

Waagenes exited the interview room. 'My client is willing to make a statement.'

'We await it with bated breath,' Hamre said.

Helleve and Solheim stood up.

'I can entertain Veum in the meantime.'

Helleve nodded, Solheim grinned and I didn't have much to say for myself. Witty repartee lay buried deep on this dark January evening.

'In fact, he could go home,' Helleve said. 'We'll contact him when the need arises.'

'It won't be for a long time then,' Hamre retorted. Nonetheless he stayed behind after the others had gone. At length he said: 'The sister found them, I understand?'

'Yes. She was in a deep state of shock. According to Helleve, she has already been admitted to hospital.'

'But what on earth made her go down to the cellar?'

I upturned my palms. 'I can imagine Margrethe and Karl Gunnar were on some kind of vengeance crusade. That was what aroused Siv's suspicions, especially after the murder of Mobekk became public. Besides, I'm quite sure it was Margrethe and Karl Gunnar who robbed a certain Lars Mikalsen of heroin with a street value of one and a half million last Saturday. They were going to use this money to make good their escape, abroad by the look of it. They just had a score to settle before they left.'

'And these drugs, where are they now?'

'Good question, Hamre. No idea. If your guys haven't stumbled across them.'

'Have you spoken to Atle about this?'

'Yes. He knows as much as I do.'

'Don't tell me you've started playing with an open deck, Veum?'

'With hands as bad as mine, yes.'

Hamre gave a wry smile. 'You've never been very good at poker, have you.'

'Not as good as you, no, I don't suppose I have.'

'Well, Veum. You can take the evening off. As Atle said, we'll summon you if we need you. Stick around. Don't go to Siberia however much we wish you would.'

He smiled his crooked smile, sighed and headed for his office with heavy steps. His next move would be a call to the public prosecutor, I guessed. A charge was a serious matter even if the main suspect did have two cold bodies in his freezer.

'I'll send you a card from Siberia then, Hamre.'

'Do that, Veum. Have a good trip.'

I sat for some moments watching the door of the interview

room where Helleve and Solheim were grilling Alf Torvald-sen, with Vidar Waagenes as the vigilant listener. I would have given half my monthly wage to be in there myself. On the other hand, that was not a huge sum of money, so it was no big deal.

As I left I patted my inside pocket, to no avail, then remem-bered my mobile phone had suffered a sudden and brutal demise out by Flesland. Instead I went to the nearest telephone booth and rang Haukeland Hospital to hear how Hege was getting on. After a lot of humming and hawing I was told she had been transferred to the Orthopaedic Department. I was also given her room number. 'But it's too late to visit her now,' the woman on the switchboard said. 'I just want to deliver some flowers,' I said, pulling out from the kerb and setting off for the hospital.

At Haukeland there was, to a certain degree, an open-door policy. If I took a lift up to the sixth floor and rushed past the duty nurse's room I could, without much difficulty, make my way to her room, which she shared with three other women. I assumed my most official face, said 'Hello, ladies' and pulled the curtain around her bed.

She seemed to be asleep. Her eyes were closed and there was a peaceful expression on her face. Sleeping, she looked much younger than she was, and now, if not before, I recognised her clearly from the time she had been in the same class as Thomas, when she had been young and innocent and on the threshold of what was to be a much more difficult life than any of us could have imagined.

'Hege,' I whispered.

She blinked and looked around, disorientated. One arm was in plaster and inside a sling, and her eyes looked a bit drugged.

On seeing me, she said: 'Varg?'

I nodded, sat on the chair by her bed, leaned forward and said in as soft a voice as I could: 'I've got something important to tell you, Hege.'

She looked at me with big eyes. 'Not ... Maggi?'

'Yes, I'm afraid so.'

'Have you found her?'

'Yes.'

She grasped my hand and pulled it close: 'Was she ...?'

I nodded. 'I'm sorry to say this, Hege, but ... yes. She's dead. Both her and her brother.'

'Oh, shit! Shit, shit, shit!' Tears came into her eyes, but it was more from fury than despair. 'The bastards! The bloody bastards!'

'Who do you have in mind?'

Then the dam burst. She let go of my hand, hid her face in her hands and cried without restraint, deep, painful sobs that wracked her whole body.

From one of the other beds in the room someone said: 'Hello! What's going on?'

'Nothing,' I said. 'Just some sad news.'

'OK.' That was enough to set her mind at rest, it seemed.

There was only one thing to do. Let her cry it out. She was not the first client of mine who had ended up in tears, and she would not be the last. My creditors had the same problem. I was a walking tear-jerker, and I seldom disappointed.

Eventually she calmed down. She groped for the box of tissues on her bedside table, snatched a handful and dried her bare, unmade-up face, looking more like a young girl and more disconsolate than I had ever seen her before. Snot and tears ran from her nose, and she looked at me with shiny, red-rimmed eyes.

'Come on,' she said in a trembling voice. 'Tell me how you found her.'

I told her about the horrific discovery in Minde, about Margrethe and Karl Gunnar.

'But … wasn't it …?'

'No. It wasn't perhaps who you were thinking of.' I told her about Torvaldsen and his car and what I had found out about him and Mobekk, that it must have been them Margrethe had refused to go with on the Friday evening, and posited my own theory that Torvaldsen had also killed Tanya.

'But what …? Why?'

'It's a complicated story, Hege, with roots going back to a difficult upbringing. We can discuss it in detail when you're out of here. Have the doctors said how long you have to stay?'

'A couple of days or so.'

'Then what will you do?'

She shrugged. 'Suppose I will have to go back to work.'

'To work, as you call it! With your arm in a sling?'

'Bound to be some men who think that's exciting. If only you had an inkling of how many weird types we meet. So that they can play doctor, you know,' she said with a mischievous grin. 'Won't get rich lying here, anyhow. You need to have your fee as well.'

'Well, the advance'll cover most of it. Besides, the outcome wasn't much to boast about.'

'No, but you did find her.'

'And more important than that, Hege. Your so-called protectors are behind bars.'

'What? You mean …'

'Both Malthus and Dalby were arrested earlier today. They've

been in for questioning all day and are bound to be charged …
with something.'

'What? But then …' For a moment she looked quite
dazed. 'But who will I …? With no one to look after me,
then …'

I leaned forward. 'Perhaps this is precisely what you needed,
Hege. A chance to get away. I can talk to Cathrine.'

'Cathrine?'

'Leivestad.'

She stared at me, big-eyed. Then she said weakly: 'Yes …
that's great. Talk to her.'

'I'll ask her to come up here and have a chat with you …
tomorrow at the latest.'

She nodded without enthusiasm.

Behind me I heard a door open. 'What's all this then?' a voice
asked. The woman in the adjacent bed must have answered
with a gesture, for the curtain was drawn and a stern dark-
haired nurse impaled me with her eyes: 'Just what do you think
you're doing here? It's way past bedtime.'

I got up and tried to appear genuinely apologetic. 'I had to
pass on an urgent message.'

'Patients have to sleep. This is a flagrant breach of our rules.
Would you please come with me?'

'OK, OK. I've passed on the message. The patient won't be
able to sleep very well tonight.'

Her expression became flintier, and I nipped past her in
case she should feel the temptation to become violent. Before
leaving, I turned to Hege. 'Get better soon, Hege. If you need
anything, you know where to find me.'

She nodded mutely and blinked.

'See. She's exhausted, the poor darling,' the nurse said and directed me out of the room, with as firm a hand as air traffic control.

She escorted me all the way to the lift, and I was not treated to the tiniest of smiles by way of a send-off. So there was not much else to do but go home. But I didn't sleep very well, either. There were still some questions I felt I didn't have a proper answer to yet.

39

A WEEK PASSED and I hadn't heard from anyone. I followed the case as well as I could through the newspapers, but not much came out there that I didn't already know.

The police appeared in court on Saturday morning and applied for four weeks' remand for Alf Torvaldsen with a ban on visitors and mail. The court reduced custody to two weeks for lack of evidence, but accepted the bans.

Newspapers across the country had big spreads on the case, but since one person had already been charged, they soon lost interest. Local newspapers had delved through their archives and found the Gimle case, although no direct link between the two cases was proved. It also appeared from the newspapers that the suspect was being questioned in connection with the murder in Nordnes, where a prostitute had been found dead in the sea. There was tangible evidence here, asserted the police lawyer, who was awaiting the results of DNA samples before the case would be presented to court in its entirety.

In a separate article I read that two men had been charged with threatening and unlawfully restraining a person the newspapers called 'a local private detective', a case that was also under investigation, although the local private detective had not yet been summoned to further interviews.

After a week I could not control myself any longer. I rang Helleve and asked if there were any new angles on the case. Helleve growled and mumbled something I didn't catch.

'What did you say?'

'Would you mind dropping by, Varg? We need to have a chat with you, anyway.'

'Thought you'd never ask. I'm as good as outside your door, Atle.'

I was, five minutes later. He showed me into his office and indicated the vacant chair.

He looked worn out. His face was drawn and pale, and the bags under his eyes darker than they usually were. 'Let's kick off with the good news, Varg. We found definite traces of Torvaldsen's DNA under the nails of the prostitute in Tollbodhopen. Furthermore, there were scratch marks on both of his hands, and not least … he has confessed.'

'Right! Everything?'

He nodded. 'By and large, as you presented it to us. But he does not admit raping Margrethe in 1988, and he claims that what he did to Margrethe and Karl Gunnar was nothing less than self-defence. They had arrived together, and he had noticed they were worked up. So he had been on his guard the whole time. When Karl Gunnar attacked him with a candlestick, he managed to wrest it out of his grip and knock him unconscious. Margrethe tried to escape, but he caught up with her and knocked her down with it as well.'

'An energetic office manager, I must say.'

'Driven by desperation, if you ask me.'

'But he hasn't given a plausible explanation as to why he didn't ring the police while the two were still unconscious, and what on earth was he thinking of when he deposited them in his freezer?'

'No. He doesn't understand how his mind was working. Waagenes is bound to plea that he was not responsible for his actions at the time of the crime.'

'It didn't sound like that when he spoke to me. He said he gave them a merciful death and was going to get rid of the bodies later.'

'Well ...' He splayed his hands. 'Waagenes has obviously changed Torvaldsen's mind.'

'And the candlestick, did you find it?'

'Yes. It was the same one *fru* Mobekk had reported missing. In fact, he had put it in the freezer as well. We found definite traces of DNA on it from Mobekk, Karl Gunnar and Margrethe, and what's more his own and Karl Gunnar's fingerprints. So, from that point of view, all the pieces have fallen into place, Varg. The forensic ones anyway.'

'And Tanya?'

'At first he claimed he hadn't had anything to do with her. But when we presented the DNA evidence he changed his statement. He claimed the trick had been nothing out of the ordinary, but she had tried to rob him and he had reacted with such force that she ...' He gave a laconic smile. 'That he accidentally killed her, as he put it. He claims that after what he had experienced with the others he was forced to get rid of the body, in the simplest possible way.'

'Nothing out of the ordinary? After killing two people a couple of days earlier, and his neighbour and drinking partner Carsten Mobekk being found murdered the same morning? He was intent on getting rid of a troublesome witness, Atle. That's how it's all connected.'

He nodded wearily. 'I suppose so. We just have to tie up the circumstantial evidence.'

'Has he admitted that he and Mobekk beat up Tanya on Friday evening?'

'He doesn't call it a beating, but concedes that perhaps they both went a bit too far.'

'And Margrethe had seen them?'

'Yes, he says Mobekk and he had been drinking on Friday evening and then they had decided to take a drive through the red-light district. Torvaldsen admitted that after his wife died he had been there often, but it seems it was the first time for Mobekk. Driving through the streets, they spotted Margrethe, and according to Torvaldsen, Mobekk had got wildly excited at the very thought.'

'He probably remembered they had done it to her once before.'

'Possible. When she refused to go along with them they picked up Tanya, and Torvaldsen maintained it was because of the frustration they felt towards Margrethe that they had been a bit too hard-handed with her.'

'Well … Why are you looking so dejected, Atle? The case seems to be in the bag.'

He looked at me pensively. 'There are still some loose threads. What made Siv go into the cellar, for example?'

I tried to recapitulate the conversation I'd had with Siv a week and a half ago. 'Don't forget that it was me who put her on the trail.'

'You?'

'Yes. I had a chat with her, must have been last Tuesday. Picked her up from work and drove her home. She told me that Margrethe and Karl Gunnar had stayed with her over Friday night. They'd said they were planning to go on their way, which they did … on Saturday. Since then she hadn't heard a word from them.'

'And you forgot to tell us this?'

'Forgot? I found this out on Thursday afternoon, and the next morning I was lured to Flesland and locked up by Malthus and Dalby. How's that case going by the way?'

He raised a hand in defence. 'Let's take one thing at a time, shall we, Varg?'

'Well … We touched on what happened to Mobekk of course, and I'm afraid I happened to mention … the finger-prints you'd found, Margrethe's and Karl Gunnar's. Hers at the crime scene, and both of theirs in the stolen car.'

His face went puce. 'You're afraid you happened to mention!' he exclaimed. 'What a damn cheek. Happened to mention! Bloody hell, Varg. Perhaps you're the one who triggered this whole chain reaction. She puts two and two together, goes to her childhood home, for some reason or other goes into the cellar and opens the freezer … and finds them there.'

'Have you … questioned her?'

'Questioned? It'll be a long time before we get the oppor-tunity. She's been admitted to Sandviken Hospital. According to the doctor in charge she's in a state of serious psychosis. It's impossible to contact her, and also in a legal sense she's beyond our reach.'

He sat glaring at me.

I said: 'What about … the other case? The robbery of Lars Mikalsen.'

He heaved a deep sigh. 'Let's take this point by point, Varg. Lars Mikalsen denies everything. The situation being what it was, we had no reason to hold him. He's already at home in Møhlenpris.'

'But …'

'We don't have a scrap of evidence. Where are the drugs, for example?'

'Well, I assume you searched everywhere.'

'We've searched everywhere they could conceivably be. But you know … They could have buried them somewhere. Put them in a safety deposit box. Sent them in a registered package to themselves. So far they haven't turned up anyway.'

'But he knew Margrethe?'

'That was more or less the only thing he admitted. That he'd had a few beers with her at Børs Café now and then. And that he knew the brother, of course. It's a small world. But he denied, in the strongest terms, that they had attacked him when he came off the Danish ferry. His line is now that it could have been a man from Østland he'd had an argument with in the bar the night before.'

'These Østlanders.'

'He flatly rejects any suggestion that he was smuggling drugs. He's never done that kind of thing, he says. *You can take my word for it.*' Helleve grinned and splayed palms. 'Again … burden of proof, Varg. We have to have the package, at the very minimum.'

'But Malthus and Dalby …'

'They deny everything, of course, as well.'

'They can't!'

'Oh no?'

'I'll testify against them. Unlawful restraint and … what lawyers call serious threats.'

He nodded. 'Fine, Varg. But how much will they get for it? Two years tops. Besides, Malthus denies all knowledge of this. He pins the blame on Dalby, which in the best-case scenario may cause the alliance to develop cracks and Dalby to start talking. But discipline in these circles is fierce. Dalby knows that if he says too much, he risks a very unpleasant period in prison. And Malthus is sitting on the resources, economic as well as legal.'

'Hell! And the pimping?'

'Will you get one of the women to testify against him? Can you present their financial accounts? It's an uphill struggle. Don't you think we've been there before, Varg? "Bergen, Bergen, Bergen," he quoted. "Norway's biggest village. Doesn't matter where you go, home is uphill." Anything else?'

'Not that I can think of?'

'Well ... then I'll have to sift my way through my piles of paper and see if I can strike gold. Have a very lively weekend, Varg. Celebrate with moderation.'

'Thank you. Not a lot to celebrate, is there.'

'No, you're right.'

I found the way down to street level and into what optimists call fresh air. January still hadn't relinquished its grip. I had a feeling that the whole town found itself in a kind of collective depression, brought on by the grey weather and the thermometer, a lethal alliance in this rain-laden town, kilometres and kilometres from all climate zones. Indeed, in a way, a climate zone in itself.

On rare occasions I wished I lived elsewhere. This was one of those. As far away as it was possible to go. But, as on most days, I didn't get any further than my office.

My letter box was empty. There were no messages on the answer machine. No one needed me.

40

SLOWLY LIFE began to stir again.

I rang Cathrine Leivestad a few times to hear how things were going with Hege. The answer was discouraging. She was on the streets again. 'We can't stop her, Varg,' she said. 'It's a free country. What she does with her body is her decision.'

I rang Thomas and told him about my meeting with his old classroom girlfriend. He did not allow himself to be affected and was more interested in telling me that Mari and he had decided to get married. 'That's nice,' I said, but still went back to Hege: 'She said you'd gone out together for a while.' 'Yes, I suppose we did. But not for long.' After a short pause he added: 'I'm sad to hear that.'

Alf Torvaldsen was brought before the magistrates' court again. This time there was no doubt what verdict the court would reach. He would be under lock and key until the trial came up, a temporary date had been set for May or June.

Kjell Malthus and Rolf Terje Dalby were charged with unlawful restraint and serious threats. The trial against them was scheduled for April, and I was already anticipating meeting them in court with mixed feelings. When I called the number for Malthus Invest an automatic message announced that the business had closed down until further notice. Enquiries could be directed to a specified number. I rang it, and a woman's voice answered: *Kristine*. I asked if Kjell was at home, but he wasn't. He was away, the woman said, before her tone sharpened.

'What did you say your name was?' she asked. 'Veum,' I said, and she cut the connection without any further ado.

At the end of March I was visited in my office by Vidar Waagenes, early one Thursday morning. He rejected the offer of a cup of coffee and sat down in my client's chair. 'I thought it would be better if you heard this from me before anyone else, Varg.'

I looked at him expectantly and motioned for him to continue.

He cleared his throat. 'Alf Torvaldsen died in his cell early this morning. A massive heart attack. His life couldn't be saved. The burden of all the accusations was too heavy to bear.'

We sat observing each other. I sensed a mute accusation in his eyes.

'He had confessed to three murders, hadn't he?'

'Yes, indeed. Under very mitigating circumstances.'

'We-ell.'

'We-ell?' He seemed affronted. 'I'm convinced I would have had a good case. A manager on the local council attacked in his own home by two dubious young people with a criminal background.'

'Neither you nor I was there when it happened, Vidar. Therefore I reserve my right to repeat my reservation: We-ell.'

'I last visited him yesterday. He was in despair that what he and his wife had considered an idealistic mission, committing themselves to three children with a very difficult home life, should have been turned upside down as it has been ... by you and those like you.'

'May I be so bold as to remind you that two of the children are dead and the third is in Sandviken Hospital for an indefinite period. That is the concrete result of their so-called idealism.'

He was about to say something, but I continued: 'And the two dead children died at your deceased client's hand.'

'It was self-defence. If the case had come before a court I'm sure the jury would have understood the tricky situation in which he found himself.'

'And what about Tanya Karoliussen? Was *that* self-defence as well?'

'She tried to rob him.'

'And that justified him killing her? But perhaps that is how it is in your world as well? The life of a prostitute is not worth as much as that of a manager on the council. A drop in the ocean, eh, Vidar?'

'You know I don't think like that, Varg. I don't have figures for all those I have defended, also from life's shady side. For me a case is a case and an individual an individual. But there are nuances in this case to which neither you nor the police have paid sufficent attention.'

'Let's say that then until the contrary is proven.'

As he left I sat back with a feeling that it would be a long time before he sent me a job again.

A couple of hours later Helleve rang and told me what had happened. I pretended I hadn't already heard. In passing, I asked what progress they had made with the investigation. He hummed and hawed, then said there was a good chance the case would be shelved until new evidence appeared.

A week later Alf Torvaldsen was buried at Solheim chapel. There wasn't a big turnout, for a variety of reasons. I didn't attend.

On a couple of evenings I drove out to C. Sundts gate and looked for Hege. I spotted her on the second. But as I pulled in and rolled down the window, she moved away as if she didn't want to talk to me. I engaged the handbrake, got out onto the pavement and followed her. When I called her name she turned and made it clear she did not want anything to do with me. At once a dark-haired man with a mass of coarse stubble appeared from a doorway and blocked my path. He asked me what I wanted, with an obvious accent. And what did that have to do with him? I replied. His face darkened. If I wanted another girl he would get me one, pronto. I watched Hege in the distance, she rounded the corner towards Strandgaten. No, thank you, I said. Did he have a business card I could have … for later use? But evidently he didn't, so I turned on my heel and went back to the car. I was furious inside. Hege had new protectors, this time of foreign origin. What annoyed me most was that there was little I could do about it. As Cathrine had said, we lived in a free country. She could do with her body what she wanted.

In April I summoned up the courage, drove to Sandviken Hospital and asked if it was possible to visit Siv Monsen. The duty doctor said it was, but we were unlikely to get much out of it, neither Siv nor I. She didn't talk to anyone. Not even the most skilled therapists had broken through her firewall. I said I would like to venture an attempt anyway. Afterwards my name was registered in the visitors' book and I was ushered to a lounge with a view of Munkebotn and Sandviksfjellet mountains. The trees on the slopes bore a touch of mauve. It was a question of days before spring would break out with green hair fluttering in the wind.

Siv sat with her back to the window, her skin so pale it could have been transparent. If you squinted, you could see right through her. She was wearing a blue and green jumper with long sleeves and dark jeans. She didn't react to my arrival in the room, and when I sat down beside her, I saw that her gaze was vacant, blank.

I said her name, but she didn't react to that, either. I tried a few standard questions. How are you? … Have you any contact with others in the ward? No response.

I looked around. A young girl sat at the other end of the room, peering at us over the top of a magazine and openly giggling. A man of my age sat in between toiling over a jigsaw. He seemed to be very fcocused and had not registered that I was there. A little woman in her fifties appeared in the doorway, scanned the room, but turned around and was gone, possibly because she had noticed a strange face.

After a further couple of attempts I gave up. I patted her gently on the hand, got up and said: 'I'll be back another time, Siv. When you're in better shape.'

On my way out, I was stopped by the doctor. 'Well? Did you make contact?'

'Not at all.'

'Thought so.'

'What's the diagnosis?'

'Catatonia, provoked by shock, combined with acute depression.'

'And what's the prognosis for the treatment?'

He looked at me with doleful eyes. 'Hard to say. It can go both ways.'

'Has she had visits from anyone else?'

He flicked through the records. 'Not many. I remember them both. A colleague from work and a friend, about the same age.'

'Nils Åkre?'

'Yes, that's right.'

'And the friend?'

'Leif Larsen.'

'Leif Larsen?' I was taken aback. 'Do they have to show ID?'

'Did you?'

'No.'

'Well …'

'Not her mother?'

'No.' He looked, if at all possible, even more doleful.

I thanked him for his kindness and went out into the spring sunshine. April is a deceptive month. All of a sudden there could be sleet in the air, a greeting from a delayed winter. I ambled down to the car and a thought struck me: I might have had summer tyres fitted a week too early.

Home once again, I checked the telephone directory for Leif Larsen. Leif 'Shetlands' Larsen, Bergen's Second World War hero, had clearly left his mark because there were quite a lot of people with that name, in Bergen alone, and I had no reason whatsoever to visit any of them. Besides, she had said that she had a male friend, hadn't she?

Towards the end of April the case against Malthus and Dalby came to court. I was called as the principal witness and did my best to avoid their eyes when I gave evidence. The Defence Counsel did what he could to sow doubt around my statement, but it was not so easy to knock me off my perch. Both received a conviction, Dalby's was more severe than Malthus's, based on a legal judgment that was too sophisticated for me to understand in its entirety. The prison sentence was not much of a deterrent: eighteen months for Dalby, twelve for Malthus. I thought to myself: eighteen months. That was what my life was worth. I would have to get into training before they were released. It was evident they themselves considered the punishment too severe.

Both appealed, and the appeal trial was scheduled for August or September. Something else to look forward to.

May passed somehow. I had a few minor cases, a couple of them for Nils Åkre. Life was back on track.

But I couldn't get the case out of my head. Back in town after the wedding in Løten I followed an impulse, drove up to Minde, parked the car and went to the house in Falsens vei.

There were new curtains on the ground floor and there was a new sign on the door. I rang Else Monsen's doorbell without getting an answer. So I rang the bell on the ground floor. The young woman who opened had a little child in her arm and looked somewhat flurried. When I explained the situation she nodded and stepped aside. 'Yes, she is undoubtedly a bit special,' she commented before I took the stairs to the first floor. 'We've just moved in.'

I knocked on the door upstairs. Only after a long wait did I hear sounds inside. There was some fiddling with the lock, and Else Monsen appeared.

She had not changed much. Perhaps there was an element of new pain visible in her face. If so, that was all. But the cigarette was in place, and if I was not mistaken she was wearing the same outfit as on the first time I visited her: beige pullover and brown trousers.

'I'm Veum. Do you remember me?'

She nodded and turned around, confident that I would follow her. We entered the sitting room. There were no changes there either, apart from the fact that she had emptied the ashtray. It was already well on the way to filling up again.

'You haven't visited Siv, I understand.'

She looked at me with a tiny scrap of surprise in her eyes. 'I never go out.'

'You don't? How do you do your shopping then?'

She held the glowing cigarette in front of me, as if to show what generally constituted her shopping. 'I have what I need delivered to the door every Friday.'

'But do you know where she is?'

She shrugged. 'Isn't she at home then?'

I sighed. 'Listen, Else. There is something I'm wondering about. When Siv came here that day in January that I'm sure you remember ... did she have something with her?'

'With her. A heavy bag.'

'A bag?'

'Yes.'

'And ... where is it now?'

'It was lying around. In the end, I put it in the cupboard.'

'Does that mean ... it's still here?'

'No, it's not here any more.'

'It's not?'

'No, her friend came to collect it.'

'Her friend?'

'Yes, that's what he said anyway.'

'Mm.'

'When was that?'

'Oh ...' She waved her hand airily, causing the cigarette smoke to settle like a silk veil between us. 'Several weeks ago.'

'Did he say his name, this friend?'

She delved into her memory, so deep that she went dizzy. 'Leif, wasn't it, think it was.'

The following day was a beautiful, hot June day. I drove to Sandviken, found a vacant parking spot and approached the same ward as on the previous occasion. There was a new doctor on duty, quite a young woman, and when I asked after Siv, she smiled and pointed to the park at the rear of the house. 'You'll find her there,' she said. 'With Leif, I dare say …'

41

THEY WERE SITTING ON A BENCH in relaxed poses, enjoying the summer day like any other lovers. She was wearing bright, airy summer clothes. Her hair was full of life, as if she had just washed it, and she had more colour in her cheeks than when I visited her in May. He was wearing light, baggy shorts and a dark red singlet. He'd had his hair cut short and had grown a moustache since I had last seen him, and the marks of the beating were gone, but I had no difficulty recognising him.

Where they sat the radiant sun filtered through the luxuriant green growth of the treetops. I felt like an interloper into Paradise as I stopped in front of them, my shadow falling obliquely across their bench. She looked up; he had recognised me from some distance. At once an air of vigilance and tension overcame him, as though he was prepared for the worst.

'Hi, Siv,' I said.

'Hi,' she said in a hushed voice without any signs of recognition.

'Varg Veum. Do you remember me?'

She nodded, with a faint smile, as at a distant memory.

'So this is your new girlfriend, Lars,' I said to Lars Mikalsen.

He shrugged, but did not refute my statement.

I looked at Siv. 'You told me you had a new friend, Siv. I should perhaps have made the link earlier.'

She wore a faraway smile, as though barely comprehending what I said.

'How are you?'

'Fine.'

'Is it all beginning to drift into the past?'

'The past,' she repeated, like an obedient child.

I was unsure how present she actually was. There was an invisible membrane over her eyes, a silk shawl protecting her from the surrounding world.

A few small birds chirped in the bushes behind them. Others pecked at the ground under some large rhododendron bushes with violet flowers. Now and then they made sporadic forays and struggled through the gravel, which surrounded them like a cloud.

'Are you perhaps ready for a chat about it?'

Lars Mikalsen half-rose from the bench. 'Veum,' he said, but I wasn't sure what he meant.

'Yes?'

'Be careful!'

'With reference to what?'

He lowered his voice. 'She's not … fine yet. It would take nothing for her to have a relapse. The doctors have not yet allowed the police to interview her.'

'This isn't an interview. I have no official status. This is a little chat in the sunshine, so to speak.'

He opened his mouth, but I interrupted him: 'But I can start with you. You haven't been admitted to hospital, I take it?'

He stood up and came over to me. 'We can talk, but let's move away. Siv …' He turned to her. In a much gentler voice he said: 'Veum and I are going to have a little chat. You just relax.'

She gave a sweet smile, and we did as he had suggested and withdrew to a spot some metres away.

'What do you want to know?'

I looked around. The main building lay bathed in sun. There were several people outside walking, others sat at tables, some with a bottle of mineral water in front of them. It was difficult to distinguish between patients, nurses and relatives.

'Leif Larsen ... what sort of name is that?'

'One I made up.'

'Useful for getting around incognito perhaps?'

'What do you want to know, I asked!'

'Let's start at the beginning, shall we. You dropped by *fru* Monsen, I heard. Collected the bag Siv had left there. Where is it now?'

He tried to retain control of his expression, but failed to hide the distaste he felt. 'None of your bloody business!'

'Well,' I said. 'They'll find it anyway once they've started looking.'

'They?' He paled visibly.

'Yes, you know ... Your debts have not shrunk since we last spoke. Malthus and Dalby may be inside, but there are others who feel you have trodden on their toes. The suppliers in Denmark, for example.' After a suitable pause for effect I added: 'Or the police.'

He pursed his lips, but it was not difficult to see: he preferred the police to the suppliers.

'Or,' I said. 'We can arrange an anonymous return of the goods. Out of consideration for Siv. I'll give you a hand, if you'd like.'

He sent me a sceptical look. Then he shook his head. 'You have no idea what you are suggesting.'

'Oh, yes, I do. Bit by bit I'm beginning to get a pretty good feel for the situation. Does she know that Torvaldsen's dead?'

He nodded. 'I've told her.'

'How did she take it?'

'Like everything else. With apathy.' In a surge of emotion he added: 'The reason she's here …' He broke off.

'Yes?'

He hesitated a few seconds more. Then he seemed to decide to lay his cards on the table. 'She feels a dreadful, heavy sense of guilt!'

I waited, but he didn't expand. 'You mean … for what happened to Margrethe and Karl Gunnar?'

He nodded. 'Yes.'

'And not entirely without reason perhaps. She had known for a long time that something was going on at Torvaldsen's. That was why she visited her mother and went down to the cellar that day. Because she'd been involved in the planning, from the very first moment.'

'No! She hadn't.'

'No?'

'She knew nothing.'

'But you said …'

'The arrangement was that we would share the money and that Margrethe and Karl Gunnar would lie low for a week and then … go abroad.'

'Really? Listen then to what I've worked out. The short version, if you like. Siv, Margrethe and Karl Gunnar had a very difficult childhood, and ever since they've been adults they – whenever they met – fantasised about how they would get even. How they would avenge themselves. And there was a lot to avenge. It was one thing that the damned committee had held the family together and prolonged the father's abuse of his two daughters for years. But quite another that two men on the committee had themselves sexually assaulted Margrethe, and now that they were showing up in the red-light district, she went to pieces. She wanted the whole thing finished. She wanted to take her revenge now. And in fact that was very convenient. You and Siv had got together and exchanged confidences. She knew about the package you were going to collect in Denmark. You told me yourself the plan was to make this the last trip, then you would do rehab and get back onto an even keel. But then you changed plans and decided to keep the whole package for yourselves. Or share it with Margrethe and Karl Gunnar. That was still a great deal more than you would have got from Malthus. Margrethe and KG were on Skoltegrunn Quay to meet you when you arrived. They drove you to Skuteviken, the package changed hands, and KG knocked you about for appearance's sake, so badly that a taxi driver intervened and drove you to A&E. Well thought out, but not quite clever enough to fool Malthus and Dalby. You were given another going-over, but obviously you kept your mouth shut.'

He swallowed and glanced at Siv. She sat with her face half-turned to the sun with the same serene smile. There was nothing to suggest that she had caught any of what we were saying.

'Margrethe, KG and Siv met at her place. She would keep the drugs there while they carried out what they had been waiting to do for many years. It was now or never, for as soon as they had shared the money they would make good their chance to leave the country ... perhaps for ever. Then they went to Falsens vei.'

'No!' he broke in. 'That's where you're wrong. Siv knew nothing about Margrethe and KG going there. She was convinced they would leave the country and that was it. That was the agreement. To Oslo, sell the drugs and then … off. But they just went missing without taking their share.'

'I see! So you were left with the whole package, in Siv's flat. That must … that must have felt like sitting on a ticking bomb.'

He looked at me, his eyes weary. 'No one knew a thing about Siv and me. Except Maggi and KG. The drugs were safe.'

He was right about that to a certain extent. I had been to her place myself, with the package in the adjacent room, in a loft storage room or wherever she had chosen to hide it.

'And what had you been planning to do with your share? Take it to Copenhagen? You wouldn't have sold it locally, I presume?'

He shrugged. 'We had our … plans.'

'Well. Let me go back to Falsens vei. What happened there we'll never know for sure, since all those involved are dead. What we feel fairly confident about is that KG and Margrethe called on Mobekk and caught him on the hop – with death as a consequence. Before leaving they messed the place up so that it would look like a burglary. But with Torvaldsen the boot was on the other foot. He was able to defend himself, and he did it so well that they ended up in his freezer. The stolen car they had used when they appeared to rob you was found by the police with KG's fingerprints on the wheel and hers on the door handle. They never got any further. Their journey stopped there, more or less where it had started.'

I looked at Lars Mikalsen. Once again it was clear a terrible battle was going on inside him. I added: 'Shall we say that more or less summarises the whole business?'

He tossed his head and threw out his arms. Then he said in a low voice: 'What did you say about sending it back … anonymously?'

'If you tell me where I can find it, then …'

'I can go with you. You won't find it on your own.'

'Of course it's impossible for me to guarantee the police won't find their way to you anyway. And you'll have to live with your relationship with the suppliers for a long time, I would guess. But, hopefully, there will be no consequences for Siv, and right now that ought to be the most important issue … for both of us.'

He looked at Siv. A tender smile lit his face, and turning back to me, he said: 'OK. Let's agree on that. Did you come by car?'

'Yes.'

'If you can give me some time with her alone, then …'

'I'll be waiting down in the car park.'

'Thank you.'

We strolled back to Siv. I held out my hand. 'I'm off, Siv.'

She looked up, reached out and gave my hand a limp shake and smiled the same, nigh on transparent smile.

'I wish you all the best. Just remember this. What happened was not your fault. The course had been set years ago, and by others, not you three children. The guilty ones in this matter are those who should have been your guardians, your biological parents and the people who committed themselves to looking after you. Most of them are gone now.'

She nodded, and in a strange way I felt as if I had been forgiven, as if it were me standing there representing all guardians from the dawn of time until today. And perhaps I was. Perhaps we were all accomplices, every last bastard who hadn't opened their eyes in time. Perhaps we were all carrying around our generation's guilt towards the weakest, the youngest and those with least protection.

I could have asked about her father's death of course. Whether she had made use of the key she had and entered the home that day as well. But I chose not to. Some questions are best left unanswered. It would not have made any difference one way or the other.

Together with Lars Mikalsen I drove to the copse in Fana where he had buried the package that never arrived at its destination in January. The same afternoon I handed it in to the police station. I told Atle Hellev I had been given an anonymous tip-off. He didn't give the impression he believed me, and of course he had good reason.

In September, Kjell Malthus and Rolf Terje Dalby stood before court for a second time. My life was still worth no more than eighteen months, but the jury extended Malthus's sentence by four months, from twelve to sixteen. I registered the result, but felt no reason to celebrate.

At approximately the same time Siv was discharged from Sandviken Hospital. On the grapevine I heard that she and Lars Mikalsen had moved to somewhere in Jutland where reliable sources informed me there was a rehab centre for drug addicts that boasted excellent results. I never saw either of them again.